Also by Jack Sheffield

Teacher, Teacher!
Mister Teacher
Dear Teacher
Village Teacher
Please Sir!
Educating Jack
School's Out!
Silent Night
Star Teacher
Happiest Days
Starting Over
Changing Times
Back to School

For more information on Jack Sheffield and his books,
see his website at www.jacksheffield.com

5B

902863530 0

www.penguin.co.uk

SCHOOL DAYS

A Teacher Series novel 1976–1977

Jack Sheffield

BANTAM PRESS

TRANSWORLD PUBLISHERS
Penguin Random House, One Embassy Gardens,
8 Viaduct Gardens, London SW11 7BW

www.penguin.co.uk

Transworld is part of the Penguin Random House group of companies
whose addresses can be found at global.penguinrandomhouse.com

Penguin
Random House
UK

First published in Great Britain in 2021 by Bantam Press
an imprint of Transworld Publishers

Copyright © Jack Sheffield 2021

Jack Sheffield has asserted his right under the Copyright,
Designs and Patents Act 1988 to be identified as the author of this work.

A CIP catalogue record for this book
is available from the British Library.

ISBN 9781787632981

Typeset in 11/15pt Zapf Calligraphic 801 BT by Jouve (UK), Milton Keynes
Printed and bound in Great Britain by Clays Ltd, Elcograf S.p.A.

The authorized representative in the EEA is Penguin Random House Ireland,
Morrison Chambers, 32 Nassau Street, Dublin D02 YH68.

Penguin Random House is committed to a sustainable
future for our business, our readers and our planet. This book
is made from Forest Stewardship Council® certified paper.

For Lily, Ava and Daisy

Contents

Acknowledgements

Sincere thanks to my editors, Molly Crawford and Imogen Nelson, for bringing this novel to publication supported by the excellent team at Transworld, including Larry Finlay, Bill Scott-Kerr, Jo Williamson, Vivien Thompson, Katie Cregg, Hayley Barnes, Richenda Todd and fellow 'Old Roundhegian' Martin Myers.

Also, thanks to my industrious literary agent, Philip Patterson of Marjacq Scripts, Newcastle United supporter and Britain's leading authority on eighties Airfix Modelling Kits, for his encouragement, good humour and deep appreciation of Yorkshire cricket.

I am also grateful to all those who assisted in the research for this novel – in particular: Janina Bywater, retired nurse, Ayton, Berwickshire, Scotland; Helen Carr, primary school teacher and literary critic, Harrogate, Yorkshire; Linda Collard, education trainer and consultant, fruit-grower and jam-maker, West Chiltington, West Sussex; Ysemay Grant Ferguson, bookseller and artist, Alton, Hampshire;

Tony Greenan, Yorkshire's finest headteacher (now retired), Huddersfield, Yorkshire; Ian Haffenden, ex-Royal Pioneer Corps and custodian of Sainsbury's, Alton, Hampshire; John Kirby, ex-policeman, expert calligrapher and Sunderland supporter, County Durham; Roy Linley, Lead Architect, Strategy & Technology, Unilever Global IT Innovation (now retired) and Leeds United supporter, Leeds, Yorkshire; Susan Maddison, retired primary school teacher, social historian and maker of excellent cakes, Harrogate, Yorkshire; Jacqui Rogers, Deputy Registrar, allotment holder and tap dancer, Malton, Yorkshire; John Wright, retired headteacher and photographer, Barrowford, Lancashire; and all the terrific staff at Waterstones Alton, including the irreplaceable Simon (now retired), the excellent manager Sam and Scottish travel expert Fiona.

Not forgetting a special thank you to the dynamic events manager, Nikki Bloomer, and the wonderful team at Waterstones MK.

Finally, sincere thanks to my wife, Elisabeth, without whose help the *Teacher* series of novels would never have been written.

Prologue

Fate . . . it comes to us all.

One's lot in life walks hand in hand with destiny.

It was Friday, 3 September 1976 when I met a striking young woman.

I was standing outside the high metal gates of New-bridge Primary School in West Yorkshire where I had been deputy headteacher for the past six years. Our newly appointed music teacher was due to arrive and the head-teacher, Jim Patterson, had asked me to look out for her.

A car pulled up across the road driven by a man wear-ing a bright red headband over his lank shoulder-length hair and smoking a roll-up cigarette. He was driving a battered Vauxhall Viva, hand-painted with psychedelic patterns and a sign on the door that read: 'MAKE LOVE NOT WAR'.

A woman emerged from the passenger seat. Medium height and slim with a mass of wavy black hair, she wore blue bell-bottom cords, a collarless white blouse and a black waistcoat stitched with yellow flowers. Over her shoulder was a cumbersome shoulder bag and she was carrying a guitar case.

The car roared away and for a moment she looked after it and sighed. It was as if for some reason she was weighed down by a millstone of memories. Then she caught sight of me, waved and gave me a cautious smile.

She crossed the road and looked me up and down while assessing my gangling six-foot-one-inch frame. My long brown hair hung over the collar of my baggy sports jacket. What I considered to be a fashionable ensemble included a wide flower-power tie, flared chino trousers and suede desert boots.

'Hello. I guess you're waiting for me,' she said.

'I'm Jack Sheffield. Welcome to Newbridge.' We shook hands. 'You must be Ms Kowalski.'

She seemed amused by my formality. 'Kowalski, yes . . . but call me Izzy.'

'Izzy? Short for Isobel?'

She grinned and shook her head. 'No, Ysemay . . . Irish mother, Polish father. Izzy is much simpler.'

'Well, pleased to meet you, Izzy . . . and call me Jack.'

'Short for John?' she asked with a mischievous smile.

I had been christened Jack but accepted the riposte. 'Touché,' I said with a grin. 'Come on, the head is expecting us. Shall I carry something for you?'

She passed over the guitar case. 'Thanks, Jack.'

I gestured towards the worn school steps that led to the entrance door of our Victorian school building.

'Fine, let's go,' she said with sudden confidence and we strode off across the tarmac playground.

Prologue

I glanced at her, aware of the intensity of her stare as we walked into school. Her grey-green eyes were the colour of moss on limestone. I was soon to discover that when she smiled her glance could light up a room. However, when she was sad, and there was a hint of that on this autumn morning, her eyes were soft with sorrow.

I had never been a believer in kismet, the notion that life is already planned and we cannot control the outcome. However, it seemed a predetermined course of events was about to run its course and an unseen fate awaited me. The academic year 1976–77 was destined to change my life and shatter my peaceful dreams.

I was a thirty-one-year-old bachelor and the unexpected lay around the corner . . .

Chapter One

The Colour of Music

'Jack, what a surprise!'

It took me a moment to gather my senses. The woman before me looked as though she had just walked off the cover of a Nordic fashion magazine: tall, slim and blonde.

'Oh . . . good to see you again. It must be . . . what, five years?'

She smiled. 'It's six. We said goodbye in 1970.'

I thought back to our last conversation. 'That's right, we did.'

She gave me a direct look. 'Jack . . . I remember it well.'

It was Saturday, 4 September and I was in a coffee shop in Leeds city centre. I had taken my mother shopping and she had gone on to meet her sister. In my own private space, I was flicking through the pages of the *Times Educational Supplement*.

I gestured to the empty chair opposite. 'Have you time for a coffee?'

'Love one.' She glanced at her wristwatch. 'I've still got an hour before I collect Sherri.'

'How is she? She must be grown up by now.'

'Fine. Thirteen and almost as tall as me.'

'Time flies.' There was a moment's pause. 'So . . . a coffee. Anything else?'

She smiled again. 'Not just now, Jack.'

I ordered at the counter and looked back at Donna Clayton as she sat at my table and opened her handbag. She appeared more self-assured now, a confident woman. I had been teaching in my previous school when we first met. Donna had been a single parent eking out a living as a hairdresser and part-time barmaid. In those days she wore tight jeans and baggy jumpers; now she looked elegant in a figure-hugging trouser suit and white blouse. Bright and determined, she had aspirations to become a teacher and I had helped her along the way. She was the same age as me but we had walked different pathways.

I put a cup of coffee in front of her and she took a photograph from her handbag. 'This is Sherri now.'

A tall, leggy teenager stared back at me, the image of her mother. 'Well, she's certainly grown. When I first saw her she was a six-year-old with pink hair.'

Donna laughed, 'Yes, a hairdressing faux pas. Happy memories, although I recall that the headteacher didn't approve. I was pleased when he moved on. It was a different school when Mrs Priestley took over: caring and supportive.'

'You must be very proud,' I said and handed back the photograph.

For a few moments we sipped our coffee in silence.

Finally Donna looked at me and said, 'So, what's happening in *your* life?' She pointed to the *Times Educational Supplement*. 'Looking for another job?'

I shook my head. 'One day maybe.'

'I knew you had got a deputy headship.'

For a few moments I waited for the question I knew she would ask. After a little more small talk it came.

'So . . . how's Penny?'

There it was. Direct as always.

'I don't know.'

I could see she was intrigued. Back in 1970 Penny Armitage had been a relationship that had briefly dominated my waking dreams.

'Sorry, Jack, I just assumed . . .'

'No. It ended as quickly as it had begun. She moved to London. Last I heard she's still there.'

Donna looked thoughtful as she settled back into her seat and stared into her cup. Around us there was the hiss of the coffee machine and the chatter of shoppers.

I went on: 'What about you? Did you enjoy Bretton Hall?'

Donna had begun a three-year teacher-training course there in 1970.

She looked up at me, more animated now. 'It was the turning point of my life. Essays, teaching practice, new friends, a sense of purpose. Great times.'

'So where are you now?'

'I was lucky. I got a job straight from college at Bracken Primary School up near Oakworth, teaching second-year juniors. I love it. It's a brilliant school.'

'I'm pleased for you. I knew you could do it.' It was rewarding to see her so excited about her work.

'I'm renting a cottage in North Beck village. It's within the catchment area for The Ridge so perfect for Sherri.'

This was our local comprehensive school. 'I'm sure she'll do well there. It has an excellent reputation.'

She nodded and smiled. 'Yes, she loves it and has some good friends.'

I noticed her hair was shorter now, a neat bob cut. It suited her.

'So what's she doing now?'

'She's in the art gallery, finishing up a school holiday project about Henry Moore. She's excited that he's a famous Yorkshire sculptor.'

'That's right, born in Castleford.'

She finished drinking her coffee and looked up again. We both knew we had been avoiding the questions we wanted to ask. I took the plunge. 'So, what about you? How's *your* life?'

She clasped her hands and rested her chin on them in contemplation. 'It can be tough at times as a single mum but I have a beautiful daughter.' For a brief moment her eyes were mirrors of an unsettled past. 'That's where my happiness lies.' She picked up her handbag. 'It's been good to see you again, Jack, but you probably have things to do.'

I was unsure what to say and stood up. We faced each other and her blue eyes looked into mine. She paused and sighed. 'Jack . . . I'll always be grateful for your support.' Then she stepped forward and kissed me gently on the cheek.

As she turned to walk away she left behind a hint of Yves Saint Laurent and a moment of loss.

'Donna,' I called after her.

'Yes?'

'Just a thought. There's a Primary Curriculum course at the Teachers' Centre in Milltown. It's in the evenings, starting on the sixteenth if you're interested.'

'Thanks, Jack. Maybe. I've got Sherri to think of.'

'Ah, yes, I understand.' But as I watched her leave, I knew I wanted to see her again.

Monday, 6 September dawned bright and clear for the beginning of a new school year. As I climbed into my Morris Minor Traveller and drove away from my bungalow in Bradley village near Skipton I felt that familiar sense of expectation. I had always enjoyed the heartbeat of the seasons and the steady rhythm of the cycle of school life with its autumn, spring and summer terms. It was the job I loved and now I wondered what was in store.

The early-autumn sunlight bathed the distant fields in a golden light as I drove south towards the cobbled streets of Milltown and the village of Newbridge on its outskirts. I turned on the car radio and hummed along to the new number one, ABBA's 'Dancing Queen'.

As I crossed the River Aire over the bridge at Hog Holes Beck, Newbridge Primary School suddenly came into view at the end of the High Street. A red-brick Victorian building with a grey-slate roof and a tall bell tower, it had been at the centre of this large village community for over a hundred years. Beyond the school gates a side street behind the main building led to a car park for the staff and visitors.

I picked up my old leather satchel, locked my car and walked towards the steps that led to the main entrance.

'Mornin', Mr Sheffield.' It was Big Frank, the caretaker, carrying his yard broom. At six feet four inches tall, forty-year-old Frank Cannon was a hard worker and a huge presence around school. 'Another year – let's 'ope it's a good un.'

'Morning, Frank. I'm sure it will be.'

Back in 1955 Frank had completed part of his National Service in Malaya. During the jungle fighting, a bullet wound to his thigh had left him with a permanent limp. He had been lucky to survive. It was his tenth year as caretaker and he was proud of his service to the school.

He leaned on his broom, always a signal he wished to impart a nugget of information. 'That new music teacher were in bright an' early. Told me she were in three days a week. Looks keen.'

'Good to hear,' I said with a smile. Frank didn't miss much.

He lowered his voice and tapped the side of his nose conspiratorially. 'Not sure 'bout that 'ippy boyfriend though. Drives like a maniac. No manners. Ah waved but 'e jus' ignored me.'

'Sorry to hear that.'

'What's a smart lass doin' wi' a layabout like that?'

'No idea, Frank. Not my business,' I replied diplomatically.

He gave me a knowing look and picked up his broom. 'They need t'bring back National Service for t'likes of 'im. That would sort 'im out.' He was still muttering as he limped towards the boiler-house doors.

*

After dropping off my satchel in my classroom I walked into the staff-room to have a final look at my school time-table, the result of hours of work on a huge sheet of squared paper. I stood back and admired it with a sense of satisfaction. Michelangelo could not have been more proud when he looked up at the ceiling of the Sistine Chapel. I was still in my private reverie when Jim Patterson, the headteacher, walked in.

Tall and genial, fifty-year-old Jim was a superb leader and I had learned so much from him. His communication skills were excellent and he worked hard to support his colleagues. Jim always *walked the job* by visiting every classroom at the beginning of each school day and speaking to every member of staff. 'Early bird, Jack,' he said with a smile and paused to look at the timetable. 'Looks good . . . very colourful.' There was a hint of irony in his voice.

'Thanks, Jim. Yes, I thought it would make it easier to identify hall times and the different lessons.'

'Well, so long as Rhonda gives it the green light you'll be fine.'

Fifty-year-old Rhonda Williams was the head of the infant department and I had a cautious relationship with her. She was fiercely proud of her Welsh heritage even though she had left Cardiff at the age of five.

Jim looked at his wristwatch. 'Anyway, things to do. Catch you later.'

Six years ago Jim had appointed me as deputy head-teacher and had given me the task of organizing the timetable. He told me I had to make sure there was an equal opportunity for all the fourteen classes to use our school hall for assemblies, physical education and the *Music and Movement* radio broadcasts while leaving time to set up and clear away school dinners. There had been a few problems but, as each year passed, I had become more proficient and finally I was confident I had taken account of every eventuality.

However, the best-laid plans of mice and men don't always work out as one would wish!

The door opened again and our school secretary, Audrey Fazackerly, walked in. 'Morning, Jack. New registers on your desk.' Short, plump and cheerful, Audrey always tried to see the good in people.

'Thanks, Audrey. Efficient as ever.'

She stared at the timetable. 'Oooh, that looks really pretty.'

'Thanks. It's meant to be easier to read.'

For a moment she was puzzled. Audrey had a keen analytical mind. 'Have you allowed extra time for Frank to put out the dining tables? He doesn't mention it but his leg is playing him up again.'

The first hint of doubt crossed my mind. 'Ah, I see,' I said hesitantly.

'Anyway, it brightens up the room,' she said with a shy smile and hurried out. There were new starters to be enrolled.

Forty and single, Audrey's life revolved around the school and local church. However, it was well known that our school secretary was a huge fan of the handsome racing driver James Hunt. She had a photo of the flaxen-haired heart-throb in the bottom drawer of her desk and in quiet moments she would stare wistfully at her pin-up, unaware that it was common knowledge among the rest of the staff.

At eight thirty it was time to go outside to welcome the parents of the new starters. A reassuring greeting by the school gate always went down well. I walked out into the sunshine and across the playground.

Standing by the wrought-iron gate I surveyed the scene. Crowds of children, sunburned and healthy after their summer holiday, were playing on the school field while mothers, clutching the hands of new starters, the rising fives destined for the reception classes, were flooding in.

Two ten-year-old girls, Susan Verity and Dawn Whitehead, were winding a skipping rope on the playground while Pauline Ackworth and Claire Braithwaite skipped in perfect unison while chanting:

> *'Rosy apple, lemon, pear,*
> *Bunch of roses you shall wear,*
> *Gold and silver by your side,*
> *I know who will be your bride.'*

I smiled and wondered if one day *I* might have a bride.

Thirty-year-old Mrs Brenda Lofthouse arrived and paused by the school gate. "Ello, Mr Sheffield. Flippin' 'eck, ah'm glad that 'oliday's over. 'E's been a right pain 'as my Colin.'

She looked down in despair at her six-year-old son and

took a final puff of her cigarette. Mrs Lofthouse was heavily pregnant and holding her aching back. Colin appeared oblivious to the criticism and continued to pick his nose contentedly. His grey flannel shorts had been recently darned and his socks were round his ankles.

I crouched down and gave him a reassuring smile. 'Are you excited your mum is having a baby?'

Colin seemed perplexed by the question. 'Don't know, sir . . . sort of.'

'What would you like – a brother or a sister?'

Colin gave this considerable thought. 'Ah'd rather 'ave a gerbil.'

Mrs Lofthouse shook her head. 'Sorry, Mr Sheffield. 'E's clueless, jus' like 'is dad.'

Colin gave his mother an angelic smile, made more endearing as his two front teeth were missing. 'Mebbe we can 'ave a kitten, Mam?'

'No! Y'bloomin' can't.'

'Why not, Mam?'

''Cause yer grandma's 'llergic.'

''Llergic?'

'Yes, she can't stand cats.'

Colin was not to be deterred. 'What if Gran slept outside?'

Mrs Lofthouse gave him a push. 'Go play wi' yer friends.' She turned to me and shook her head. 'Kids – who'd 'ave 'em?'

I felt sorry for this hard-working lady as she walked back to the council estate. She was clearly exhausted.

A reluctant Billy Oldroyd was the next to walk in. As usual his mother, Mrs Phoebe Oldroyd, held his hand and the eight-year-old boy cringed as she bent down to kiss him on the cheek. 'Now work hard, Billy, and be good.' She smiled at me: 'Morning, Mr Sheffield,' and hurried off to catch the bus into Milltown where she worked in a shirt factory.

'Welcome back, Billy,' I said.

'Morning, sir.'

'What's wrong? You don't look happy.'

'I'm not keen on all this *kissing*, sir. My dad kisses my mum when he leaves for work and it puts me right off my porridge.' He put his hands in his pockets and ambled into the playground to find his best friend, Tony Entwhistle.

I was still smiling when there was a screech of brakes and a battered Austin 1100 pulled up. Mrs Kathy Swithenbank yelled at her twin daughters on the back seat: 'Come on, you two, I'll be late for work.'

The ten-year-old identical twins, Stacey and Tracey, tumbled out with frowns on their faces. 'Not *our* fault,' grumbled Stacey.

Kathy wound down her window. 'You need to get organized,' she shouted.

'Well, y'should have yelled at us earlier,' retorted Tracey.

As she roared away the girls gave me a big smile. 'Morning, sir,' they said in unison.

'Good t'be back,' said Stacey.

'An' we're in *your* class now, sir,' added Tracey for good measure.

Don't I know it, I thought.

The two tall and athletic girls suddenly sprinted on to the playground and joined in the skipping game.

*

It was a few minutes before nine o'clock when I walked back into school. In the hall Izzy was sitting at the piano. Her long hair covered her face as she leaned forward and her slender fingers caressed the keyboard with a light touch.

I watched her for a moment. 'Morning, Izzy. I see you're settling in.'

'Hi, Jack. Just getting ready for my first lesson.'

'That's great. It's in Miss Jolley's reception class.'

She looked puzzled. 'Oh, I assumed it would be in the hall. It just said "Music" on the timetable.'

'No, hall times are in blue.'

She smiled. 'So what colour is music?'

'It hasn't got a colour.'

'Really? How about yellow? That's cheerful.'

'Yellow is for art and craft lessons.'

She held up the hem of her maxi dress and her eyes twinkled. 'How about this? Mint green.'

'Green is for the school field.'

She nodded. 'Yes, I suppose it would be.'

'Sorry,' I said.

'Only teasing, Jack.'

'If there's anything you need, don't be afraid to ask.'

'I won't, Jack. I'm not shy.' She stood up and began to collect her music.

I watched her stride confidently to her first lesson. There was something fascinating about this woman.

At nine o'clock I rang the school bell and the villagers of Newbridge knew that another school year had begun.

After I had completed the registers, the children in my

16

class, the top juniors who would be eleven during the school year, were full of news. 'We were queuing f'water, sir, from a tap in t'street,' said Gary Cockroft. 'Every mornin' ah were there wi' a bucket.'

It had been the worst drought in the UK since the 1720s and measures had been introduced to distribute precious drinking water. During the heatwave a record temperature of 35.9 degrees had been recorded in Cheltenham.

'Ah saw Big Ben on t'news, sir,' said Stacey Swithenbank. 'It's damaged.'

'Won't be running f'nine months,' added her sister for good measure, and so it went on.

It was a busy morning, making sure everyone had a reading book, exercise books, a dictionary and a Berol pen along with a tin of Lakeland coloured pencils. We began a writing exercise with mixed results as few had picked up a pen during the past six weeks. Either way, it was a positive start and I emphasized that they must set an example to the younger ones and be on their best behaviour. I had found it was always best to start with high expectations.

Monitor jobs were organized and Susan Verity was allocated the job of bell-ringer. When she rang it after morning assembly the children filed out into the playground while the staff gathered in the staff-room.

Audrey had been busy and a neat row of coffee cups greeted us. Soon there was the usual hum of conversation. The two sports teachers, twenty-seven-year-old Katy Bell, a county-standard netball player, and twenty-four-year-old Tom Deighton, a keen footballer and a fast bowler for the Newbridge 1st XI, were checking out a sports-equipment catalogue.

Celestine Jolley, our timid reception class teacher, was deep in conversation with Audrey about the film stars Ali MacGraw and Steve McQueen, now a married couple.

'I hope she's happy with him,' said Celestine. 'I've heard he wants a wife who will cook and clean for him.'

'Well, I'd volunteer,' said Audrey.

Celestine looked aghast. 'But what about equality of the sexes?'

Audrey smiled. 'Yes, Celestine ... but we're talking about *Steve McQueen* here.'

They shared a secret smile before Audrey picked up an old copy of *Woman* magazine from the pile on the bookshelf and they were soon engrossed in the recipe page.

Meanwhile, Diane Hardisty, who taught one of the third-year junior classes, was telling Izzy that she thought the recent Notting Hill Carnival ought to be banned as it had ended in violence.

'My boyfriend was there,' said Izzy. 'He said he loved it.'

Suddenly the looming presence of Rhonda Williams was before me. The head of the infant department was not a woman to be crossed. Stocky, with short black hair and a severe fringe, she often had the demeanour of a bull terrier. 'I need to make some changes to the timetable, Jack,' she said. 'Hope you don't mind.' Rhonda was always polite but firm. 'Nothing too dramatic, just making sure the infant classes could team up occasionally for one of the new *Music and Movement* radio broadcasts.'

I had learned from past experience not to be confrontational with her. 'That's fine, Rhonda,' I said quietly. 'Let's have a chat at lunchtime and see what we can do.'

Suitably placated, she wandered off to discuss with

Celestine and Audrey the recipe for a strawberry walnut gateau.

School lunches were free for staff who sat with the children so, shortly after twelve o'clock, I found myself on the same table as Celestine and a group of lively children.

As usual the dinner lady, Mrs Rita Starkey, patrolled the tables. It was said she had a bark like a farmyard dog and a stare that could stop a clock at ten paces. Although she had the persona of a stormtrooper in a pink pinny, Mrs Starkey was highly regarded in spite of her charisma bypass. Jim tolerated her because she kept order.

'GARY COCKROFT,' she yelled and silence descended. 'There's no puddin' if y'don't finish yer dinner.'

'Why, Miss?'

"Cause ah said so.' Mrs Starkey always had an answer for everything.

'But ah don't like carrots, Miss.'

Mrs Starkey was going red in the face. 'Carrots mek y'see in t'dark.' She regularly dispensed pearls of wisdom amid her admonishments.

Gary looked perplexed.

'Don't make that face. If t'wind changes, you'll stay like that.'

'What?'

'Don't say *what*. Say pardon.'

'Sorry, Miss.'

'An' put that knife down, you'll 'ave someone's eye out.'

Mrs Starkey's dicta ruled our dining room and we all breathed a sigh of relief when she moved to cast a steely gaze over another table.

Meanwhile, Celestine held up a small plastic pencil case and gave it to seven-year-old Henry Dewhirst. 'This must be yours, Henry. It's got your name on it.'

'Cor, thanks, Miss, it were a present for m'birthday. Ah lost it in assembly.'

'Well, keep it safe from now on.'

'Yes, Miss.'

It was later during our meal of spam fritters, chips and peas followed by jam roly-poly pudding and custard that Tony Entwhistle suddenly spoke up. 'Ah think you're a good looker, Miss.'

Celestine's cheeks flushed. 'Oh, Tony, that's very kind.'

'You're like my mum, Miss. She's a good looker as well.'

'Well, thank you, Tony,' said Celestine, somewhat surprised but secretly pleased.

'Yes, Miss, 'cause when ah lose m'football socks she can allus find 'em.'

The penny dropped. 'Ah, I see,' said a slightly deflated Celestine.

By afternoon break it was clear my timetable was going down like a lead balloon. Tristan Lampwick, a rather presumptuous twenty-two-year-old literary buff in his probationary year, said, 'Never mind, Jack. "It was the best of times, it was the worst of times." '

The fearsome Rhonda was hovering and Tristan stepped back hurriedly. 'It's more a tale of two *departments*,' said Rhonda curtly, 'rather than a tale of two *cities*.'

Across the room I saw Izzy looking at me with a sympathetic smile.

*

At the end of school ten-year-old Jeremy Prendergast, a quiet and studious boy, came up to me. 'Thank you for a good day, Mr Sheffield.'

'That's very thoughtful of you, Jeremy,' I said. He was clutching his new reading book, *Swallows and Amazons*, the Arthur Ransome classic. 'Definitely one to enjoy. It's a wonderful story.'

He gave a shy smile. 'I read every night in bed, sir. It's like having a friend.'

I knew how he felt.

Dawn Whitehead and Susan Verity were now firm friends. 'I'm going to Susan's house to watch *Go with Noakes*,' said Dawn enthusiastically.

'He's our favourite,' added Susan.

Apparently John Noakes of *Blue Peter* fame was racing on a yacht in the Channel Islands.

'Well, enjoy it, girls, and see you tomorrow.'

''Bye, sir,' they chorused. At that moment they were completely unaware their friendship would continue for the rest of their lives. Such are the bonds that are formed during school days.

When all the children had left I began to tidy my classroom. Suddenly Audrey popped her head around the door. 'Message for you, Jack.'

'Oh, yes?'

'A teacher rang.' She checked her spiral-bound notepad. 'A Miss Clayton . . . says she's booked into the Primary Curriculum course in the Teachers' Centre.'

'Thanks, Audrey.'

I smiled.

Once my classroom was sorted, I walked across the hall to the stock cupboard and saw Izzy in conversation with our Chair of Governors, the Revd Grayson Huppleby. I wandered over to join them. A kindly fifty-eight-year-old, if a little old-fashioned, Grayson was a regular visitor to school. He was the vicar of St Luke's Church in Newbridge and ran the local youth club with Audrey. A quirky academic, he was also a Latin aficionado.

'I always call in to meet new members of staff,' he said. 'It's important you settle in well.'

'Everyone has been very helpful,' said Izzy.

'Ah . . . *"in die enim bona venimus"*,' he said with a smile.

'Yes,' said Izzy with a knowing look. 'We've both come on a good day. I did Latin at school.'

'Really, well . . . good for you,' said our surprised vicar.

Grayson looked up at me. 'Just welcoming our new music teacher, Jack. Another Latin scholar.'

'Yes, Ms Kowalski has many talents.'

Izzy studied me for a moment, a whimsical smile on her lips.

'I've seen your new timetable, Jack, and I noticed Ms Kowalski is in for three days. It's important we make the most of her obvious expertise.'

Izzy glanced at me again. 'Fortunately Jack has sorted all that for me.'

I owe you one, I thought.

The rather stilted conversation ebbed and flowed. Izzy told Grayson that she had trained at the City of Birmingham College in Edgbaston and now worked in three schools in the area as a peripatetic music teacher. 'I'm hoping to start up a school choir here in Newbridge,' she said.

'That should be wonderful and perhaps we could hear them in church at Christmas.'

'Perhaps,' said Izzy cautiously.

Grayson glanced up at the hall clock. 'Well, must go to prepare for my confirmation class. Pleased to have met you, Ms Kowalski. *Valete, amici mei.*'

'And farewell to you as well,' said Izzy without a hint of hesitation.

They shook hands and Grayson wandered off to talk to Jim in the head's office.

'Impressive,' I said. 'You handled him well.'

'Thanks, Jack. It was good of him to take time to call in, even if the Latin wasn't really necessary.'

Izzy looked at the clock. It was twenty minutes to five. 'I'm not being collected until five o'clock.'

'There's time for a coffee if you like,' I suggested.

She smiled. 'I'd like that.'

'In that case, *carpe diem* . . . and don't ask. That's about my sum total of Latin apart from my school motto.'

'And what was that?'

'*Virtutem petamus.* We seek virtue.'

She grinned. 'How disappointing.'

The staff-room was empty. I guessed everyone was busy in their classrooms.

'What do you think of Newbridge?' I asked as we settled facing each other.

She sipped her coffee thoughtfully. 'Really good. Nice atmosphere. Lots of potential for music.' Then she studied me for a moment. 'What about you? Are *you* happy here?'

Her direct questioning reminded me of someone else.

'It's a terrific school, mainly thanks to Jim. He selects

his staff very carefully to produce a team with many talents.'

'And what are *your* talents, Jack?'

'I just enjoy teaching. It's a pleasure for me to come to work. I guess English is my forte but I try to be a decent all-rounder.' I glanced at the clock. 'Who's picking you up?'

'Steve, my . . . boyfriend.'

'*Boyfriend*?'

'I'm not sure it will last.'

There was a pause while the old clock on the wall with its Roman numerals ticked round towards five.

'Sorry about that, Izzy,' I said quietly.

'I'm not,' she said in a determined voice and stood up. 'He's a bit crazy. Keeps saying he's into *sex, drugs and rock and roll*.'

I stood to face her. 'And I'm guessing that's not your scene.'

She gave me a mischievous look. 'That's right . . . I'm not into drugs.' She walked away with a confident step. 'Goodnight, Jack. See you tomorrow.'

I stared after her, captivated by this intriguing woman.

It was close to six o'clock and Jim and I were in the staff-room making a few final amendments to the timetable. The sticky labels were moved around until all the various requests had been accommodated.

'That should keep Rhonda happy,' said Jim as he stood back and took in the kaleidoscope of colour. 'I see art and craft is orange now.' Jim was always perceptive.

'Yes, it made sense.'

He smiled as he turned to leave. 'I saw you talking to Izzy. Quite a character. Looks like a really good appointment.'

As I drove home it struck me that life could be incongruous. For the past few years I had dated a few women but there had been nothing serious, no lasting commitment. I had drifted along, enjoying my work, playing rugby, reading books, pottering in my tiny garden and making meals that were either undercooked or burned. It was a simple, steady existence. What was lacking was a partner, a love life, a woman who was intriguing and exciting.

Then, like buses, two had come along at once.

I was looking forward to meeting up with Donna once again and hoped Izzy would see the timetable when she arrived in the morning.

I had made yellow the colour of music.

Chapter Two

Honour among Thieves

'Jack . . . don't you simply love Prokofiev?'

Neville Wagstaff almost swooned as we listened to *Peter and the Wolf*.

It was a special day for forty-year-old Neville. Our new sound system had arrived and he had brought in one of his precious LP records. The wonderful sound of the London Symphony Orchestra echoed around the hall. 'One of my favourites,' murmured Neville wistfully.

Neville, short, slim and prematurely balding, was one of the kindest men I had ever met. He loved teaching and used his various passions, including music, stamp collecting and cooking, to support his work. Next Monday in morning assembly his class of second-year juniors would be performing a dramatization of the famous story of the boy and the wolf with a supporting cast of various animals.

Until today Neville had always brought in his old sixties Dansette record player to support his lessons. From now on life would be different. It had taken many PTA bring-and-buy events, jumble sales and the occasional dance night to raise the funds for this state-of-the-art equipment. 'We're at the cutting edge of modern technology,' said Neville proudly. 'Isn't it wonderful?'

Jim Patterson walked across the hall with Big Frank in attendance. Jim was holding an invoice for a Linn Sondek LP12 turntable plus two large speakers. Our caretaker had helped to unload the early-morning delivery while Neville and I set it up on one of the dinner trolleys.

'So, what do you think, Neville?' asked Jim.

'Perfect, simply perfect. We'll make good use of it, starting this morning in assembly.'

Jim tapped the metal dining trolley thoughtfully. 'We could do with something more permanent than this.'

'I could knock up summat,' said Frank. 'Ah've a lot o' spare Contiboard an' a set o' castors in m'shed.'

Neville was thrilled. 'That's very kind.' He stroked the plastic lid of the record player gently. 'It deserves something special.'

'Thanks, Frank,' said Jim. 'Then we can wheel it in the stock cupboard overnight.'

I looked at the hall clock. 'Almost nine, I'll ring the bell.'

It was Thursday, 16 September and all seemed well in our world.

At morning break I was on duty while pale shafts of autumnal sunshine lit up the playground. It was relaxing leaning against the school gate, sipping coffee and watching the children. The boys were on the school field kicking a football about while the girls were skipping and playing two-ball against the wall.

It was almost time for the bell when Mrs Pauline Poskitt hurried in through the school gate with her eight-year-old son. 'Ah'm sorry our Joe's late, Mr Sheffield, but 'e went out wi' 'is dad las' night an' 'e were up 'til all 'ours.'

She pinched the end of her cigarette between finger and thumb and put it into the pocket of her coat. Then she tightened the knot of her headscarf that covered her curlers. 'Go on, gerrin t'school,' she said gruffly and pushed the boy towards the school entrance. Bristle-haired Joe was keen to get away and ran off. He was welcomed by his friends as the bell rang for the end of morning break.

'Thanks, Mrs Poskitt. We must make sure Joe doesn't miss school too often. He's a good boy and I've been told by Mr Wagstaff he's making real progress now with his reading.'

'Well, that's good. Ah do m'best but it's been 'ard when it were jus' me.'

The significance of her words struck a chord. 'I heard your husband has been released.'

'That's right, Mr Sheffield. My Norbert 'as served 'is time an' learned 'is lesson.'

'I certainly hope so.'

Norbert 'Nobby' Poskitt was a likeable rogue but also a renowned local burglar and often in trouble with the police.

'Mind you, Mr Sheffield,' said Mrs Poskitt proudly, 'everyone knows 'e never steals from 'is own, only them posh folks on t'other side of t'valley.'

'I see,' I said cautiously.

As she wandered off, she called over her shoulder, 'Ah know 'e 'as 'is faults, Mr Sheffield, but 'e gave me my Joe so 'e can't all be bad, can 'e?'

It seemed a strange conversation but Mrs Poskitt was utterly sincere.

As I walked across the playground I glanced back and saw two teenage boys across the road. They were local skinheads, dressed in scruffy jeans, heavy boots and 'Proud to be British' T-shirts. I had seen them around from time to time in Milltown with the rest of their gang, shouting out neo-Nazi slogans and causing mayhem. They were staring up at the school. When they saw me they scowled and sauntered away.

At lunchtime the teachers were relaxing and Tristan Lampwick was excited. He was going to Stratford to see the Royal Shakespeare Company's production of *Macbeth* starring Ian McKellen and Judi Dench.

'It's in that super theatre called The Other Place,' said Tristan. 'Can't wait.'

'I love Judi Dench,' said Audrey as she served up mugs of tea. 'I saw her in *Cabaret* back in 1968.'

Celestine Jolley was reading her *Woman's Own* and an article about the film star Liz Taylor. 'At least Judi Dench is settled with a nice husband. Poor Elizabeth Taylor is struggling to cope without Richard Burton.' She sighed deeply and muttered, '*Rejection* is a terrible thing.'

A few of the ladies on the staff looked at her with concern. There seemed to be more to that remark than met the eye.

Meanwhile, Katy Bell was reading her morning paper and lifted the mood. 'How about this, girls,' she said. 'There's an article here about Tom Jones.'

Rhonda's eyes lit up. 'Now there's a *real* Welshman. What does it say, Katy?'

'He's going to star in a Hollywood movie called *The Stud*. He'll be acting alongside Joan Collins.'

'She's a lucky woman,' said Rhonda wistfully.

'The film sounds a bit racy,' said Katy.

Rhonda pursed her lips and shook her head. 'In that case his mother won't approve.' The Welsh chapel that had been a focal point of her parents' upbringing occasionally shone through.

Tristan appeared to be at a loss, wondering how we had moved from *Macbeth* to a Hollywood sex romp. He sighed and called in briefly to the stock cupboard before wandering back to his classroom to put out the Cuisenaire counting rods for his maths lesson. Some days were better than others and this wasn't one of them.

At the end of school Jim called into my classroom. 'Good luck tonight with your talk, Jack. I'm sure it will go well. Sorry I can't be there. Shame it clashes with our governors' meeting.'

I looked up from marking Claire Braithwaite's long division. 'Thanks, Jim. Looking forward to it.'

'I've just had County Hall on the phone. Emily Featherstone confirmed she will be doing the introduction and there'll be technical help for your overheads. She said she's expecting a large attendance for the first teachers' meeting of the academic year.'

'Good news. I like Miss Featherstone. You may recall she interviewed me.'

Jim nodded and smiled. 'I remember it well. We're lucky to have her. Always supportive and talks sense. Anyway . . . let me know if I can do anything to help.'

When I drove home from school to shower and change for the evening event I found myself thinking about Donna. I was looking forward to seeing her again: it would be good to rekindle the friendship. However, her life had moved on and it seemed unlikely I would be part of it.

At six fifteen I left Bradley village again. It was a beautiful evening and, beyond the hedgerows, the last of the ripe barley swayed in the fields, russet gold in the early-evening light. The Teachers' Centre was already filling up when I arrived and I arranged my acetates for the overhead projector before sitting down behind a long table and facing the audience. There was a hubbub of chatter as teachers caught up with local news following the summer break. It was almost seven o'clock when I saw Donna hurry in and find a seat on the back row. She looked elegant in a neat cotton shirt and skirt. I saw her looking around the delegates and her surprise when she saw me at the speakers' table. She gave a hesitant wave and I smiled back.

Peter Wright, our local Primary Education Adviser from County Hall, stood up, tapped the microphone and surveyed the audience. 'Good evening and welcome to our first course of the academic year. I should like to extend a special welcome to teachers who are new in the area.' He nodded towards a few of the fresh-faced newcomers. 'This is a six-week course entitled "The Impact of Plowden". There is no doubt the Plowden Report of 1967 had a huge impact on our education system and that's our focus this evening. We shall begin with a plenary lecture from Miss Emily Featherstone, Deputy Education Officer, followed by two ten-minute contributions from Yvonne Stapleton, headteacher of Willow Green Infants, and Jack Sheffield, deputy headteacher of Newbridge Primary. After the refreshment break there will be group discussions and a final Q and A. So thank you for your attendance and I do hope you find the course informative and helpful. Feedback will be appreciated.'

Everyone settled for Miss Featherstone's lecture. A few keen young teachers, recently arrived from college, were on the front row, pens poised. The more experienced filled the seats at the back of the hall and looked forward to the tea break and exchanging ideas with colleagues, often the most valuable part of a teachers' meeting.

Miss Featherstone was an excellent speaker and spoke about the impact of Plowden and how we had moved from rote learning and a one-way style of pedagogy to a more child-centred approach. I was content in the knowledge it was the form of teaching we used at Newbridge. As she came to a rousing conclusion I glanced out of the window. The sun was setting and the backlit clouds were a fiery orange. The last rays lit up the room and I saw Donna in a shaft of light with her head bowed, deep in thought.

Yvonne Stapleton gave a short positive talk about teaching in a deprived area and the importance of support from Social Services. It was well received and then it was my turn. I felt confident speaking about 'Cross-Curricular Activity' and how topics can embrace meaningful maths and English along with science, art and drama. I spotted

Neville Wagstaff at the end of a row nodding his support. He was sitting next to a young man I didn't recognize with long wavy hair, high cheekbones and florid cheeks. There was a ripple of applause as I finished, followed by the scraping of chairs as teachers headed for the tea urn and Bourbon biscuits.

I joined the queue and suddenly Donna was by my side. 'Well done, Jack. I didn't realize you were going to be one of the speakers.'

'It could be you one day,' I said with a smile. 'Emily Featherstone is always on the lookout for teachers to share good practice.'

'What makes you think my work would be recognized in that way?'

'Because I know what you're like and I'm sure you're a good teacher.'

'Do you?' she asked coyly. 'Are you sure?'

'Of course.'

'Wishful thinking.'

We collected two mugs of strong tea and the obligatory biscuit and found a place to talk away from the throng. 'I'm pleased you could make it,' I said. 'I imagine it's difficult to get out much.'

'Yes, but that goes with being a mum.'

'I guess so.'

I decided to take the plunge. 'Have you time for a drink afterwards? There's a nice pub across the road.'

She looked disappointed. 'Sorry, Jack. I can't be late. Debbie is a friend of mine on the staff and lives close by. She said she would sit with Sherri but I'll need to leave straight after the Q and A.'

'Oh, I see.'

She smiled. 'Of course Sherri insists she doesn't need *baby-sitting*, as she calls it, but I feel more secure if there's an adult with her.'

'I understand.' I didn't, in fact: I was surprised at the way she seemed to be mollycoddling a thirteen-year-old. But of course it was not my place to comment.

A bell rang. 'Looks like it's time to take our places. Good to see you again, Jack.'

I watched her walk back to her seat and felt that familiar feeling of emptiness.

At the end of the evening the delegates headed for the car park, but Neville paused to talk to me. 'Well done, Jack. Super talk.'

'Thanks, Neville.'

He gestured to the man with him, the wavy-haired chap who had been sitting alongside him during the meeting. 'This is David Lovelock. He teaches French up at the secondary school.'

David was slim and youthful, and looked distinctive in an oatmeal cord suit and red knitted tie. We shook hands.

'Pleased to meet you, David.'

'Likewise, Jack. I've heard a lot about you.'

Neville smiled. 'We're both in the local Philately Society. David has a wonderful stamp collection.'

'That was one of my hobbies when I was at school,' I said. 'I wish I had continued.'

'You must come to one of our meetings,' said David enthusiastically. 'We go from one member's house to another each month. It's great fun.'

'Thanks,' I said.

'Come along, David,' said Neville, 'we must let Jack get on.' I smiled as they both hurried away in animated conversation, pleased that Neville seemed to have found a friend and fellow philatelist.

However, as I drove home, stamp collecting was far from my mind and I wondered if Donna would come to next week's meeting.

On Friday morning my telephone rang and I hurried barefoot into the hallway.

'Mr Sheffield, sorry t'ring so early.'

I looked at my wristwatch. It was 6.30 a.m. and the dawn had only just begun to light up this corner of Yorkshire. 'What is it, Frank? Is there a problem?'

'We've 'ad a break-in.'

'Oh no! Any damage? Anything missing?'

'You're not gonna like this. It's t'new sound system. All gone. Broke in t'back door and forced open t'stock cupboard. Ah've rung t'police.'

'Have you told Mr Patterson?'

''E's on 'is way.'

I took a deep breath. 'Thanks, Frank, I'll be there as soon as I can.'

A policeman was talking to Jim and Frank in the school hall when I arrived.

'We've got the details now, thanks, Mr Patterson,' he said as he replaced his notebook, 'and we'll check the stock cupboard door for fingerprints, but I can't say I'm hopeful.'

Jim sighed. 'Well, do your best and thanks for coming in so quickly.'

As he wandered off, Frank shook his head. "Scuse my French, Mr Patterson, but ah 'ope they catch the bastards. Stealing from kids . . . lowest of the low. Ah know what ah'd do to 'em.' He walked slowly back to his store cupboard, muttering and clenching his huge fists.

'That's exactly how I feel,' said Jim. 'We need to tell the staff as soon as they arrive to see if anything else is missing.'

'I'll see to that,' I said.

'They will be so disappointed,' he said, 'especially Neville. He'll be heartbroken.'

On his way home for his morning break Frank stopped on the High Street and called into the local shop, Snoddy's Stores, for cigarettes. The bell above the door rang as he walked in.

The shop owner (and would-be entrepreneur), forty-eight-year-old Gilbert Snoddy, was serving Pauline Poskitt.

Gilbert knew his customers well and slapped a packet of twenty Embassy Envoy on the counter. 'Forty pence, please, Pauline.' On the side of the packet it read: 'Middle Tar. Every packet carries a government health warning'. Gilbert saw her hesitate. 'Yer all right wi' these, Pauline, 'speshully wi' y'bein' in t'family way, so t'speak, 'cause they're *middle* tar, not like t'strong stuff you've 'ad in t'past.'

Pauline shook her head, 'Ah were thinkin' o' changing m'cigarettes. My Norbert sez ah should start smokin' Black Cat No. 9 'cause they're *low t'middle* tar.'

'Fair enough, luv, an' they're *filter-tipped*, so they're safe,' said Gilbert with a knowing nod.

'That's good to 'ear,' said Pauline.

'An' they're a lot cheaper, only thirty-three pence f'twenty.'

Pauline looked at the coins in her purse. 'Well, in that case ah'll tek two packets.'

'Meks sense, Pauline.' Gilbert reached for a second packet. 'An' 'ow's young Joe?'

'Growin' out o' shoes like there's no t'morrow an' allus inter mischief.'

'Teks after 'is dad then,' added Gilbert with a grin.

'Y'right there. Trouble allus finds 'im.'

'Ah've 'eard 'e's out now.'

'Yes, an' 'e's turned over a new leaf.'

And pigs might fly, thought Gilbert. He glanced up at Frank. 'Usual?'

Frank nodded, rummaged in his pocket, fiddled through his loose change and counted out thirty-seven-and-a-half pence.

Gilbert put a packet of twenty Players No. 6 on the counter.

'Thanks,' said Frank.

'Ah saw t'police outside school,' said Gilbert. 'What's 'appened?'

Frank shook his head. 'Break-in.'

'Oh 'eck,' said Pauline. 'Owt missin'?'

'Only t'bran'-new record player that we saved up for.'

'That's awful,' she said. 'Tekkin' from kids. What nex'?'

'No honour among thieves,' recited Gilbert.

'My Norbert would never 'a done that.'

'Yer right there, Pauline,' said Gilbert. 'Nobby never stole from his own.'

When Frank walked out on to the High Street and lit up a cigarette he paused and looked back at the school. 'Bastards,' he muttered.

At the end of the school day Nobby Poskitt walked through the school gates. Built like a stocky middleweight boxer, he had a swagger about him as he approached the boiler-house doors. Big Frank saw him coming. He closed the doors after Nobby had stepped inside. Nobby took out his packet of cigarettes. 'Fag?' Frank nodded and Nobby produced an expensive Dunhill lighter from his leather jacket. They lit up and puffed contentedly.

'Now then, Nobby. Ah'm guessin' you've 'eard t'news.'

'Tell me 'xactly what's gone missing.'

'A record player, top o' t'range by all accounts, an' a couple o' big, 'efty speakers.'

'An' you'll need 'em f'Monday, so Pauline sez. Our Joe's in a play. Summat abart chasing a wolf. Sez 'is teacher's proper upset.'

'They're *all* upset, Nobby. Parents as well. They saved up 'ard.'

Nobby weighed this up. 'Leave it wi' me, Frank. Ah'll sort it. What y'doin' t'night?'

'Nowt special.'

'Meet me outside T'Black 'Orse at closing time. Bit o' extra muscle'll come in 'andy.'

'Sounds like y'know summat.'

'Jus' kids, Frank. Need teachin' a lesson. Don't want no thievin' in our village.'

They finished their cigarettes and then Nobby walked away like a prizefighter while Frank went to empty the waste baskets from each classroom. He worked quietly. There were some things you needed to keep to yourself and this was one.

Meanwhile, it was a gloomy group of teachers that walked out to the car park. The theft of the sound system had dominated the conversation in the staff-room. Poor Neville had been distraught, Celestine had blamed it on the influence of violent television drama such as *The Sweeney* while a more forthright Rhonda had suggested that back in Wales the culprits would have been castrated.

'G'night, Mr Sheffield,' called out Big Frank after he had swept my classroom.

'Goodnight, Frank. Let's hope the police have some success.'

Frank kept his thoughts about the local constabulary to himself. He was thinking about a different kind of law enforcement.

Later that evening, back in Bradley village, I left home and walked down the High Street. The temperature had dropped and the first log fires were burning while wood smoke spiralled into a starlit sky. The trailing pelargoniums in the hanging baskets outside The Eagle had blackened and the warmth of the saloon bar was welcome. I nodded to the regulars, found a corner table and reflected on the day over a pint of Tetley's Best Bitter.

The loss of the sound system had been a devastating blow. A copy of today's *Daily Mirror* had been left on the bench seat next to me. I flicked through the pages but gave up after the first three articles provided little solace. Whilst my love life was non-existent it struck me it could have been worse. A husband in Upper Warlingham, Surrey, had not shared a bed with his wife for four months because his mother-in-law wouldn't let him in the house. Meanwhile, a £200,000 top-security detention centre was being built in Brentwood, Essex, for the youths who were out of control. I thought back to the gang of skinheads in Milltown that dominated the town centre these days and made life miserable.

I wondered if the police had made any progress but guessed they might have other things on their mind, particularly those serving in Tottenham Court Road Police Station where it was reported a thief had stolen eighteen pounds in five-pence pieces from their billiards room.

As it was Friday evening I settled down with my usual takeaway supper: fish, chips and mushy peas. I was enjoying it with my feet up on the sofa while watching an episode of *The Good Life*. Richard Briers and Felicity Kendall had been leading Penelope Keith and Paul Eddington a merry dance when the phone rang.

'Hi, Jack. Hope I'm not disturbing you.' It was Donna.

'Hello, Donna. No, of course not.' This was unexpected. 'Good to hear from you.'

'I have an invitation for you . . . but don't get too excited.'

'Let me guess, it's a school dance.'

'Sadly, no. I did say don't get excited. It's our school bring-and-buy sale tomorrow afternoon and I wondered if you would like to call in. All the staff are ringing round their friends trying to boost the numbers.'

'What time does it start?'

'Two thirty.'

'That's a shame. I play rugby on Saturday afternoons.'

'Oh, it didn't occur to me you would still be playing.'

'Why? Too long in the tooth?'

She laughed. 'Well, if you are, so am I.'

'Maybe another time,' I said.

'Yes, maybe.' She sounded disappointed.

'Shame it's not in the morning. I'm free then.'

There was a pause but she didn't take the bait. 'Never mind, Jack.'

'So, see you at the next teachers' meeting.'

'Sadly, Debbie's not available for next Thursday so I'll have to stay in with Sherri and give it a miss.'

'Well, perhaps the week after.' I was clutching at straws.

'Hope so, Jack. I'll do my best. Sorry to have interrupted your evening.'

'You didn't. It was good to hear a friendly voice.'

'Yes . . . me too.'

She sounded sad as the conversation petered out and we ended the call.

That night I was unsettled. There was a lot on my mind.

On Monday morning, when I walked out to my car, there was a special quality to the light as a golden hue lit up the September mists that cloaked the fields. My emerald-green Morris Minor Traveller with its wood frame and bright chromium grille was my pride and joy and I paused to polish the AA badge with the sleeve of my sports jacket. Next to the driveway the scent of the yellow floribunda roses was fragrant and, beneath my feet, fallen leaves swirled in an eddy of wind. The season was moving on and teardrop cobwebs shivered in the hedgerow.

When I pulled into the school car park Big Frank was waiting for me, his face wreathed in smiles. 'Mornin', Mr Sheffield. Ah'm glad yer in early. Ah've gorra nice s'prise.'

We walked into the hall where Jim Patterson and Neville Wagstaff were plugging in our sound system. Once again it was perched on a dining trolley. Jim was beaming with satisfaction while Neville looked as if all his Christmases had come at once.

'Ah rang Mr Wagstaff first thing,' said Frank. 'Ah knew 'e would be pleased.'

'This is wonderful,' I said. 'Did the police recover it?'

'No,' said Neville. 'Frank thinks the thieves had a prick of conscience and returned it.'

Jim cast a knowing glance towards Frank. 'Either way, it's great news.'

'Suddenly it were back 'ere,' said Frank, the picture of innocence. 'Ah found it as soon as ah came in, an' ah rang t'police.'

In morning assembly Neville's class provided a most entertaining performance. They clearly loved the story of 'Peter and the Wolf' and brought it to life in the inimitable style of young children.

Around a dozen parents had managed to call in and watch their children perform. It was rare to have fathers turning up but to my surprise Norbert Poskitt was sitting next to his wife and he nodded in appreciation. Mrs Poskitt had been thrilled to see young Joe, who was perfect as the cat leaping around to the sound of a clarinet. Tony Entwhistle was a creditable duck to the accompaniment of an oboe while Melanie White responded to the light refrain of a flute by flapping around as a bird. All the while a contented Neville stood guard next to the sound system, adjusting the volume to create atmosphere and smiling as the children recreated the timeless story.

Jim stood up at the end and praised the children for their excellent assembly. He also thanked Neville and drew attention to our new audio system that had been used so successfully. 'Thank you to all the parents and members of the PTA who have supported us over the years,' announced Jim, 'and for providing such a valuable educational resource to improve the work of our school.' Meanwhile, Norbert nodded in appreciation of the headteacher's words.

Gradually, class by class, the children and teachers filed out of the hall. As I was walking back into my classroom I saw Big Frank and Norbert Poskitt out of the window. They were deep in conversation by the school gate. It concluded with Frank tapping Norbert on his shoulder and shaking his hand.

Whatever they were smiling about, it was clearly a job well done.

At morning break I was on duty. Audrey had mentioned to me that Izzy had telephoned to say she had been delayed.

The local bus pulled up outside school and I saw her get off carrying a heavy shoulder bag. There was no sign of the painted Vauxhall Viva.

I waited in the centre of the playground to greet her. She approached me with her head bowed. I was shocked as she glanced up. Her eyes were red with crying. She gave me a hesitant look and shook her head. 'Don't ask, Jack. *Please . . . just don't ask.*'

Chapter Three

The Price of Wisdom

It was a pale autumn morning on Monday, 4 October and the season was turning. When I walked out to my car a faint pink glow in the east caressed the distant hills and fallen leaves, amber and gold, were scattered at my feet. As I drove out of Bradley and over the Leeds–Liverpool canal, spiders' webs laced the hedgerows and wisps of wood smoke hovered over the rooftops. It was a familiar journey, south through Milltown with its back-to-back terraced houses and then beyond to the sprawling village of Newbridge with its bustling High Street.

I was early and, as I walked into the playground, I saw Big Frank talking to Mrs Deborah Finch. Her six-year-old son, Vernon, a sickly child, was holding his mother's hand. Mrs Finch had a reputation for mollycoddling the boy. It was rumoured she rubbed his back and chest with cam-phorated oil every night.

''E's neither use nor ornament,' I heard her say as I approached. She nodded towards her husband, Arnie,

44

who was standing some distance away by the school gate, smoking a cigarette and looking thoroughly dispirited. He was wearing a suit that might have fitted him before his beer belly got in the way.

'That's 'is weddin' suit,' she said sadly. 'These days 'e only wears it when 'e's in court.'

'Good morning,' I said.

'G'morning, Mr Sheffield,' said Frank. 'Mrs Finch wants t'drop off young Vernon early.'

'That's fine, Mrs Finch. We'll look after Vernon.'

'Thank you, Mr Sheffield. Ah wouldn't ask but my Arnie's in front of t'judge this morning.'

'I'm sorry to hear that.'

'Yer not t'only one.' She sighed as if the worries of the world were on her shoulders. Then she looked down at her son and for a moment was distracted by his big toothy smile. She appeared to be thinking out loud. 'Ah'm sure one day 'e'll grow into them teeth.'

'They allus do,' said Frank with a reassuring smile. He gave me a knowing look and I guessed he was thinking the same as me. The last time we saw teeth like that was when Red Rum was in the winning enclosure at Aintree.

'Well, we 'ad better be off.' She crouched down and gave Vernon a hug. 'Be a good boy an' go wi' Mr Sheffield.'

'Ah want t'go wi' you, Mam.'

'No, y'can't.'

'Please, Mam.' He began to sniffle.

'Stop yer moanin' an' groanin'. It's silly.'

'Well, *you* moan an' groan, Mam. Ah've 'eard you.'

'What y'on abart?'

'Moanin' an' groanin', Mam. That's what y'do when m'dad's out and Uncle Terry comes round.'

Mrs Finch's face flushed and she looked up at us. 'Tek no notice of 'im. Daft as a brush. Jus' like 'is dad,' and she hurried away to the school gate.

Frank gave me a conspiratorial wink but said nothing.

I spotted a couple of our latchkey children, who had been dropped off by their working parents and would have to go back to an empty house at the end of school. 'Vernon, would you like to go and play with your friends on the field?'

'Yes, please, sir,' and he ran off.

'That Arnie's in real bother this time,' said Frank. 'It's t'bosses at t'supermarket that are tekkin' 'im t'court.'

'Why's that?'

'Well, 'e worked in Grandways labelling food. Then 'e changed labels round on tins o' dog food – swappin' 'em wi' tins o' best-quality beef stew. Friends got t'beef an' management were eatin' dog food. Bosses found out and 'e were sacked!' He grinned. 'Nowt so queer as folk, Mr Sheffield.'

'You're right there, Frank.' He set off for the boiler house and I walked into school.

In the entrance hall a distraught Izzy was talking to Audrey.

'Talk to the head,' said Audrey. 'He will help.'

'Thanks. I just need some time to sort it out.'

I saw Izzy tap on Jim's door and walk into his office. Her face was etched in concern.

'What's happened?' I asked.

Audrey shook her head. 'She'll tell you when the time's

right, Jack. It's tricky and I'm walking on eggshells.' She turned quickly and went back into her office.

In the school hall the Revd Grayson Huppleby was preparing to lead our morning assembly. He was propping up some large pieces of card that spelt out the word 'HARVEST'. I had seen this visual aid in previous years. When he removed the letter 'H' and rearranged the rest he could spell the word 'STARVE' and go on to talk about the starving people of the world.

'Good morning, Grayson.'

'Ah, hello, Jack.' He glanced up from pinning a map of the world on our portable noticeboard. 'It's that time of the year again.'

The annual harvest festival service was due to take place the following Sunday in St Luke's Church and it was always well attended.

'Yes, looking forward to it.'

'You've heard this one before, of course, but it always goes down well.' He studied me for a moment. 'You look concerned . . . and it's not about my assembly.'

I remained silent.

'Sometimes, Jack, I fear we are living in a mad world.' He nodded sagely, '*Mundus furiosus,*' he murmured. Grayson always found an inner peace with his Latin.

I decided to speak up. 'I've just passed Ms Kowalski in the entrance hall.' I considered his reaction. 'I'm concerned.'

Grayson was always perceptive. 'I guessed that was it.'

'I want to help but she refuses. Doesn't want to talk about it.'

He put his hand on my arm, ushered me to the side of the hall and spoke quietly: 'Jack, sometimes it's difficult to make the right decision. We have finite minds in a world of infinite possibilities. I have to content myself with the Book of Job, chapter twenty-eight, verse eighteen.'

'You've lost me.'

'It says, "The price of wisdom is above rubies".'

I nodded. 'I guess it is but surely we have to rely on past experiences and good advice.'

'And *intuition*, Jack. What does your heart tell you?'

'Simply to try to do the right thing.'

'So do it.' He patted me on the shoulder, smiled and walked back to the front of the hall.

Back in my classroom I thought about his words: *do the right thing*, whatever that might be.

It was shortly before nine o'clock and I was deep in thought at my desk when Katy Bell walked in. Katy taught the other top junior class and we liaised regularly on a whole range of matters.

'Hey, new haircut,' I said approvingly. It was surprisingly short on top with long strands around the neck.

'Just a different style, Jack. It's called a "lion" cut. To be honest it's easier in the shower after netball.'

It was certainly striking. 'Looks good.'

Katy was from Hornsea on the east coast of Yorkshire where she had begun her teaching career at Withernsea Primary School. She had been happy except for the open drain that had run through her classroom. While she was there she had written a school play based on Jason and the Argonauts, which had still to meet its public. Since then she had moved on to Newbridge. Her salary was £3,309 per annum and she was content in her work in the West Riding of Yorkshire.

Katy had enjoyed a string of boyfriends but none had come up to her expectations, including the latest, ironically named Jason, who, in spite of his flowing golden locks and capacity for mythical adventures, had proved to be an untrustworthy two-timer. Now she rented a two-bedroom cottage in Skipton all to herself and Jason had left on another voyage of discovery.

She put a typed sheet of notes on my desk and gave me a wry smile. 'Is it too soon to mention Christmas?'

'Well, we are still a week away from the Harvest Festival but go ahead.'

'I was thinking about our two classes teaming up for the annual Christmas entertainment.'

'Sounds good to me. What's the theme?'

'Christmas through the ages. Four playlets with, say, up to fifteen pupils in each so everyone has a speaking part. Something special for their last Christmas in Newbridge. The infants always do a Nativity, so we could perform a Dickensian Christmas, maybe two more set in the fifties and sixties when their parents were young and on up to the modern day. Just an idea at present but if I work on it we could start rehearsals after half-term.'

'Brilliant. Thanks, Katy. What can I do to help?'

'Let me think about it. In the meantime, I thought I would discuss the music with Izzy.'

I responded with caution: 'We would just have to pick the right moment.'

Katy paused, 'Jack . . . I know what's going on. I spoke

to her last Friday. Her boyfriend needs kicking into touch but, apparently, it's complicated.'

'I'm keen to help.'

'Maybe you need to keep your distance for the time being.' She glanced at her wristwatch. 'Anyway, nearly time for the bell. Thanks again. We can progress this later.'

As she hurried out I guessed she meant the Christmas drama and not the one unfolding in Jim's office.

I was soon immersed in the morning maths lesson and the properties of triangles followed by a series of Schonell Reading Tests, so it was with surprise that I heard someone practising the opening bars of 'We Plough the Fields and Scatter'. I leaned out of my classroom door and saw Celestine at the piano. The children in her class were sitting cross-legged in front of her. It meant Izzy would not be playing in assembly and I wondered about the outcome of her meeting in the head's office.

After Susan Verity rang the bell for assembly we all filed into the hall for Grayson's harvest assembly. Rhonda walked over and whispered in my ear, 'Jim's busy, Jack. Shall I do the usual announcements?'

I nodded my thanks. My mind was elsewhere.

At morning break Rhonda was sipping coffee and looking thoughtful.

'Thanks for taking the lead this morning, Rhonda.'

'I guessed you were preoccupied. Don't worry. We're all concerned about Izzy. She's putting on a brave face and doing her music lessons. I've had a word. She'll get there in the end.'

'Where is she now?'

'With Audrey having a tête-à-tête in the office.'

'I see,' I said . . . but I didn't.

Meanwhile, Diane Hardisty, our scientist on the staff, was talking to Tristan Lampwick about their favourite films.

'Well, mine is *Love Story*,' said Diane. 'I thought Ali MacGraw was wonderful with Ryan O'Neal. It was so very sad. I cried at the ending. I can still see him sitting on that bench alone in the snow. It broke my heart.'

Tristan thought he would keep to himself that *his* favourite was the film that took most money at the box office last year. He had seen *Jaws* three times and hummed the theme tune every time he had a bath.

'I agree,' he said through gritted teeth. '*Love Story* was wonderful.'

Diane gave him a sad but sincere smile, pleased she had such a sensitive colleague on the staff.

At lunchtime in the staff-room there was still no sign of Izzy.

Katy was reading an article in the *Daily Mirror* by Rachel Heyhoe Flint, the England cricketer. 'Hey, ladies, how about this? The Women's Cricket Team have been allowed to play on the hallowed turf of Lord's Cricket Ground!'

'About time too,' said Rhonda. 'Load of male chauvinists in their ivory towers.'

'Can women actually *play cricket*?' asked Tristan as he hurried out.

'And there speaks another one,' shouted Rhonda as the door closed.

'Very interesting,' said Katy with a wicked smile. 'She says here that they're not all pint-swilling lesbians!'

'Oh dear, language please,' said Celestine. 'Mixed company present.'

Neville Wagstaff, slightly bemused, looked up from his *XLCR Stamp Finder and Collector's Dictionary* before returning to the rare stamps of British Guiana.

It was almost 4.15 p.m. and Pauline Ackworth and Claire Braithwaite were deep in excited conversation as they packed their bags. They had just finished the after-school netball practice with Katy Bell.

I looked up from marking books. 'Are you in a hurry, girls?'

'Yes, sir,' said Pauline. 'Claire says you can win a prize on *Blue Peter.*'

'That's right, sir,' said Claire. 'It's a competition for the best Silver Jubilee picture. It's on tonight after *Jackanory* and we're going to plan what to do.'

Next year's Silver Jubilee celebrations seemed a long way off but I guessed it was never too soon to launch a few activities for children.

'G'night, sir,' they shouted as they ran off.

I smiled at the excitement of youth. Claire was captain of netball and the tallest girl in the school. She was a hard worker and I admired her enthusiasm. Life was exciting for an eleven-year-old when a lifetime of possibilities stretched out before her. Then there was a knock on my door. It was Katy. She was still in her tracksuit and there was a hint of concern on her face.

'Jack, I've just seen Izzy getting ready to leave.'

'How is she?'

'Not saying much. Steve will be picking her up soon. I thought I would walk out with her to the gate.'

I stood up. 'I'll come with you.'

She shook her head. 'That might not be a good idea.'

'Do we know any more about what's happening?'

'Something to do with her boyfriend. To be honest, I think she's a bit confused and maybe a little frightened.'

'Then I'm coming too.'

Katy gave me a stern look. 'Jack, I've seen you play rugby.'

'What's that supposed to mean?'

She gave me a friendly punch on the shoulder. 'You know very well what it means . . . behave!'

I picked up my old sports coat from the back of my chair, slipped it on and followed her out.

The three of us were standing by the school gate and Izzy had said barely a word. Then a familiar Vauxhall Viva appeared round the corner and pulled up with a screech of brakes. Steve opened the car door, got out and leaned on the bonnet.

'Hurry up. Put y'stuff in the back. Boot's full.' He eyed Katy warily while I was standing further away, acting the part of a passive observer. 'What's this . . . a welcome committee?'

'These are my friends on the staff.'

Steve stared at us but said nothing.

'We're just making sure Izzy is OK,' said Katy pointedly.

Steve looked Katy up and down. 'Y'need t'get back to yer rounders match, darling.'

Katy took a step forward, 'Actually, it's netball.'

'Well, ah'm not into girlie games.' He looked at Izzy. 'We need t'get going.'

Katy moved forward another pace. 'We were concerned about Izzy.'

Steve's eyes narrowed. 'No need.'

Katy glanced across at me and there was an imperceptible shake of the head. 'Well, we don't want her upset. And for your information I'm *not* your darling.'

Steve took a last drag of his roll-up cigarette and flicked it at her feet. 'In that case, you don't know what you're missing.'

Izzy stepped away from the car. 'Sometimes, Steve, you disgust me.'

He glared at her. 'Get in the car.'

'I'm not sure I want to.'

He grabbed her by the arm. 'I said *get in the car.*'

It was time to act. I stepped forward and grabbed Steve's wrist, twisted it until he let go and towered over him. 'Do that again and I'll break your arm.'

'Let him go, Jack,' said Katy, trying to stand between us. 'He's got the message.'

Izzy was looking frantic. 'What's happened to you, Steve? You didn't used to be like this.'

'Make up your mind,' he said. 'Are you coming or not?'

Katy put her arm around Izzy's shoulders, 'Listen,' she said quietly, 'you can come back with me.'

Izzy looked surprised.

'Don't worry: I've got two bedrooms and it's just for tonight. Come on. We can get some food in the pub and then you can get organized tomorrow.'

Izzy breathed deeply. 'Thanks, Katy.' She looked at Steve. 'You had better go.'

He shook his head. 'There's plenty more like you.'

I put my hand on his shoulder and squeezed. 'Time to leave.'

He brushed it away but didn't look me in the eye and I knew I had the measure of this man.

He climbed back in his car, mouthed, 'Screw you,' through the window and drove away.

We stood there as a cool breeze ruffled Izzy's hair. She turned to face the wind, held back her head and breathed deeply. Slowly a hint of colour returned to her cheeks. She looked at Katy with a relieved smile. 'Where do you live?'

'A couple of miles from Jack, up in Skipton.'

Katy lived in a lovely cottage behind the High Street near the canal basin. I had been there with the rest of the staff in the summer and we had sat outside one of the pubs and watched the colourful narrowboats drift by.

Katy was her usual assertive self. 'Jack, why don't we meet up at The Cock & Bottle?'

'I know it. On Swadford Street. Great pub. Fine, see you there.'

We walked back to our cars and set off in convoy. As I drove north, on the radio Brotherhood of Man were singing 'Save Your Kisses for Me'. When I parked in Skipton it was after six o'clock and getting close to sunset. Above me the sky turned a fiery red.

The Cock & Bottle was a perfect venue and within a short walk of Katy's home. It was a traditional pub with a stone fireplace and a wood-beamed ceiling. Katy had parked outside her cottage and they both arrived within a few minutes of me. We found a spare table and decided on the Monday special on the blackboard. It was sausage and mash and I ordered at the bar. Izzy was looking more relaxed now and she and Katy were deep in conversation when I returned with a tray of drinks, orange juice for Katy, a gin and tonic for Izzy and a pint of the local Champion real ale for me.

Around us the pub was filled with farmers, market traders and a walking group, along with a few visitors who had ventured from their narrowboats. A group of young men were playing darts and had selected ABBA's 'Mamma Mia' on the jukebox.

While we ate little was said and time seemed to move slowly like the shadow of a sundial. Katy and I were both cautious but slowly Izzy opened up. I bought a second round of drinks after our meal and she sat back and sighed: 'Thanks to both of you. I'm really grateful.'

'You're better off without him,' said Katy without hesitation. 'He was no good for you.'

Izzy nodded. 'It was good at first. Lots of fun. A bit wild. Guess I was rebelling against my parents. Then I moved in with him. It was in August he seemed to change. He'd been to the Knebworth Music Festival with some of his friends. Steve was a big fan of the Rolling Stones and they were one of the headline acts. While he was there he moved on from his usual angel dust to LSD and, lately, one or two more experimental drugs. His personality changed.'

'In what way?' I asked.

'I think you've guessed.'

It was after nine o'clock when we stood on the pavement and said goodnight. 'See you tomorrow, Jack,' said Katy.

Izzy paused and looked at me. 'Thanks, Jack.' Then she stretched up and kissed me gently on the cheek. 'You're a good friend,' she whispered.

I watched them walk away under the street lamps.

As I drove the two miles back to Bradley, above me in the vast firmament the clouds were sprinkled with silver from the light of a cold crescent moon. When I finally pulled up outside my home, on the radio Elton John and Kiki Dee were singing 'Don't Go Breaking My Heart'.

I sat there until the record ended and thought of Izzy Kowalski.

On Tuesday morning as I drove towards Newbridge the smoke from a hundred chimney pots smudged the powder-blue sky. Katy was waiting for me in my classroom. 'Guess what? I've got a new flatmate.'

'Izzy?'

'Yes, I'm really pleased and it will help with the rent.'

'That's good.'

'We talked until late and it seemed the logical solution. We're collecting her stuff after school.'

'What about Steve?'

'We won't have any trouble, Jack. You scared him off.'

'So I have my uses.'

She got up to leave. 'You could say that.' Then she paused by the door and gave me a knowing look. 'And who knows . . . one day you may understand women.'

As I sat down at my desk it occurred to me that Katy

was a great colleague and the annoying thing about her was that she was usually right.

It proved to be a busy day. The local Primary Adviser, Peter Wright, had called in to discuss our English and science schemes of work. Apart from teaching our classes it dominated the day for Diane Hardisty and myself.

I saw little of Izzy apart from catching sight of her in Rhonda's classroom. She was strumming her guitar and singing in her beautiful mezzo-soprano voice. A new copy of her *Okki-tokki-unga* music book was propped on a stand, open at number 33, 'I'm a little teapot'. The children were singing verse two:

> *'I'm a tube of toothpaste on the shelf;*
> *I get so lonely all by myself.'*

I smiled. I knew how it felt.

At the end of school Grayson called into my classroom as Peter Wright was leaving. 'Good afternoon, Peter,' he said.

'Grayson, good to see you. How are you?'

'Fine, thanks. Will I see you at woodwork class tomorrow evening?'

'Yes, I'll be there. Should finish my bookcase with a bit of luck.'

I looked up in surprise. I had no idea they both went to the same evening class. They shook hands and Peter set off for the car park and his Triumph 2000.

'Lives alone, Jack, and makes the most beautiful furniture.' Grayson studied me for a moment. 'I've been speaking to Jim. He's been following the news of Ms Kowalski with great interest. Her situation would appear to have been resolved.'

'Yes, I hope so.'

'So I called in to say well done. Your intervention worked.'

It was when he left that I thought back to Grayson's words.

Wisdom really did come at a price.

Chapter Four

Buddy Holly Spectacles

Perfect . . . absolutely perfect, I thought.

My eyesight had deteriorated gradually over recent years and, while I could read without difficulty, my long sight wasn't quite right. An optician in Skipton had checked me out and solved the problem. It was Friday, 29 October and as I looked out of my bedroom window I could see everything clearly.

It had been a reluctant dawn but now bright sunshine lit up the land and a gauze of mist was clearing from the distant hills. The trees beyond the hedgerows bared their skeletal souls and stood out with sharp clarity against a powder-blue sky. The season was moving on and, outside, russet leaves swirled across the road. The floribunda roses in the garden next to The Eagle had blackened with the arrival of early frosts while tiny creatures sought out the red hips of dog roses. Winter was coming and on this bright autumn morning I was full of anticipation.

I walked into the bathroom wearing my new spectacles

and looked at myself in the mirror. In the optician's it had been a hasty choice and I had selected the first frames that seemed to fit. It was only when I saw my reflection that the penny dropped. The heavy black frames reminded me of someone. Back in 1959 the first record I had ever bought was 'Heartbeat' by a late, great American singer-songwriter. He was staring back at me now.

It was Buddy Holly.

When I set off I turned on my car radio. Noel Edmonds introduced Thin Lizzie singing 'The Boys Are Back in Town' and I hummed along. Driving to school had suddenly become a pleasure and my vision was perfect. On the back of the bus I was following I could read every word of the advertisement for Fry's Chocolate Cream and on Newbridge High Street the poster in the doorway of Snoddy's Stores read: 'Light up the sky with Standard Fireworks'.

The previous evening I had polished my Morris Minor Traveller and Big Frank gave it an approving look as I parked in the car park.

'Yer car looks good, Mr Sheffield,' he called out. 'Younger generation don't know what polishin' is these days. When ah were in t'army y'could see yer face in m'toecaps.' As I walked closer he leaned on his broom. 'Flippin' 'eck. New specs.' He smiled. 'Well . . . good luck t'day, Mr Sheffield. You'll need it.'

'Thing is, Frank, I can see perfectly now. They've made a big difference.'

'Y'can say that again,' he said with a grin and wandered off to check the boiler.

*

It was a surprise when I walked back into the entrance hall where Katy Bell was talking to Tom Deighton. Our athletic young sports teacher was hobbling on crutches.

'Tom, what's happened?'

'Hi, Jack. Looks worse than it is. Just taking the weight off my right leg. My Achilles went last night during football training.'

'And we've got Bracken Primary turning up for netball and football matches this afternoon,' added Katy.

'What can I do to help?'

'We were hoping you could referee, Jack.'

It was usual for the sports teacher of every school to be the referee for their home games.

'No problem, Tom. I've got my sports gear in the car.'

'Thanks, Jack, and, by the way, impressive new specs.' The smile on his face suggested otherwise. He chuckled as he hobbled to his classroom.

'Take no notice,' said Katy with a grin. 'They suit you.' She stared at me and then nodded. 'Bit like Robin Day on the telly.'

'I'll take that,' I said. The renowned television journalist was famous for peering over his spectacles and making life uncomfortable for leading politicians.

'Should be a good couple of games, Jack. Bracken Primary are like us, one of the top teams in the area.'

'By the way, how's it going with Izzy?'

'Fine, a good flatmate. We get on well although she has some interesting friends.'

'Interesting?'

She smiled. 'Well, a bit crazy to be honest. Colourful,

loud and musical. She was talking about singing with a couple of the guys in The Cock & Bottle.'

'Well, she plays well and has a great voice. Could be a good idea.'

'And extra cash, Jack. She never seems to have much.'

'I wish her luck.'

Katy glanced at the clock. 'Are you doing assembly this morning?'

'Yes, usual stuff about the firework code and I'll mention the sport as well.'

'Fine, see you later and thanks again for helping out.'

I called into the school office where Audrey had opened her bottom drawer and was staring wistfully at her signed photograph of James Hunt. Last weekend he had become Formula One World Champion. I had since learned that, above her bed in her tiny cottage on the High Street, a huge poster of her hunky flaxen-haired Adonis kept her company on lonely nights.

She closed the drawer quickly, her face flushed, and looked up. 'Good morning, Jack.' Then she blinked, 'Oh . . . spectacles.' There was a moment's pause. 'They suit you,' she added kindly.

'Thank you, Audrey. I really needed them. I hadn't realized how my eyesight had deteriorated.'

'Yes, it creeps up on you. So, how can I help?'

'I'm taking morning assembly and I wondered if you had the firework code posters.'

'Yes, I'll get them for you.' She got up, opened her huge wooden cupboard and took out a large cardboard tube.

'Thanks, Audrey. We would be lost without you.'

'That's kind. Anyway, here are the posters.' She gave me a curious smile. 'You remind me of someone famous now you've got those spectacles.' She pursed her lips. 'It will come to me.'

Back in the entrance hall, Jim appeared from his office looking concerned. 'Jack, do you mind going down to the gate and checking all is OK? Just had a call from Milltown Police. Sergeant Moxon was ringing round local schools and shops to say that Wormley guy was out and about again and exposing himself. Might be worth checking he's not hanging around in Newbridge.'

Gordon Wormley was well known. Once a respectable single man and Chairman of the Newbridge Book Club, he had lived his life with a hunger for books. They were his secret companions, almost a literary love affair. Each night they provided a solace for his troubled soul. However, Gordon went off the rails after the group discussed D. H. Lawrence's *Lady Chatterley's Lover*. He read it at home while drinking a bottle of whisky and was later dismissed from the club after exposing himself in the doorway of Boots the Chemist.

Predictably a few of the less discerning villagers now referred to him as Flash Gordon.

At the school gate the children were excited. It was the last school day before the half-term holiday and Hallowe'en and Bonfire Night beckoned. My new spectacles certainly provoked a lot of interest. Tony Entwhistle and Billy Old-royd stopped in astonishment. 'Hey, sir. You've got glasses,' said Tony.

'Just like Brains in *Thunderbirds*,' added Billy, clearly trying to impress.

'No, 'is are blue,' said Tony.

'Oh yes,' acknowledged Billy, 'but if they were blue, sir, you'd look just like him.'

The boys were keen for me to resemble one of their favourite superheroes. They walked on to the playground discussing whether any other members of the International Rescue team of Thunderbirds puppets – namely, Scott, John, Virgil, Gordon and Alan – wore glasses.

Jeremy Prendergast, ten years old and bespectacled, was thrilled that his teacher was also wearing spectacles. 'Sir, I like your glasses. Just like Clark Kent. When you take them off you could be Superman. That's what I do.' He stretched out his arms and pretended to fly on to the playground.

Pauline Ackworth and Claire Braithwaite were convinced Elton John had a similar pair while Mrs Deborah Finch said it made me look more intelligent. I think she meant well.

However, not everyone was preoccupied with my new image. Mrs Doris Crabtree and her ten-year-old daughter, Kirsty, stopped to talk to me. 'Go on,' said Doris, 'y'can tell yer teacher.'

Kirsty looked up. 'We might be movin', sir.'

'Really? That's news.'

'My Danny 'as gone t'Selby t'day, Mr Sheffield,' said Doris. "E's lookin' f'work in t'new coalfield.'

'I read about it in yesterday's paper. The Duchess of Kent is doing the official opening later today.'

'That's right. Danny sez there'll be four thousan' new jobs.'

'It's a new era for coal, Mrs Crabtree. It said on the news they'll produce ten million tons of coal every year for the next forty years.'

'Ah 'ope so. That's jus' what we need . . . a job f'life.'

It had been a cause for celebration for the government. Tony Benn, Secretary of State for Energy, had been particularly vociferous when he announced that 'King Coal' was being restored to his throne.

'Well, I wish you luck, Mrs Crabtree. I hope it works out for you.'

She gave me an anxious look. 'We need this job, Mr Sheffield. Ah worry when there's no money comin' in an' m'work at 'Unter's Mill pays a pittance.'

She gave Kirsty a kiss on the forehead and walked to the bus stop and I was left to ponder on the difficulties in the lives of others.

At lunchtime I called into Tom's classroom. He was sitting at his desk marking maths books.

'How are you?' I asked.

'Fine. Everyone's been helpful and Audrey is bringing a school lunch for me.'

'Anything else you need?'

'There is something, Jack. Can you get a bag of oranges from the shop for half-time in the football? They need cutting up and we give a quarter to each boy. Audrey will give you some petty cash.'

'Yes, I'll go straight after my lunch.' I looked at him. He wasn't his usual ebullient self and was obviously in discomfort. 'How are you getting home?'

'My girlfriend is picking me up after the game.'

'Fine. Catch you later.'

When I walked into Snoddy's Stores Gilbert was serving Mrs Sylvia Ackworth.

'What's it t'be, Sylvia?'

'A tin o' Heinz Spaghetti Bolognese an' another one o' Heinz Ravioli please, Gilbert. Ah'm goin' all Italian. My Eddie likes a bit o' foreign.'

'Comin' up, Sylvia,' and Gilbert slapped two tins on the counter. 'An' what about a nice sweet course? Mebbe a tin o' pears.'

'Sounds lovely.'

Two more tins appeared as if by magic.

'What's that, Gilbert?'

'Summat special,' he said, ever the entrepreneur. 'A nice tin o' Nestlé's Cream an' ah'll tell y'a secret.' He leaned forward as if he was passing on the plans for the D-Day invasion. 'F'*thick* cream jus' put it in t'fridge for an 'our. Then, wi'out shakin' it, pour off the whey and yer left wi' t'thickest cream on God's earth.'

Sylvia was clearly impressed. 'Well y'can't say fairer than that.'

She paid and hurried back to the fabric shop at the end of the High Street where she worked as an assistant.

Next in the queue was Mrs Marie Whitehead, mother of Dawn in my class and a renowned local gossip. 'Just a loaf an' a tin o' peas, please, Gilbert.' She stared after Mrs Ackworth as the bell rang over the door and shook her head. 'Ah'll tell y'summat f'nowt.'

'An' what's that, Marie?'

'She treats 'er 'usband like a skivvy.'

'Does she?'

Marie nodded. 'Mind you, they say 'e's a sandwich short of a picnic so no s'prises there.'

'Ah see,' said Gilbert and looked at me. 'Sorry t'keep y'waitin', Mr Sheffield.'

Mrs Whitehead didn't take the hint. She paid and Gilbert counted out the change from the till. 'Well, ah'll get off,' she said. She put the coins in her purse and the shopping in her bag but it was clear there was more to come. 'Problem is she teks after 'er sister.'

'Really?' said Gilbert. 'What's she like?'

'Sex-mad.'

'Oh, ah see.'

She lowered her voice, 'Ah'm not one f'gossip, Gilbert, but ah've 'eard she likes a bit o' 'anky-panky . . . so they say in T'Black 'Orse. In fac' they say there's not much she doesn't know in t'bedroom department.'

'Ah thought she worked in soft furnishings,' replied Gilbert with feigned innocence.

Mrs Whitehead looked puzzled as she left and Gilbert gave me a wink.

'Just a bag of oranges for the football team, please, Gilbert.'

'It's usually young Mr Deighton who comes in f'these.'

'He was injured at football training.'

'Nothing serious, ah 'ope.'

'No, he'll be fine with some rest.'

'Oh well, pass on m'best wishes.' He put eight oranges in a bag. 'On the 'ouse, Mr Sheffield,' he said when I offered to pay.

'Thanks, Gilbert. That's very generous.'

'Got t'support t'football team,' he called after me. 'Ah were t'school goalie back jus' afore t'war. Could've been a professional but ah weren't tall enough. They called me t'pocket rocket.'

'That reminds me, I'll be back for some fireworks.'

'Big boxes are t'best value, Mr Sheffield,' he called after me.

When the bell went for afternoon break the boys and girls in the top two classes who were playing football and netball hurried away to unpack their sports gear from their duffel bags. Those not in either team could go outside to watch. Meanwhile, I changed into my tracksuit, collected my rugby boots from my car and walked on to the school field. The football match was due to kick off at 3.00 p.m. and a crowd of parents had begun to gather. I gave my spectacles a good polish with my handkerchief before putting them back on.

I shook hands with Mike Foster, the teacher from Bracken School; it was clear he and Tom were good friends. Both played for Newbridge United, the local football team. 'Thanks for running the game, Jack,' said Mike. He was taller than me and played centre half while Tom was the centre forward and top goal-scorer.

I was used to refereeing games and tried to support both teams as they passed the smaller size four ball around the pitch. It was clear the boys were well coached and there was little to choose between them. At half-time, with the score 1–1, they collected their piece of orange and Tom gave a team talk to the Newbridge lads. The same was happening further down the touchline and it was obvious that there was a friendly rivalry between the teams. Even so, appropriate manners prevailed and the parents were in good spirits as they cheered the boys back on to the pitch for the second half.

But then Gary Cockroft scored a second goal for Newbridge and I heard a harsh voice shout, 'C'mon, ref. It were off-side.'

Two scruffy men were standing on the far touchline away from the other parents. Each was swigging from a can of beer.

I glanced in their direction and one of them gave me a V sign. 'C'mon, Bracken. Yer playin' against twelve men.'

I was becoming annoyed but realized I had to remain professional.

With five minutes to go the netball match on the playground ended and Katy and the girls in their brightly coloured bibs walked over to the field to watch the football.

It was when I blew my whistle for a foul by one of the Bracken boys that the trouble started. 'Gerra grip, ref. Yer bloody rubbish.'

'Yurra cheatin' bastard,' added his friend for good measure.

That was it. The final straw. I blew my whistle and stopped the game. I didn't want the boys to hear this abuse.

I walked over to Mike Foster. 'We need to deal with these guys or I'll have to abandon the game.'

'Sorry about this, Jack. One of them is a parent. We banned him a while back. Don't know the other one. I'll see if I can shut him up while you finish the game.'

Mike didn't have much luck but the game was nearly over and we made it to the final whistle.

Mike came back and shook hands with Tom. 'Good game, Tom. You deserved to win.'

They returned to the playground to check that each boy was collected by a parent.

Meanwhile, the two strangers strode across the pitch to confront me.

Katy put a hand on my chest. 'Jack, don't rise to the bait.'

'I could flatten them both,' I muttered.

'I know . . . but you mustn't.'

'Yer bloody clueless,' yelled one.

'Yurra four-eyed git,' shouted the other.

'NO HE'S NOT!' shouted a female voice. 'That's no way to behave in front of the children, Mr Snaith. Now be sensible and get off home before you cause a scene.'

The two men stepped back in astonishment at being confronted by this tall, determined woman. It clearly worked and they sloped off.

'Well done,' said Katy. 'You see, Jack, it just needed the *female* touch.'

I stared in surprise. 'Donna, what are you doing here?'

She smiled. 'I've just taken over netball. Jill Snedley is on maternity leave.'

Katy looked at us curiously. 'You know each other?'

'Yes,' I said. 'Donna was one of the parents at my last school.'

'And Jack helped me to become a teacher,' added Donna.

'Sounds a good story,' said Katy. She nodded towards Kirsty Crabtree, who was standing close by with her mother. 'Anyway, must have a quick word with Kirsty's mum; I've heard they're moving house. Pleased to have

71

met you, Donna, and good luck with the netball. Contact me any time if I can help.'

They shook hands and Katy walked back to the playground.

I looked back at Donna. She was wearing a tracksuit that emphasized her slim figure. 'Good to see you again.'

'You too, Jack. Couldn't miss the chance to come to your school.'

Parents were drifting away, some on foot, others in cars.

'Are you hurrying off?'

'Not specially. My car is here in your car park and I'll need to get changed at some point.'

'What about Sherri?'

'She's away. My mum collected her for a sleepover with friends.'

There was a pause as we stood there facing each other. It was getting dark and the last rays of the dying sun dipped below the golden rim of the Pennine Hills.

'Maybe we could get a bite to eat.'

She gave me that familiar direct stare. 'Why not?'

'Where would you like to go?'

'Not my village, people talk.'

'Is that a problem?'

'Not really . . . but we have a choice.'

'Well, there's The Eagle in my village.'

'What's local? I passed a couple of pubs on the High Street.'

'Yes, there's The Black Horse but that can be a bit rough.' In the near distance the bright orange lights of The Crooked Billet were shining. I pointed it out. 'That one is much better, Donna, and serves decent meals. We could walk from here.'

'Fine. Can I get changed in school?'

'Yes, I'll show you where. I've got some clearing up to do in my classroom so let's meet in the entrance hall.'

It was much later when we finally walked down the High Street. Donna looked great in a green denim skirt, an oatmeal polo-neck jumper and a stylish brown leather coat. Her blonde hair curled softly over her ears. She wore the merest hint of lipstick and her cheeks were flushed in the cold night air. When we walked into The Crooked Billet the television behind the bar was on with the sound turned down, while on the jukebox Dusty Springfield was singing 'I Only Want To Be With You'.

We found a corner table where we could talk. I ordered a glass of red wine for Donna and a half of Chestnut for me plus two of the specials: beef pie, mashed potatoes and carrots with piping hot onion gravy. It was a feast on a cold night.

When we had finished our meal we sat back and relaxed.

'Thanks for your intervention at the football. You certainly put that idiot in his place.'

'I've come across him before. An abusive drunk. I didn't know his friend.'

'If he behaved like that up at Wharfedale they would kick him out.'

She nodded, sat back and sipped her wine. 'So, you're still enjoying your rugby.'

'Yes, but at thirty-one there're a lot of young bucks wanting to take my number-six shirt.'

She smiled. 'We're getting older now, Jack. Turning thirty was significant for me. Life started getting serious.'

I sighed deeply and stared into her blue eyes. 'I know what you mean.'

She spoke softly: 'What are you thinking?'

'Just how we used to be.'

Donna sighed and shook her head. 'Words have consequences, Jack.'

'What do you mean?'

'You said there was someone else. Someone special.'

'We were younger, much younger. We're different people now.'

'Yes, we are. I have a good job and a teenage daughter.'

'You're lucky.'

'I suppose I am.'

'What about her father?'

'Barty Withinshaw? Just a wild time in my life. I was seventeen and off the rails.'

'Does she ever ask?'

'Occasionally. Wants to know what he was like.'

'What do you say?'

'That he was good-looking and fun; well, most of the time. I don't tell her that he was a lying cheat and sometimes unpleasant.'

'I see.'

She stared down at her wine and looked thoughtful. The television above the bar flickered on silently, but no one seemed to notice. 'So what about you, Jack? Are you still in your bungalow up near Skipton?'

'Yes, I'm pleased I made the move. I'm in a lovely village and the Dales are on my doorstep.'

'I go to the coast occasionally with Sherri. She loves it . . . Bridlington, Scarborough, Whitby.'

'We're lucky living here. God's Own Country.'

'So they say . . . well, most days.' She looked at her watch. 'Anyway, I ought to be getting back.'

I decided to speak up. 'Maybe we can meet up again now the teachers' course is over.'

'Maybe,' she said quietly and she put on her coat.

As we were leaving Bryan Ferry was singing 'Let's Stick Together' on the jukebox and I wondered if Donna was thinking the same.

Outside the night was cold and we walked briskly back up the High Street towards school. I paused for a moment to glance in the brightly lit television shop window while Donna walked on and was a few yards in front of me. As she passed the betting-shop doorway a man suddenly stepped out in front of her and pulled open his raincoat. Beneath it he was wearing a pullover and shoes and socks. Nothing else. All that nature endowed, and there was little of it, was revealed for all to see.

Donna's reaction was both swift and unexpected. She burst into laughter. 'Put it away, you silly man. It's pathetic.'

Gordon Wormley was stunned and closed his coat quickly. With an astonished look at Donna and a frightened gasp as he spotted me close behind he ran off down the street.

Donna had handled the moment well but I guessed she might be upset. 'Are you OK?' I asked quietly.

'I'm fine.' She gave a sad smile. 'Pity that he feels the need to do something like that.'

'Oh dear,' I said.

'What?'

'Just thinking about my new specs.'

Donna looked puzzled, 'Why?'

'Well, they give me absolutely perfect vision and that was something I would have chosen not to see.'

'Yes, not a pretty sight. Will you tell the authorities?'

'Definitely. The head told me the police had been in touch to warn us that Flash was on the prowl again. Fortunately I know the sergeant at Milltown police. An old rugby friend. I'll ring now from school.'

'Flash?'

'His name is Gordon.'

'I get it.' She shook her head and smiled. 'Perfect name.'

As we stood in the car park the school seemed still and sepulchral, a monochrome world of light and dark under the dim crescent moon. Above our heads a barn owl, like a pale spirit of the night, flew by towards the school bell tower.

Donna took out her keys and unlocked her Mini Clubman Estate. 'Well, thanks, Jack. Good to talk.'

'Yes, for me too.'

There was a moment's hesitation as we looked at each other. Then, unexpectedly, she leaned forward and kissed me on the cheek. 'Goodnight, Jack.'

'Goodnight, Donna.'

She sat in the driver's seat and looked up at me. 'And, by the way . . . love the Buddy Holly spectacles.'

I watched her drive away and smiled.

Chapter Five

Ashes in the Wind

It was an iron-grey morning on Friday, 5 November and I had driven into Newbridge to help with the PTA Annual Bonfire. There was a large area of spare ground beyond the school football field and during the past week parents and villagers had built a huge bonfire. All the staff supported the event and, traditionally, Audrey and Rhonda and members of the PTA organized refreshments. Izzy and I were on the list to serve on the hot soup stall. Last night Jim had telephoned to ask me to collect a few more rockets on the way in and I pulled up at the top of the High Street.

When I walked back towards Snoddy's Stores I met Rhonda and Audrey carrying large shopping bags.

'Good morning. Do you want a hand?'

'Morning, Jack,' said Rhonda. 'No, we're fine. It's just the bread buns for the sausage rolls.'

'And we've ordered another basketful for your soup stall,' added Audrey.

'Thanks. Jim asked me to get a few more fireworks.'

'OK,' said Audrey. 'See you later.'

'Forecast is good, no rain,' said Rhonda. 'This mist will clear so we'll be fine.'

'By the way, Jack,' added Audrey with a wry smile, 'it's Gilbert's daughter looking after the shop . . . so good luck.'

Outside the stores and beneath a huge poster that read 'Remember, remember the fifth of November, gunpowder, treason and plot', Tony Entwhistle and Billy Oldroyd were staring in the window at the display of fireworks. The two boys were excited.

'What y'got so far, Billy?' asked Tony.

'Loads,' said Billy with a smile. 'Two Roman Candles, a Silver Rain, Coloured Fire, Catherine Wheel and a rocket.'

'That's brilliant. Ah'll bring mine t'your 'ouse,' said Tony. 'Ah've got some real noisy ones, a Jack in the Box, a Fireball an' a Super Sonic Bang.'

'Flipping heck,' said Billy, clearly impressed.

Tony counted his change. 'M'mam wants me t'get summat for m'little sister.'

'Sparklers for girls,' said Billy with utter conviction, 'definitely not bangers.' Tony nodded knowingly in agreement. In Newbridge male chauvinists started young.

I followed them into the shop while they bought a packet of sparklers and, in their view, a *gentle* Silver Fountain. Even at the tender age of eight the two intrepid friends had clearly established the pecking order of gender-related fireworks.

Short, plump and uninterested in life around her, seventeen-year-old Michelle Snoddy was behind the counter. The current number-one record, Pussycat's 'Mississippi', was playing on her Sony transistor radio propped on the shelf next to a box of Smith's Square Crisps.

When she saw me she turned down the volume. "Ello, Mr Sheffield.'

'Good morning, Michelle. How are you today?'

'Jus' middlin'. Nowt special. M'dad's doin' deliveries,' she said by way of explanation. It was well known and much to Gilbert's dismay that Michelle was never keen to work in the shop. In fact, to be precise, Michelle was never keen to work. She continued to file her nails as she waited for me to speak.

'I'd like a box of fireworks, please. I saw one in the window at two pounds.'

She nodded towards the display case on the other side of the shop. "Elp y'self,' and turned up the volume once again.

I selected a box of Standard Fireworks and two huge rockets at the exorbitant price of fifty pence each. When I took them to the counter Michelle took out her Casio calculator. She was clearly struggling as she tapped in the numbers.

'It's a box at two pounds, Michelle, and two rockets at fifty pence each.' I put three pounds on the counter and waited an age for her to reach the same amount after a couple of failed attempts.

'Yeah, that's, er, three poun'.'

She put the money to one side instead of entering it into the till and turned the volume up even louder. I left her applying mascara and humming along to the Wurzels singing 'The Combine Harvester'.

*

Back in the school hall, fifty-five-year-old Mrs Clarissa Peacock, Honorary Chair of the PTA, was holding forth and Jim was listening patiently. She was dressed in a grey winter coat and a black hat complete with an impressive six-inch pin. Tall and with a sallow, truculent face, she often spoke as if she had swallowed an alternative dictionary. Her long-suffering husband, the diminutive and brow-beaten Gerald, as always, was by her side. He had the demeanour of a whipped dog. There was no doubt that Mrs Peacock considered herself to be a cut above the proletariat in Newbridge village. After all, as she constantly reminded us, her father had been the manager of the Midland Bank in Milltown.

'I can assure you, Mrs Peacock,' said Jim with the patience of a saint, 'that Miss Fazackerly has been her usual efficient self and has produced this list.'

Clarissa proceeded to study it with an occasional shake of the head. 'I have no wish to prevaricate but to put so young a man as Mr Lampwick in charge of such a popular stall as Bonfire Toffee could be interpreted as an incautious decision.'

Gerald leaned over and glanced at the list. 'Well, my dear, it would appear he has Mr Wagstaff alongside him on the Yorkshire Parkin stall, which would deter any ambiguity of purpose.'

It was at times like this that Jim and I were aware we were in the presence of a couple who spoke a different language.

Mrs Peacock gave her husband a withering look. 'My husband has a capacity for equivocation.'

Gerald knew when he was beaten, 'Apologies, everyone. I have become accustomed to the fulminations of

Mrs Peacock,' he responded bravely, 'but I am sure she is right.'

Clarissa gave him a look that would have turned most men to stone. However, Gerald, though hen-pecked, had a core of stoicism. During the war they had lived in Stoke Hammond in Buckinghamshire and Gerald had worked at the Hoover factory. When he returned home each evening he had walked with his briefcase over his head for fear of falling shrapnel. Such was the sharpness of his wife's tongue, there were days when he would have preferred to have slept in the office air-raid shelter. Now they wandered off with Mrs Peacock muttering and Mr Peacock following in her wake.

'How on earth does she get voted in every year as Chair of the PTA?' I asked.

Jim sighed. 'It's a mystery. I think she canvasses for votes and it's tough to say no to her. Fortunately the rest of the PTA do a great job.'

As I walked into the staff-room it occurred to me that I had learned so much from Jim. He always showed calm and assured leadership and was sympathetic to the needs of each member of staff. He was also a past master at dealing with awkward parents.

In the staff-room Izzy and Katy were admiring Neville's huge tin of scrumptious parkin. Sticky, moist and tasty, it was perfect for cold nights and bonfires.

'Have a sample,' said Neville, clearly proud of his creation. He collected half a dozen small plates from the staff-room cupboard and sliced up a few generous pieces.

'Delicious,' said Katy. 'You must give me the recipe.'

'Well, I use oats of course to make sure it's *traditional* Yorkshire parkin and there's plenty of treacle, ground ginger and nutmeg.'

'Perfect, Neville,' said Izzy. 'You have a rare talent.'

Neville blushed. 'It's just that I've always loved cooking and baking. I find it satisfying.'

Rhonda and Audrey came in. 'Oh, what have we missed?' said Rhonda.

Audrey smiled. 'Ah, Neville's parkin. If it's as good as last year we're in for a treat.' She prepared some steaming mugs of coffee while we relaxed amidst the camaraderie of friends.

By mid-afternoon all was ready and the staff departed. The school was quiet once again as we sought refreshment and an opportunity to prepare for the busy evening ahead. It was a time of contrasting conversations.

Izzy and Katy were sitting in The Cock & Bottle in Skipton, drinking draught beer and eating fish, chips and mushy peas. The television behind the bar was on low volume for those who wanted to listen to the BBC's *Pebble Mill*. However, Izzy and Katy were discussing a topic that was popular with both of them: namely *men*.

'I'm seeing Mike Foster tonight at the bonfire,' said Katy.

'I think you've mentioned him,' said Izzy.

'He's the teacher from Bracken School. I met him last month. He plays football with Tom.' It was as if she was thinking out loud between the beer and the food. 'A really nice guy. Unexpected. Small steps. You know how it is. We just went for a drink and hit it off.'

Izzy smiled. 'Sounds good.'

'He may stay the night.'

Izzy gave a wicked grin. 'I promise not to get in the way.'

Katy looked across the table at her friend. Izzy looked more relaxed these days, hair dishevelled but clearly content with her life. 'So what about you? Steve is long gone, thank goodness. Anyone on the horizon?'

Izzy put down her knife and fork and drained her glass. 'Not sure, to be honest. There is someone but it's probably a non-starter. Even so, I do like him.'

'Go on.'

Izzy cupped her hands under her chin and stared out of the window. 'Not sure.'

'Why?'

'Well, I think he likes me but I don't want to spoil a good relationship.'

'In what way?'

'He's almost *too* nice. Steady and safe.'

'So *definitely* not your type.'

'It's just he's a good guy, completely the opposite of Steve. Good-looking in a quirky sort of way.'

'Go on then, I give in.' Katy picked up the glasses and stood up. 'I'm going to get another couple of drinks. So put me out of misery and tell me. Who's this mystery man?'

There was a long pause.

Izzy took a deep breath. 'Well . . . it's Jack.'

Katy sat down again and shook her head.

It was an impulse. Back in Bradley village I picked up the phone and rang Donna.

It took a while for an answer. There was chatter in the background.

'Hello?'

'Donna. It's Jack.'

'Hi, this is a surprise.'

'How are you?'

'Fine. Sherri has a friend from school staying over. We've got a few fireworks to set off in the back garden. What about you?'

'I'm helping out with our PTA Bonfire in Newbridge. It's usually a good event. If you want to get out with the girls you're welcome to come along.'

'Ah, I see. Might be tricky with a couple of teenagers in tow.'

'I understand but maybe you would all enjoy it.'

'Thanks, Jack. I'll talk to them.'

'And it would be good to see you.'

There was a slight pause. 'As I said. Not sure what the girls will want to do. Can we leave it for now?'

'Of course. Just turn up if you change your mind.'

'OK, Jack. Sorry but must rush. I've got some soup on the stove.'

'That's what I'll be serving tonight at the bonfire.'

'Well, good luck and thanks for ringing. Bye.'

I replaced the receiver and walked into my silent kitchen.

Audrey and Grayson were in Audrey's cottage drinking tea from china cups and enjoying slices of her Dundee fruit cake.

'Well, I do think we are well prepared for this evening,' said Grayson.

'The staff and PTA have worked very hard,' said Audrey.

Grayson sipped his tea and looked at the sideboard next to him. 'Those are wonderful.'

On a series of shelves above the sideboard Audrey had a collection of hand bells. They were an eclectic mix of designs in brass, glass, porcelain and pottery. It had been an interest for most of her adult life and included many visits to the cathedral cities of England. Most weekends she would dust them carefully and rearrange them. It was a labour of love.

'Thank you, Grayson, they really are my pride and joy.'

'And the paintings are exceptional.'

The walls of her tiny lounge were filled with a selection of colour-by-numbers paintings. Frans Hals's *The Laughing Cavalier* hung alongside John Constable's *The Hay Wain*. Pride of place above the mantelpiece was given to Leonardo's *Mona Lisa*.

'I'm halfway through *The Last Supper* at present.'

'Really?'

'Yes, but I'm struggling with the right colour for Judas Iscariot's face.'

Grayson wasn't sure whether to offer a suggestion or simply move on. He chose the latter. 'It's important to have a creative hobby.'

'Yes, I do try and it's good to leave school behind for a short while.'

'I'm sure it can dominate your life on occasions.'

'Perhaps, but I see it as my Christian duty to help the children and support Newbridge.'

'Of course,' said Grayson, hoping there might be

another slice of the delicious cake coming his way. 'Just think, Audrey,' he mused, 'when we were young we believed in a Christian Commonwealth.'

'I sometimes think we were dreamers but I don't lose hope.'

'Faith, hope and charity,' said Grayson recalling 1 Corinthians 13.

Audrey poured another cup of tea through her silver tea strainer. She added milk from a china jug and two lumps of sugar while they settled back once more.

'Wonderful cake,' said Grayson appreciatively and with no little anticipation.

'Thank you but not in the same league as Neville's, of course. His cakes are a work of art.'

'It's good that *he* has hobbies as well.'

'And ones that benefit school. He's started to do cookery lessons with the children in his class. They made an apple tart last week. It was a sight to behold.'

'That's very gratifying.' He stirred his tea thoughtfully. 'I heard a story about Neville from one of our congregation. Just idle gossip, I presume, but nevertheless it can be a little unsettling.'

'What do you mean?' asked Audrey, even though she knew exactly what he meant.

'Just rumours about his personal life.'

'Neville is one of our finest teachers,' said Audrey firmly. 'I do hope you said as much to whoever it was.'

Grayson's face flushed and he drank his tea quickly. 'I'm sure I did.'

The clock on the mantelpiece chimed four times and Audrey smiled gently. 'More tea, vicar?'

'Er, yes, please.'

She didn't offer a second slice of cake.

Meanwhile, Rhonda and Celestine were in The Copper Kettle Tea Rooms on Newbridge High Street enjoying a quiche salad and a pot of tea.

'I do like your outfit, Celestine,' said Rhonda. 'Really suits you.'

'Thank you. I saw it in my *Woman's Weekly*.' Celestine had unbuttoned her knitted cardigan to reveal a stripy cheesecloth shirt that went well with her cotton twill skirt. 'I thought I would make a bit of an effort for tonight.'

'I've gone for warmth,' said Rhonda bluntly. She was wearing a tweed two-piece suit over a thick polo-neck jumper. 'It's from my catalogue.'

'Oh, which one?'

'Empire Stores.'

'I have Kay's Catalogue,' said Celestine with pride. 'It has a thousand pages.'

Rhonda was unimpressed. 'Well, mine is fastest for delivery, gives you a hundred and four weeks to pay plus ten per cent cash commission.'

Celestine knew when to concede defeat. 'Shall we finish off with a hot buttered crumpet?'

Rhonda smiled. It was good to be top dog of the infant department.

At precisely seven o'clock it was Jim's task as headteacher to light the bonfire. He held a long stick with rags that had been soaked in petrol tied around the top. He walked forward with great ceremony as if he was about to light the

Olympic flame. After thrusting it into the centre of the brushwood at the base, he stepped back quickly as the flames rose through the stacked timbers.

It coincided with the first of Tom Deighton's rockets. With a roar and a bang it lit up the ink-black sky in an explosion of colour. Around three hundred people had turned up for this annual event, mainly parents, grandparents and children, and the atmosphere was friendly and relaxed. Billy Oldroyd was thrilled to hear from Joe Poskitt that Guy Fawkes was a Yorkshireman. However, he was less enthused that his mother had forced him to wear a multi-coloured balaclava along with a long scarf that would have rivalled the one worn by Tom Baker in *Doctor Who*.

Sylvia Ackworth was the first in the queue for a cup of soup and a bread roll. 'What's the soup?' she asked bluntly.

'Chicken, Mrs Ackworth,' answered Izzy.

'Nowt else?'

I stirred the steaming contents of the huge cauldron, a contribution from the local Scout group. 'No, that's all we've got.'

'It comes with a free bread roll,' said Izzy eagerly.

'Ah'll jus' 'ave a bread roll then.'

She picked one up from the wicker basket and walked away.

'Maybe we need to improve our sales technique,' I said and Izzy gave me a dig in the ribs.

It always struck me that this was a strange celebration: remembering the night in 1605 when Guy Fawkes and his fellow conspirators attempted to blow up Parliament. However, it was an opportunity to spend time with Izzy, who was always good fun these days.

Soon we were doing a roaring trade on our hot-soup stall. Izzy looked good in a green duffel coat and her Doc Marten boots. The firework display continued and parents wandered off to watch the spectacle as rockets lit up the sky and a giant Catherine Wheel whirled on the cross-bar of the football posts.

Izzy moved closer as we sipped our mugs of chicken soup. Her shoulder brushed against my arm. 'Like the perfume,' I said.

'Charlie by Revlon, Jack. Good of you to notice.'

'I like it.'

She studied me for a moment. 'You're different to other men I've known. You *notice* things.'

'Thanks.'

'And you listen.'

'Really? Isn't that normal?'

'Not usually with men.'

'I'll take that as a compliment, shall I?'

She put down her soup and turned to face me. 'If you don't mind me asking, why haven't you got a partner?'

'Who says I haven't?'

'I would know,' she said with a mischievous smile.

'Perhaps I've never found the right one.'

She stared up at me. 'Like me. I've not had much luck.'

'You will one day, Izzy. You're a dynamic woman. I guess Steve turned out to be a disappointment.'

She nodded. 'He was.'

'Then you're better off without him.'

'Very true – and he's found someone new, so I've heard.' She sighed. 'I pity her.'

'I suppose it depends on what you're looking for.'

There was a long pause and her grey-green eyes remained looking up into mine. 'Perhaps someone like you.'

This was unexpected.

Suddenly our private reverie was disturbed. 'Two soups, please, sir,' asked a smiling Susan Verity with Gary Cockroft in close attendance. We watched them walk away into the darkness.

'They look close,' said Izzy.

I shook my head. 'But they're only eleven.'

'Nothing wrong with boys and girls being really good friends, Jack, even at eleven.' She smiled and squeezed my hand.

It was at that moment Donna arrived and I wondered if she had noticed.

I hoped she hadn't.

'Hi, Jack, three soups please.'

'You made it. Good to see you.'

'I've got Sherri and her friend with me. They're loving it.' She pointed towards the two tall teenagers engaged in conversation with a few girls they recognized from school.

I began to ladle hot soup into large mugs. Donna was looking curiously at Izzy. 'Donna, this is Izzy, our music teacher.'

'Hello, Izzy, pleased to meet you.'

'Likewise,' said Izzy and leaned over the trestle table to shake hands. 'You obviously know Jack.'

Donna gave a wry smile. 'Yes, we go back a long way.'

Izzy nodded with cautious acknowledgement.

'Donna,' I asked, 'do you want a hand with the soup?'

'We're fine, Jack.' She called out to the girls and they hurried over.

'Sherri, do you remember Mr Sheffield? He was very helpful to us when he taught at Heather View.'

Recognition gradually dawned and Sherri smiled. 'Yes, sir. I was sad when you left.'

'Good to see you again, Sherri.'

She picked up her mug of soup and passed another to her friend. 'This is Georgie. She's a friend from school.'

'Are you enjoying The Ridge?' I asked.

'It's brilliant,' said Georgie. 'We've got great teachers.'

'Are you doing music?' asked Izzy.

'Yes,' they both chorused. 'With Mr Valentine,' added Sherri.

'I know him,' said Izzy. 'You're lucky.'

Donna took out her purse. 'No, these are on me,' I said.

'Thanks, Jack. Catch you later. Come on, girls. Let's enjoy the fireworks.'

I turned to Izzy. 'Donna teaches at Bracken.'

Izzy stared after her.

By mid-evening we had sold all the soup and cleaned up. I was carrying our trestle table back to a farm trailer when I heard Donna calling out. 'I enjoyed the evening, Jack. Many thanks for the invitation. The girls loved it.'

'Thanks for coming. It was good to see you.'

'Do you need a hand clearing up?'

I looked around the field. There were twenty or thirty parents and PTA members carrying tables, pots and plates. 'Thanks, but it looks like it's all in hand.'

'Well, we ought to get off.' There was a moment's hesitation but with two teenagers in attendance Donna decided to forgo a peck on the cheek.

'I'll ring,' I said as they set off.

'Do that,' she said and they disappeared into the darkness.

On Saturday morning I looked out of my bedroom window. A weak sun was hidden by leaden clouds and a cold mist covered the distant land. Tom and I had offered to help Jim and members of the PTA to do some clearing up on the bonfire field. After a shower I rummaged in my sock drawer. There were miscellaneous cards and letters tucked away in the back corner and I took them out. There was my last birthday card from my mother, an Easter card from my Aunt May and a couple of receipts from the rugby club.

At the bottom of the pile I found what I was looking for. It was an envelope I had not looked at for many years. Inside was a photograph. It was from Donna and dated 24 July 1970. I remembered it well. It had been my last day at Heather View Primary School. Donna had received a letter of acceptance for her teacher-training course. I stared at this younger version of her. She was wearing a smart two-piece business suit and standing outside Bretton Hall College. The message on the back read: 'Thank you, Jack, for changing my life. Love, Donna x'. I took it downstairs and propped it on my hall table.

After a bowl of warming porridge, as an afterthought, I picked it up and put it in the pocket of my duffel coat.

There were around ten hardy souls on the bonfire field when I arrived. Jim was working with Big Frank collecting spent fireworks in a bucket. Rhonda and a few parents were picking up litter while Audrey was taking down the posters and signs from the fence.

I decided to tidy up the bonfire area. I worked alone and felt comfortable with that. There was a lot on my mind. I recalled that Grayson had once said to me that everything passes and we are but fleeting shadows on this earth. It was at times like this I reflected on my life. I had always enjoyed solitude: my own company, a good book and a glass of wine. Often I found peace there, but there was always an underlying need for companionship, a friend to share experiences, perhaps even a lover.

Suddenly a breeze sprang up and chilled my face. The charred branches that remained of our bonfire crackled in the wind and a cloud of ash flew into the air and across the field. I watched it disperse into a pewter-grey sky until it disappeared into the distance. Then I took out the photograph from my pocket and stared at it.

On this cold, grey morning my thoughts were like ashes in the wind.

Chapter Six

Granny Two Cats

It was Friday, 10 December and on the high ground of the Pennine Hills the first snow of winter had fallen. As I ate a hurried breakfast the new number one, Showaddy-waddy's 'Under the Moon of Love', was on the radio. I gave a wry smile. Meanwhile, a busy day was in store. The infant classes were due to present their Christmas entertainment and it was the staff Christmas party this evening.

It was also the day I met a remarkable lady called Violet Birtwhistle.

When I stepped outside I paused and took in the scene. The land was cold as iron, still as stone and the rising sun was gilding the distant hills with a rim of golden fire. In the hedgerows, frost sparkled on the holly berries with a diamond light as I drove with caution out of the village.

Newbridge High Street looked like a Lowry painting with stooped figures in winter coats striding out under a pewter-grey sky. Winter was coming and the smell of wood smoke was in the air. Outside Snoddy's Stores a poster read: 'Suck a Spangle. Get Happy', and I wished it was as simple as that.

I arrived at school to see the children, undeterred by the cold, their breath steaming in the freezing air, playing their games and sharing stories of Christmas; it was good to witness their excitement and zest for life. As I hurried towards the entrance hall I caught sight of Pauline Ackworth. She was waving her arms frantically.

'Sir, sir!' she yelled. 'Ah've jus' seen a cat go into school.'

I stopped abruptly. 'What did you say, Pauline?'

'Mr Cannon were shakin' salt on t'steps an' t'door were open an' that's when ah saw it. It were a cat, sir, black an' white.'

'Thanks, Pauline.'

'Can ah 'elp, sir?'

'Let me check first to see what's happened.'

It was then that I spotted a lady walking briskly through the school gates. She strode across the playground towards me. Tall, smartly dressed and with greying hair, she called out, 'Excuse me. Are you one of the teachers?' Her voice was refined and authoritative.

'Yes, I'm Jack Sheffield, the deputy head.'

'I'm sorry to trouble you, Mr Sheffield. I'm Mrs Birtwhistle and I'm hoping you may be able to help me.'

'Of course. I'll do my best.'

Behind her blue eyes there was a sharp intelligence. This was an astute lady.

'It's my cats, Mr Sheffield. They went missing this morning when I was lighting the fire. It's not like them to wander off. I was worried if perhaps a dog had chased them or they had been scared by traffic.'

'Well, you may be in luck. A girl in my class saw a black and white cat running into school a few minutes ago.'

'Oh, that *is* encouraging news.'

'So you have more than one cat?'

She rummaged in her leather bag and held up a photo of two black and white cats that looked identical. 'Here they are. I have *two* cats, Bertie and Harold . . . and I love them both.' She sighed wistfully. 'I've been showing this to shoppers in the High Street but no luck until now.'

'Shall we go into school and see if one has been found?'

'Yes, please.'

In the entrance hall Big Frank smiled in recognition when he saw Mrs Birtwhistle. ''Ello, Violet,' he said. 'Ah did wonder if it might be one o' your cats.'

'Good morning, Frank,' said Violet. 'How is your leg these days?'

'Still limpin' but ah don't complain.'

'That's not what your mother says,' Violet replied with a smile. She turned to me. 'Frank and I are neighbours.'

I looked at Frank. 'So . . . any sign of a missing cat?'

He shook his head. 'Not yet but we're all lookin'.'

The office door opened and Audrey appeared. 'Oh, hello, Violet. Are you coming to see your Amy this afternoon?'

'Definitely. I wouldn't miss her first Nativity. My Sarah has got the afternoon off from school so she will be here as well.'

Audrey looked up at me. 'Mrs Birtwhistle is Sarah Hardcastle's mother.'

The penny dropped. 'Ah, of course, I know your daughter . . . a domestic science teacher at The Ridge. I spoke to her on our last parents' evening.'

Mrs Birtwhistle smiled. 'Yes, my husband and I were very proud when she became a teacher.'

I looked at Audrey. 'Mrs Birtwhistle has lost her cats and one of them was seen running into school.'

'Oh dear,' said Audrey. 'Don't worry, I'm sure they will turn up.'

'We'll do our best to find them,' I said.

'Thank you, Mr Sheffield.' The concern was still etched on her face.

Audrey laid a hand on her arm. 'Would you like to come into the staff-room, Violet? You could have a cup of tea while you're waiting.'

'That's very kind.'

The staff-room door closed behind them.

'Lovely lady,' said Frank quietly. "Er 'usband passed on a few year back. Lives alone now.'

'She showed me a photo of her cats. It's clear she loves them.'

'Ah know.' Frank grinned. 'Locals call 'er Granny Two Cats.'

Suddenly Rhonda appeared. She was holding a black and white cat. Celestine was in close attendance. 'This dear little thing was in Celestine's Home Corner,' said Rhonda.

'It was under one of the cushions,' added Celestine, clearly thrilled with the discovery.

'Mrs Birtwhistle will be delighted,' I said. 'She's in the staff-room with Audrey.'

'I know Violet,' said Celestine. 'Helps out at St Luke's.'

When they walked in we heard the delight in Mrs Birt-whistle's voice: 'Oh, Harold. My dear Harold!' The relief was palpable.

Frank grinned. 'One down, one to go. Ah'll 'ave a look in m'boiler 'ouse.' He wandered off as the staff-room door reopened midst excited chatter.

'I'll take Harold home now, Mr Sheffield, and settle him down. Then I'll continue my search. Many thanks for your assistance.'

'A pleasure, Mrs Birtwhistle. I do hope you find Bertie.'

'Perhaps someone could let me know if he turns up in school. Miss Fazackerly will know my number. Either way, I shall be back for the Nativity.'

She stroked the cat lovingly and walked back to the school gate.

By morning assembly it appeared the search for Bertie Birtwhistle had ground to a halt. Jim related the story of the disappearing cat to the children, much to their interest.

'I could go home for some cat food, sir,' said Pauline Ackworth.

'Sir, sir,' said an excited Dawn Whitehead, 'our cat comes if y'shake a box o' biscuits.'

Suggestions came in thick and fast.

'Pity we've no mice, sir,' said a phlegmatic Colin Loft-house. 'Our cat drags them in.'

It wasn't a pleasant image but Jim smiled and thanked the eager little boy.

*

At morning break it was good to retreat to the sanctuary of the staff-room and enjoy hot coffee and the busy hum of cat-free chat.

Diane Hardisty was concerned that Princess Margaret and the Earl of Snowdon had gone their separate ways while Tristan was surprised that Jimmy Carter of Georgia had been elected the President of the United States.

Rhonda was complaining bitterly about squatters moving into homes that didn't belong to them. 'Thirty thousand of them now in England and Wales. There are a couple on my sister's street in Cardiff and the police can't shift them unless they're causing criminal damage.'

However, it wasn't long before Bertie Birtwhistle drifted back into the conversation.

'I do hope Violet finds her cat,' said Audrey. 'She really is a special lady. I hate to see her so sad.'

Celestine nodded in agreement. 'She's coming back into school this afternoon to see her granddaughter. Little Amy Hardcastle is playing the part of Mary. She's such a sweet little girl. Violet will be thrilled to see her.'

'I don't know her,' said Tristan.

'Mrs Birtwhistle helps out at our church events,' explained Celestine. 'Retired now after a lifetime of service in the NHS. She worked in the East End of London at Mile End Hospital.'

'I've heard of it,' said Rhonda. 'It used to be a workhouse.'

'That's right,' said Audrey, 'and because of that it carried the stigma of poverty. Violet was a ward sister in the Mercer Ward caring for elderly patients. Many were poor and disadvantaged.'

'A brave lady,' said Celestine. 'I do hope we can find Bertie for her.'

Katy was catching up with the story. 'Bertie?'

'Named after her late husband,' said Audrey. 'Harold Albert Birtwhistle, died a few years ago of cancer. He was in the navy in World War II, a petty officer on the Atlantic convoys. Then worked as a builder until lung cancer caught up with him. She was heartbroken.'

'Oh dear,' said Katy as the bell went for the end of morning break.

Rhonda stood up and clapped her hands, 'Come on, everybody, final preparation time. The birth of Jesus awaits,' and we all hurried back to our classrooms.

Back in class Pauline Ackworth raised her hand.

'Yes, Pauline.'

'Jus' thinkin', sir. What was it like at Christmas when you were our age?'

'It was very different. We didn't have the sort of presents you get now.'

'What did you get, sir?' asked Gary Cockroft.

Where to begin, I thought. 'Well, I remember Christmas 1953. I was eight years old and I woke up to find a parcel and a stocking at the foot of my bed.'

All the children were silent and eager with anticipation. 'Go on, sir,' said Stacey. 'What was in the parcel?'

'And the stocking,' added Tracey.

'In the stocking was a satsuma, some nuts and a three-colour torch.'

'What's a satsuma, sir?' asked Danny Bishop, a new admission from Leeds.

'It's like an orange but smaller an' really juicy,' said Susan Verity.

'Thank you, Susan, that's right and in those days it was very rare. I tried to make it last all day.'

'What was the torch like, sir? That sounds good,' said Susan.

'There was a switch and you could change the light from red to yellow to green.'

'Bit like traffic lights, sir,' said Dawn Whitehead.

'That's right, Dawn. Well done.'

'What about the parcel, sir?' asked Claire Braithwaite.

Their attention was absolute. Every child waited for my reply.

'It was a book.'

'What was it, sir?' asked Jeremy Prendergast.

'*Five Go Off to Camp* by Enid Blyton.'

The Swithenbank twins weren't impressed. 'But what was your *big* present, sir?' asked Stacey.

'Yes, sir,' added an impatient Tracey, 'you *must* have had something else . . . like a bicycle.'

'No, that was it and bicycles were too expensive.'

There was a pause while they considered the implication.

'So were your mum and dad *poor*, sir?' asked Stacey.

'Didn't they have much money?' added Tracey.

'They had enough,' I replied cautiously.

Fortunately Jeremy changed the subject.

'The book was a good choice, sir. I read *Five Go Off to Camp* and I enjoyed their adventures so I went with my mum to Milltown Library and read the rest of the series.'

'That's really good to hear, Jeremy. I read my copy in bed at night by the light of my three-colour torch.'

Billy Gubbins from Barnsley suddenly waved his hand in the air.

'Yes, Billy.'

'Nineteen fifty-three was a long time ago, sir.'

'That's right, it was the year of the Queen's Coronation.'

'An' nex' year will be t'Silver Jubilee,' added Billy.

'That's right. So how many years ago was the Coronation?'

'Twenty-five minus one, sir,' said Billy quick as a flash.

'Well done, Billy.'

The little boy beamed with pleasure.

'I watched it on television. It was the first time I had ever seen a television set. I went to a neighbour's house because we didn't own one.'

This statement was met with complete astonishment.

'How did you watch football?' asked Gary Cockroft.

'By going to the games or watching the highlights at the cinema.'

There was a communal shaking of heads.

'What did you do when you got home after school, sir, if there was no telly?' asked a bemused Pauline Ackworth.

'I played outside with my friends.'

'But what about in winter when it's dark?' asked Dawn Whitehead.

'We sat round the fire and listened to the radio.'

'Like *Top of the Pops*,' suggested a hopeful Pauline Ackworth.

'No, there wasn't a *Top of the Pops* then.'

I watched their faces. Those long-ago times of post-war austerity were beyond their comprehension.

'I think I'd rather live *now* than then, sir,' said a phlegmatic Susan Verity.

'I'm sure you would, Susan.' I glanced at my watch. It was time to move on. 'Right, boys and girls, take out your maths books please.'

Billy Gubbins smiled. 'I like maths, sir.'

'Why is that, Billy?'

'Well, it means if you were eight in 1953 . . . I know how old you are.'

Sometimes you just have to smile.

The school dinner of liver and onions was a hurried affair. Apart from Mrs Starkey telling Tony Entwhistle 'I want, never gets' in a strident voice, all went smoothly. Soon Tom and I were helping Frank and Jim to arrange the wooden stage blocks we had borrowed from The Ridge.

Izzy arrived carrying her music stand and guitar. She set up her music books and then I helped her push the piano to the side of the stage.

'Good luck, Izzy. If it's like yesterday it will be brilliant.' The Junior Christmas entertainment organized by Katy had gone really well.

She gave me that familiar mischievous smile. 'Party tonight, Jack. Looking forward to it.'

'I heard you're singing with your group.'

'Yes, Jim arranged it. We're doing a set at some point. A few favourites.' She propped her guitar on a stand. 'Rhonda said you've invited an old friend.'

'Yes, Donna, the teacher from Bracken.'

There was a flicker of recognition. 'Well, save me a dance,' she said as she walked back to the infant classrooms.

The Nativity was due to commence at two o'clock and by one thirty the children in my class had arranged chairs in rows. First to arrive was Violet Birtwhistle with her daughter, Sarah. The likeness was striking.

'We're early birds, Mr Sheffield,' said Violet.

'Hope you don't mind,' added Sarah. 'It's a special day.'

'Of course. Take a seat.'

They sat at the right-hand side of the front row. Rhonda arrived carrying Jesus's manger and placed it carefully in the centre of the stage. She walked over to join us. 'Hello, Mrs Birtwhistle, any news of Bertie?' she asked quietly.

'Sadly, no, but I remain hopeful.'

Sarah squeezed her hand. 'It will be fine, Mother.'

Suddenly there was a crash as the hall doors burst open. Mrs Deborah Finch dashed in, panting and with tousled hair sticking out as if she had been electrocuted.

'Ah've got our Vernon's 'alo,' she gasped.

She was clutching her handbag and holding a cardboard halo wrapped in some old tinsel. It was clear she had run all the way to school and appeared to be in distress.

'Sit down, please, Mrs Finch, and catch your breath,' said Rhonda.

She swayed and sat heavily on a chair behind Violet.

Looking round, Violet suddenly moved into professional mode. She held Mrs Finch's hand. 'How are you feeling, my dear?'

'Dunno. Dizzy. Can't remember.' She was pale and there were beads of sweat running down her forehead.

Violet felt her pulse. It was rapid.

Rhonda crouched down. 'I recall Mrs Finch is on insulin.'

'My mother is a nurse, Mrs Finch,' said Sarah.

Deborah Finch didn't seem to comprehend.

Violet spoke calmly: 'Have you eaten today, Mrs Finch?' She shook her head. 'Dunno.'

Violet stared into Mrs Finch's eyes. They appeared vacant and her head was rocking from side to side. 'Let's get Mrs Finch into another room. We must act quickly. This can lead to convulsions and loss of consciousness,' she said quietly.

'Staff-room,' said Rhonda. She lifted the stick-thin Mrs Finch from her chair and we helped her into the seclusion of the staff-room.

Violet spoke quietly. 'She has hypoglycaemic symptoms, sweating, pale and possibly hungry. Her heart rate is high.' She glanced up at her daughter. 'Sarah, look in Mrs Finch's handbag. She may be carrying glucose tablets.' Then she turned to me. 'Mr Sheffield. Something sweet to drink, please. Sugar in hot water will do.'

Rhonda glanced up at the cupboard next to the sink. 'There's an iced fruit cake. Shall I cut a slice?'

'Yes, please,' said Violet. 'My guess is she will have taken insulin but has forgotten food in her haste to help her son.' She felt her pulse again. 'We need to control her heart rate. It's over one hundred beats per minute.'

For the next few minutes we followed Violet's lead. 'It's working,' she said. 'No need for an ambulance.' She felt the pulse once more and nodded.

It was now five minutes to two and we heard Izzy

playing some introductory Christmas music on the piano. I walked to the front of the hall where Jim was preparing to introduce the Nativity and clearly wondering what had happened to Rhonda. He listened carefully. 'Thanks, Jack.'

Katy had taken charge of the top two classes, who were sitting cross-legged on the floor in front of the parents. The seats that had been occupied by Violet and Sarah were now occupied. Teachers were sitting next to the children in their classes while Celestine arranged the infant children on the stage.

Rhonda delivered the tinsel halo to Vernon Finch who, thanks to his mother's persistence, was word-perfect for his role of Angel Gabriel and unaware of his mother's distress.

I found three spare chairs and propped them against the wall bars at the side of the hall. Violet and Sarah walked in slowly with a much-recovered Mrs Finch and took their places just as Jim welcomed everyone and introduced one of the most eagerly awaited events of the school year.

As the timeless story unfolded many mothers shed a tear watching their five- and six-year-olds dressed in tea-towel headdresses and long white shirts tied with dressing-gown cords. Little Amy Hardcastle looked perfect in her blue shawl as the Virgin Mary and carried a small doll wrapped in 'swaddling clothes' or, to be more precise, one of her mother's best towels.

Mrs Finch was alert once again and looked on expectantly when the diminutive Vernon, as the halo-clad Angel Gabriel, stepped up on a box to deliver his speech.

Celestine held a copy of the script as she sat at the side of the stage and was proud that, up to now, no prompting had been required.

'You shall have a baby,' announced Vernon in his best dramatic voice. He looked down at Mary and the slightly self-conscious Colin Lofthouse who, as a male chauvinist Joseph, had no intention of holding a girl's hand. 'And his name will be . . .'

There was a dramatic pause. Members of the audience held their collective breath. A few moments later Celestine, as official prompter, repeated the line: 'And his name will be Jesus.'

Vernon was staring at the manger. He nodded at Celestine, took a deep breath and tried again: 'And his name will be . . .'

The single word 'Jesus' was mouthed by countless parents, every teacher and Henry Dewhirst who had been last year's Angel Gabriel.

A little louder this time, Celestine said, 'JESUS!'

Vernon looked imploringly at Celestine while Amy Hardcastle stood up and pointed at the manger. A head had appeared above the blanket.

'There's a *cat* in our manger, Miss,' said the Angel Gabriel.

'It's Bertie,' said a surprised Virgin Mary, recognizing her grandmother's pride and joy.

'BERTIE!' exclaimed Violet. She hurried towards the stage, swept up the cat from the manger and hurried back to her seat. 'It's a miracle,' she murmured.

The audience nodded in agreement. Virgin births were fine but a cat in the manger was definitely in the realms of a supernatural phenomenon.

Undeterred, Vernon finally completed his line: 'And his name shall be Jesus.'

At the end there was thunderous applause, more from relief than anything else, and everyone was pleased that the Saviour of Mankind wasn't named Bertie.

After the performance parents collected their children and drifted home. Violet stayed to have a brief word with Mrs Finch about managing her lifestyle to create a balance between insulin and glucose. Finally Deborah Finch gave Violet a hug and they departed as friends.

'Well done,' I said. 'It looked serious for a time.'

Sarah beamed. 'All in a day's work for my mother.'

Violet smiled too. 'Thank you, Mr Sheffield, for all your assistance today.'

'A pleasure, Mrs Birtwhistle, and I'm delighted you have been reunited with your cats.'

I watched them leave. It really was good to know that Bertie, after his starring role in the Nativity, would spend the evening with his twin brother.

I was also in awe of Granny Two Cats.

Chapter Seven

A Decision for Donna

That evening was the staff party and I had agreed to pick up Donna from her home in North Beck village. Shower, shave, suit and tie followed in quick succession before I set off again into the darkness.

She answered quickly when I tapped the door knocker of the ancient cottage.

'Hi, what happened to you?'

'I got here as quickly as I could.'

She smiled and touched the swelling above my eye. 'No, I meant this.'

'Oh, yes, I tripped up getting out of the shower.'

'There's a cut as well. You need a plaster.'

'Thanks.'

'So come in. Let's get you sorted first and then I'll get my coat.'

She set off upstairs. 'Hey, you look great,' I shouted after her.

When she reappeared with some antiseptic cream and

a box of plasters she grinned. 'Thanks . . . and you seem to have made an effort.'

I raised my eyebrows in faux disbelief. 'My mother used to say, "Don't mock the afflicted." I've never really been into fashion. This is my best suit by the way.' It was my grey three-piece I used for parents' evenings and funerals.

'You look fine, Jack. Good to dress up for something special.' She leaned forward and straightened my flower-power tie.

I glanced into the kitchen at the end of the hallway. 'No Sherri?'

'No, she's at my mother's for the weekend.'

The school hall was full of light, colour and sound when we walked in. The staff party was an event that Jim had organized before I arrived as deputy headteacher. Each year at the end of the penultimate week of term the staff gathered in the school hall to enjoy a relaxing evening of refreshment and dancing. We were encouraged to bring a partner and it was always interesting to see who turned up.

Jim's wife, Elizabeth, a tall, elegant civil servant who worked for the Home Office, was arranging a tray of vol-au-vents. Katy, in a striking floral maxi dress, was with Mike Foster. They looked relaxed together as they filled two bowls of punch, one non-alcoholic.

Rhonda's husband, Bryn, a retired Welsh miner, much older than her but full of engaging stories, was in conversation with Tristan, who had come alone.

Tom Deighton and his current girlfriend, a nurse from Milltown Hospital, were filling bowls with Disco's Crisps and Frazzles along with plates of sausage rolls and large slices of pork pie. Meanwhile, Audrey and Celestine were completing a hemispherical masterpiece of cheese and pineapple on sticks to complement countless slices of Christmas cake.

I delivered my can of Watney's Party Seven to Jim, who was on the impromptu bar. 'Thanks, Jack. We can open this now if you like. I'm ready for a pint.'

I looked around. 'Going well.'

'Yes, Neville and his friend have ringfenced the record player and seem to be doing a good job.' Neville had invited his philatelist friend, David, who was putting on Chicago's 'If You Leave Me Now' after vetoing Neville's insistence for Beethoven's Symphony No. 9 to 'add a bit of class'.

Donna and I were sitting with Diane Hardisty, who was clutching a Babycham in one hand and her new boy-friend in the other. Paul, a smart, shy, balding chemist from Leeds University, seemed a little over-awed by the occasion.

Suddenly Izzy arrived and waved to me from across the hall. 'Hi, Jack, can you give me a hand?'

Her appearance was striking. She was wearing tight blue jeans and a red crop top under a tie-dyed jacket. 'There's a lot of gear in the van. The guys would appreciate the help.'

Katy had arranged with Jim for Izzy and her Cock & Bottle folk group to kick-start the evening while we enjoyed drinks and nibbles.

The two members of her backing group were distinctive. Benny, with the buttons of his collarless shirt undone, a medallion necklace and tight green cord trousers, was on bass guitar. Nigel played the violin. He wore a black ensemble: shirt with the collar turned up; waistcoat; bell-bottom pants and platform shoes. Both sported a droopy moustache and shoulder-length hair. They seemed to have a lot of amplifiers, cables and microphone stands.

Finally Jim stood on the stage, tapped the microphone and smiled. 'Good evening, everybody, and welcome to our annual staff Christmas party. We're kicking off with something a little different. Many thanks to Izzy, our music teacher, for bringing along her new folk group from The Cock & Bottle up in Skipton. They've agreed to entertain us with a few songs. So, a big hand please for the Three Locks.'

Izzy strummed away on her rhythm guitar while Benny and Nigel provided perfect accompaniment. They were surprisingly good and performed some old Bob Dylan classics including 'Blowing in the Wind' and 'The Times They Are A-Changin'' along with a few modern numbers. ABBA's 'Fernando' showcased Izzy's voice beautifully and the applause was well merited.

I walked over to her. 'Well done. That was terrific. You've a great voice.'

She squeezed my hand. 'Thanks, Jack. That means a lot.' She glanced at Donna, who was chatting with Katy Bell. 'I see you brought Donna along.'

'Yes, she's a good friend.'

She gave me that direct stare once again and, on impulse, grabbed my hand. 'You promised me a dance.'

We held each other and swayed from side to side. I have never been the best dancer and bumped into Jim and his wife. I apologized and he grinned and raised his eyebrows. David Essex was singing his 1975 number one, 'Hold Me Close', and the centre of the hall filled up with couples. From the corner of my eye I saw Donna looking at us curiously. Izzy noticed it too. 'I don't want to interfere, Jack. Donna is obviously special.'

'Not a problem,' I said.

'I never did thank you properly for helping me to get Steve out of my life.'

'He wasn't the man for you, Izzy.'

I looked down into her eyes and couldn't understand why she would have stayed with a man like Steve. It seemed that for her it was still a tainted memory and lived alongside her like an unwelcome shadow.

'I know that now,' she murmured and, as the record finished, she rested her head on my shoulder.

There had been a day when I dreamed of this moment but times had moved on and I was with Donna now. It occurred to me there were no easy solutions to relationships, simply an endless sea of shifting tides.

With a final squeeze of my hand she walked back to her singing partners and poured a gin and tonic for herself.

David was clearly taking the lead as impromptu disc jockey and when ABBA's 'Dancing Queen' came on I felt slightly embarrassed by my uncoordinated efforts. In contrast, Donna was a great dancer. 'I'm better on a rugby field,' I murmured apologetically in her ear.

'Relax and enjoy,' she said with a grin. 'This is a great night. I wish we did it at our school.'

I was more comfortable when Rod Stewart's 'Sailing' gave me the opportunity to hold Donna close and smooch around the dance floor as the lights were dimmed. It was good to relax in our private space. Tristan was making the most of the alcoholic punch while, on the next table,

Rhonda was halfway down a bottle of Blue Nun and Bryn was supping beer as if it was going out of fashion. It was only when Tom Jones started singing 'Delilah' that Rhonda dragged him on to the dance floor.

As the evening progressed Donna and I engaged in conversation with most of the staff while the music played on. Next to a crate of Corona Pop, Celestine was sitting with Audrey sipping American Cream Soda and Dandelion & Burdock.

Donna nodded towards them. 'Jack, ask them for a dance.'

Reluctantly I agreed. Audrey, in particular, was a wonderful dancer, and taught me a basic quickstep as we skated around the hall. Celestine was more sedate and we moved serenely to Engelbert Humperdinck's 'The Last Waltz'.

Finally David selected Shirley Bassey's 'The Party's Over' for the last dance of the evening. Donna rested her hands behind my neck as we moved around the floor. I glanced across at Izzy who was doing the same with the tall, lean and slightly inebriated Benny. She gave me a wistful smile.

After clearing up and saying goodnight we all wandered out to the car park. As we drove back to Donna's cottage she seemed very quiet, but when we got out of the car she smiled as I held her hand. We walked to her front door and stood there hesitantly.

'Thanks,' I said. 'It's been a lovely evening.'

'I enjoyed it too.' She kissed me on the cheek.

'Well, it's late and you're getting cold.'

She smiled again. 'Just like that night in Lotherswicke village back in 1970 when I was stuck in the snow.'

'I remember it well.'

'It was when you said there was someone else.' There was a hint of sadness in her voice.

'That was over . . . a long time ago.'

She looked pensive.

'What is it?'

'I'm thinking of Sherri.'

'She's a great girl. Growing up fast.'

'I'm wondering what she would think of us . . . now.'

'I guess she would understand if her mother wanted to go out occasionally with a friend.'

'Is that what you are, Jack . . . a friend?'

'You know I want to be more than that.'

'What are you saying?'

'I'm saying . . . I could stay.'

She sighed. 'You've probably forgotten, Jack, but I said that to *you* once.'

'I know.'

We stood there outside her door in the sylvan shadows. There was moonlight on her face.

Finally she made a decision.

She kissed me softly on the lips, held my hand and led me inside.

A bar of pale light lay on my face as I awoke from a pleasant dream. I was warm and comfortable until realization slowly dawned that I was in a strange bed. I opened my eyes and stared at the empty pillow beside me. Donna was no longer there. I sat up and stretched. Memories of a wonderful night with this beautiful woman filled my thoughts. I glanced at the bedside clock. It was early and a reluctant dawn caressed the land on this sleepy Saturday morning.

There were sounds from downstairs and the clatter of crockery and, for a moment, I was sad that I wasn't waking up with Donna by my side. I looked around the tidy bedroom. Everything seemed to have its place with the exception of my clothes scattered on a chair in the corner. On a chest of drawers was an oval mirror, a bottle of scent and a framed photograph of Sherri in her school uniform. On the walls were paintings of places that marked the pathway of Donna's life, some clearly Sherri's work, including a picture of the main mansion building of Bretton Hall where Donna had trained to be a teacher. I smiled at the memory as I recalled it was my suggestion she went there.

I pulled on my trousers and socks and dragged my buttoned shirt over my head; then I walked down the narrow staircase to the kitchen. There was the smell of frying bacon. Donna had her back to me, standing in front of the gas cooker; she looked different . . . jeans, baggy denim shirt and tousled hair.

'Hi,' she said simply.

'Morning. You're up early.'

'I thought some breakfast would be a good idea.'

'Thanks. Sounds good.'

'How do you like your eggs?'

'Whatever you prefer.'

She cracked two eggs with expert ease and added them to the pan. I wanted to put my arms around her but wasn't sure if it would be welcome, so I sat down at the pine table.

'Can I do anything?'

'Cutlery in the top drawer.'

It was strange: everything felt very matter of fact. Two slices of bread popped up in the toaster.

Soon we were facing each other across the table and enjoying our early-morning feast. We were sipping tea when I asked, 'What would you like to do today?'

She gripped her mug in both hands and considered me steadily. 'I'm not collecting Sherri until six so we could go out somewhere, maybe for lunch or afternoon tea.'

'Is there anywhere special you would like to go?'

'York would be good but it's a bit far.'

'Particularly if you have to be back for Sherri.'

She stared out of the window at the frosty snowscape. 'And driving might be difficult.'

'Somewhere closer then.'

She glanced up at the clock. It was just after nine. 'How about Harrogate? We could be there in an hour.'

'Harrogate is a great idea. Let's do that.'

I kept glancing at her as we cleared away. She seemed relaxed but there had been no mention of last night. It was as if she was moving on quickly and with purpose, afraid to get involved or commit. Had I been able to read Donna's mind, I would have discovered that I was right.

We drove away in my car through Skipton and on the A59 past Bolton Abbey. Donna, wrapped up in a warm coat and fur boots, turned on the radio. As I negotiated the hills and bends on the snow-covered road over Blubberhouses, Diana Ross was singing 'Love Hangover'. There was little conversation. Both of us seemed content with our own thoughts as we approached the North Yorkshire spa town of Harrogate.

We parked on Montpellier Hill. 'So what would you like to do first?'

'I would love to go to Bettys.'

'So would I. That would be a real treat.'

We walked into the centre and arrived outside Bettys Café Tea Rooms, noticeably without the expected apostrophe in 'Bettys' on the large ornate sign, and stared in the window. Earlier in the year it had relocated from Cambridge Crescent to its new prestigious corner site in Parliament Street and it looked very grand with its Christmas decorations.

It was always special walking into the timeless tea rooms and a bygone era of white linen tablecloths and silver service. A waitress wearing a starched white apron and a neat cap showed us to our table. We ordered sandwiches, scones and tea. Soon the setting before us was perfect with a silver teapot, a matching sugar bowl, silver tongs and a tea strainer. The centre of the table was dominated by three tiers of sandwiches, warm scones and delicate filo pastry cakes.

'Perfect,' said Donna with a smile.

There was no rush and, as the clock ticked on to midday, we chatted about school, Donna's plans for Sherri and my rugby – today's game had been cancelled owing to the snow. The fruit scones filled with citrus peel, almonds and cherries were delicious. Neither of us mentioned the time we had spent together last night. It was almost as if it had never happened.

*

It was early afternoon before we left after buying a box of home-made Brontë biscuits and a small iced Christmas cake. Donna took my arm as we walked around the town and under the bright Christmas lights. We visited the Royal Pump Room Museum in the Montpellier Quarter with its mineral springs and crunched through the snow-covered Valley Gardens.

We finished up in the Old Swan Hotel and, while we enjoyed a drink in the bar, Donna read the brochure about the disappearance of Agatha Christie. It was here in Harrogate that she was reputed to have stayed. The famous creator of Hercule Poirot had died earlier in the year and the hotel was full of posters of this remarkable lady.

'She must have been so unhappy, Jack, and what a strange story.'

'So . . . it's fifty years ago.'

'Almost to the day. It says here that it was on a cold December night in 1926 that she went out in her beloved Morris Cowley Roadster and didn't return home for eleven days.'

'I wonder what really happened.'

'I guess we'll never know but what a legacy she has left behind. Over sixty detective novels and *The Mousetrap* is still running in London.'

'Maybe we ought to go down there to see it,' I added hopefully.

There was a long pause. 'Perhaps,' she said quietly as she replaced the brochure and finished her drink.

I looked at my watch. 'It will be dark before four. Maybe we should think about making a start for home.'

'We could stop at Bolton Abbey for some fish and chips if you like.'

'Great idea. Let's do that.'

As we drove slowly out of Harrogate I reflected on the day. It had been good to spend time with Donna and she seemed relaxed if a little quiet. As we approached Bolton Abbey the Walker Brothers were singing 'No Regrets'.

It was cosy sitting in the car eating fish and chips out of newspaper: the windows steamed up and we felt as if we were in our own private little world. Then the snow began to fall again, and the temperature dropped suddenly. A severe winter's night was in store.

It was after five o'clock and pitch dark when we arrived outside Donna's cottage and we sat there for a moment while I wondered what would happen next.

'Thanks for today, Jack. Really enjoyed it.'

'So did I. A good idea to go to Harrogate. Bettys was special.'

She looked at her watch. 'I need to collect Sherri so I had better get a move on.'

'Can I help? Shall we go in my car?'

'No, I'll be fine. It's not far. I'll go in mine.'

'So, I'll ring, shall I?'

She was taking her car keys out of her handbag and sounded a little distracted: 'Yes, fine . . . do that.' Then she leaned over, kissed me on the cheek and got out of the car. She waved as I drove away.

I didn't turn on the radio as I returned home. My thoughts were focused on our special day. It had been one to remember.

Chapter Eight

Where Angels Fear to Tread

Her name was Alice Cripps and she was seventy-seven years old.

Known in the community as 'Awkward Alice', she was by far the most anti-social resident of the Eternal Peace Residential Home in Newbridge. Born at the end of the last century, she had seen many changes in her life, not least a faithless husband, an embittered sister and the death of her two sons in the Second World War. So it came as no surprise to the other so-called *inmates*, as she called them, when she conducted a noisy altercation with her neighbour and Social Committee Secretary, the well-meaning and patient Miss Gladys Slack, a relative youngster at the age of seventy-one.

'But children really *make* Christmas, Alice,' pleaded Gladys. 'It was kind of the headteacher to make the offer once again.'

'Tell him charity begins at home.'

Gladys took a deep breath. 'The children come every

year and their singing is beautiful . . .' She could see that Alice was in a particularly difficult mood and decided not to say any more. She recognized when a conversation was over. 'I'll bring your coffee and biscuits,' she said, crept out and closed the door quietly.

Back in the common room there were excited voices and the rattle of crockery. The visit of the Newbridge Primary School choir was always a special event. It was Wednesday, 15 December and, outside the tall windows of this Edwardian building, a crisp frost covered the lawns and neat shrubbery.

Before school we had all gathered in the staff-room. 'Don't forget tonight's meeting, everyone,' said Jim. 'Four o'clock sharp, please. Lots to discuss. Christmas parties, end-of-term reports and so on. Also, keep in mind the last time we highlighted bullying. I'll raise it again in tomorrow morning's assembly.'

'I'm not aware of any bullying,' said Tristan.

Everyone looked at him and recalled he was the new-comer. 'A fair point, Tristan,' said Jim patiently. 'This is something we discuss every year. The aim is to raise awareness.'

'Ah, I understand,' said Tristan. His hair was dishevelled and he appeared preoccupied.

Jim pressed on: 'Even though there's been no evidence of bullying, it's important we help children understand what it is so they can stop it happening. Then perhaps you could follow this up in a class discussion.' Jim looked up at the clock. 'So, anything else before we ring the bell?'

'Neville's brought a cake,' announced Audrey.

'It's for the meeting,' said Neville.

Jim smiled. 'Well, there definitely won't be any absentees.'

Neville blushed profusely but knew his magnificent coffee nut cake was one of his best. For the last four years his baking bible had been *The Homepride Book of Home Baking*, the first metric book of flour cookery in Britain, and this particular recipe was always a success.

After lunch Katy and I gathered the thirty children in the top two classes who formed the school choir. Jim had volunteered to teach the children who remained behind and Izzy was coming along to play the piano.

It was an annual event and always successful. The children were divided into pairs to engage in conversation with one of the residents. It was an idea Jim had discussed with Miss Slack and had been well received. The elderly folk loved the opportunity to regale the children with stories of times gone by. The added bonus of excellent refreshments was also welcome. It was a fifteen-minute walk down the High Street and past the sports fields. I led the way with Katy and Izzy bringing up the rear. Predictably the children were completely oblivious to the bitter cold while I shivered inside my duffel coat.

The building was at the end of a long driveway beyond the local cricket ground and the gravel crunched beneath our feet. As we approached, I spotted eager faces peering out of the windows. The executive director, Mrs Vivien Beecham, a tall, imposing lady in her fifties, and the smiling Miss Slack were there to greet us.

'Good afternoon, Mr Sheffield,' said Mrs Beecham. 'Lovely to see you again.'

'Thank you, Mrs Beecham. You will recall Miss Bell who came last year, and this is Ms Kowalski, our new music teacher, who will be playing the piano.'

They shook hands and we walked inside.

'Thank you so much for bringing the children,' said Miss Slack. 'They always bring joy into our hearts.'

The benevolent Mrs Beecham looked at the children, rosy-cheeked after their brisk walk. 'Boys and girls, hands up if you like orange juice and chocolate cake.'

Thirty-one hands shot in the air: namely all the children plus a smiling Izzy.

We followed them into a large dining area where the children took off their coats and sat at tables while four ladies in neat aprons served refreshments.

'Mr Patterson rang to confirm the arrangements regarding the chatting after the carols,' said Mrs Beecham.

'And we're all looking forward to it,' said Miss Slack.

'A few of the children are a little nervous,' added Katy.

'Understandably so,' said Mrs Beecham, 'and we shall do our best to put them at ease.'

Twelve ladies and three men were seated around the common room in large, comfortable high-back armchairs and they all enjoyed the concert. There was a baby grand piano next to a huge and brightly decorated Christmas tree. Izzy opened her copy of *Carol, Gaily Carol* and played beautifully while the twins, Stacey and Tracey Swithenbank, captured everyone's hearts with their duet of 'Little Donkey'.

At the end everyone joined in with 'Hark, the Herald

Angels Sing' which gave Miss Slack the opportunity to describe the children as *angels* in her vote of thanks. This was followed by more tea and cake and animated conversations between the children and the residents. Predictably, some of the children were more forthcoming than others.

'Did you fight in the war?' asked Jeremy Prendergast.

'An' did you beat the Germans, sir?' echoed an eager Gary Cockroft.

Sixty-eight-year-old William Nightingale proceeded to return to memories of 1942 and relate the story of the second Battle of El Alamein to the awestruck boys.

'Is this a bit like being in prison?' asked a bemused Pauline Ackworth to the benign seventy-year-old Fanny Boot.

'I've never been in a prison,' said Fanny, 'but if it was like this I would be very lucky. Everyone is so kind.' Suddenly she frowned as a balding, beefy man strode past wearing grubby overalls and carrying a toolbox. 'Well, almost everyone,' she added.

Katy and I were talking to Mrs Beecham when suddenly we were rudely interrupted by a heavily built man wearing oil-smeared dungarees.

'Ah've done that stickin' winder in Cripps's room.'

'That would be *Mrs* Cripps, Mr Birtle,' corrected Mrs Beecham.

He remained silent, glowered and walked away.

'That's Mr Birtle. He's our temporary maintenance man until Mr Giles returns from visiting his sister in Scotland. She's unwell.'

'I expect you'll be pleased when Mr Giles returns,' said Katy pointedly. The demeanour of Mr Birtle conflicted with the obviously friendly ethos of this caring home.

Mrs Beecham nodded but said nothing.

Miss Slack hurried over to us, a smile on her face. She had spotted Alice Cripps in conversation with the Swithenbank twins. 'Mrs Beecham, good news. Alice decided to join us to meet the children while Mr Birtle repaired her window.'

'That *is* good to hear,' said Mrs Beecham. 'I was beginning to get concerned about her.'

I glanced at my watch. 'I think the children would stay here for hours if they had the chance but we shall have to leave shortly.'

Miss Slack looked at Alice Cripps, still in conversation with the Swithenbank girls. 'Perhaps a few more minutes, Mr Sheffield.'

Meanwhile, the twins asked the sort of direct questions one would expect of ten-year-olds.

'We 'ave school dinners, Miss,' said Stacey.

'What's yours like?' demanded Tracey.

'Probably the same as yours. Some are good and some not so good.'

There was a pause as the two girls stared into the lined face of Alice Cripps.

'We were a bit frightened of comin' 'ere, Miss,' admitted Stacey.

''Cause of everyone bein' old an' mebbe a bit scary,' continued Tracey.

Alice smiled for the first time. She felt an empathy with

these two girls. They reminded her of her own life long ago when she lived in Manchester.

'There's no need, girls. It was good of you to come and cheer us up. Your singing was wonderful.'

'So . . . do y'like it 'ere?' asked Stacey.

'An' 'ave y'got a telly?' said Tracey, scanning the room.

'Yes, we have a television room but I don't go there often.' There was a pause. 'And I like it here most of the time . . . but not always.'

'Why d'you keep rubbin' y'wrists?' asked Stacey.

'Is it 'cause yer old?' added Tracey, who, according to her mother, was never backwards in coming forwards.

Alice Cripps stared into the young faces of these girls and remembered what it had been to be young with a lifetime that stretched out in front of her. She glanced across the room and spoke quietly.

The staff meeting after school went well. Jim thanked everyone for their hard work and was pleased with the standards achieved by the children. He also confirmed the last afternoon of term was an opportunity for the children to play games. Audrey said the distribution of end-of-term reports was in hand and Rhonda thanked Izzy for her support with the infant Nativity. Katy and I reported back on another successful visit to the retirement home.

'It went well,' said Katy, 'and, although there were a few who were a little fearful of meeting strangers, we were soon made to feel comfortable.'

Conversation ebbed and flowed and Izzy invited everyone to come along to hear her sing on Christmas Eve in The Cock & Bottle. Finally Jim closed the meeting with a reminder about the safety of the children as they left school on these dark nights.

It was late when I rang Donna. Wednesday evening was her rehearsal night for the North Beck Amateur Dramatic Society. Mainly for Sherri's benefit, she had joined this eclectic group of would-be thespians for the annual village pantomime on New Year's Eve. It was *Aladdin* this year and Sherri had a part. Reluctantly, Donna had agreed to take on the role of assistant props manager.

'Hi, Donna, just ringing to confirm we're still on for Christmas shopping in Leeds next Monday.'

'That's fine, Jack. I'll be in the coffee shop around eleven while Sherri and her friend do their own shopping. Just a bit preoccupied here at the moment. I'm trying to make a Chinese kimono. I don't suppose you have any sewing skills?'

'Sadly, no, but if I can help in any other way ... I'm here.'

There was a long silence. 'I know,' she said quietly.

Last weekend had been special. We were both thirty-one years old and our teenage days were far behind us. Even so, making love to this beautiful woman had been a voyage of discovery.

When I awoke on Thursday morning a wolf-grey canvas of sky lay heavy over the sleeping earth with the promise of more snow. While eating a hasty bowl of Oat Krunchies I listened to Radio 2 burbling away in the background. Terry Wogan was introducing Leo Sayer singing 'You

Make Me Feel Like Dancing' and I thought back to the staff party and my time with Donna.

Thursday morning's assembly proved to be eventful. Jim talked at length about being kind to others. 'How can we show this at Christmas?' he asked.

A flurry of hands appeared.

'Buying a present, sir,' said Henry Dewhirst.

'Makin' a card,' added Pauline Ackworth.

'I'm sewing a peg bag for my mother, sir,' said Claire Braithwaite.

'These are wonderful ideas, boys and girls,' said Jim. 'Now let me ask you something else.' He paused for dramatic effect. Jim could hold the attention of a large audience like no one else I knew. 'Does anyone know what *bullying* is?'

There were fewer hands this time.

'Being unkind,' suggested Gary Cockroft.

'Well done, Gary.'

'Not being nice,' suggested Tony Entwhistle.

'That's right, Tony, but bullying is *more* than that. Does anyone know what I mean?'

Jeremy Prendergast raised his hand and offered a tentative answer. 'When someone is not nice to the same person . . . again and again.'

'Correct. Well said, Jeremy. Always tell a teacher if you can.'

Susan Verity spoke up. 'My mam says all bullies are cowards, sir.'

Jim smiled. 'Your mother is right.'

The assembly came to a close and we returned to our classrooms. Katy and I spotted the Swithenbank girls in a whispered conversation. 'What is it, girls?' asked Katy.

'Well, we were jus' thinkin', Miss,' said Stacey.

'About yesterday, Miss, wi' Mrs Cripps,' said Tracey.

'Mrs Cripps?'

'Yes, sir. One of t'ladies in t'retirement 'ome,' said Stacey. 'Me an' Tracey were talkin' to 'er.'

Tracey nodded vigorously. 'An' she told us 'bout this nasty man.'

Katy glanced at me.

'I'll follow this up,' I said, 'and get back to you.'

When the bell went for morning break Katy called into my classroom. 'Stacey and Tracey have been very helpful,' I said.

'That's good to hear,' said Katy and gave me an enquiring look.

'I think we must go to share something with Mr Patterson.'

The four of us set off for the headteacher's office.

Jim was sitting at his desk when we tapped on the door and walked in. He smiled. 'How can I help?'

'Now, girls,' said Katy reassuringly. 'Don't worry, you're not in trouble. Just the opposite. Mr Patterson was so pleased to hear about your wonderful duet yesterday at the retirement home.'

'Yes, well done, girls. We're all very proud of you and I shall pass a message of thanks to your mother.'

'Thank you, sir,' the girls chorused.

'Now . . . there is something else,' I said. 'The girls have been telling me about a conversation they had with a lady called Mrs Cripps. Could you tell Mr Patterson what you told me, please?'

As always the twins were direct and honest. 'That's right, sir, it were about bullyin',' said Tracey.

Stacey agreed. 'Jus' like y'said in assembly.'

'I see,' said Jim. 'Can you tell me about it?'

'Well, Mrs Cripps was unhappy at first,' said Tracey.

'Then she seemed t'settle down an' tell us things,' added Stacey.

'There's a new man there, sir.'

'Called Mr Birtle.'

''E's unkind an' grabs 'er wrist when she won't get up quick enough.'

'She's got bruises.'

'We saw 'em.'

'On *both* wrists, sir, an' 'e does it again an' again.'

Jim immediately appreciated the import of this message. 'Thank you, girls, you've been very helpful. Now you can go out to play.'

They ran off unconcerned to join their friends.

Jim scribbled a note. 'I'll ring Mrs Beecham.'

'I remember the man they're talking about,' I said. 'A new temporary handyman, by all accounts.'

'And pretty rude, I recall,' said Katy. 'Clearly wants following up. Sounds like this lady is scared to speak up. The girls provided an unlikely outlet.'

Jim was taking all this in his stride. 'I'll get back to you.'

'Thanks,' I said and we turned to leave.

'If necessary,' said Jim, 'I'll alert Di Matlock.'

The formidable Mrs Matlock was our Education

Welfare Officer. She had links with Social Services and I knew her from my previous school.

At lunchtime Jim asked Katy and me to call into his office. 'Well, a lot has happened since my call. Mrs Beecham acted quickly. This Birtle guy has been sent packing. More cases of bullying and physical abuse came to light when she investigated. She was really grateful to the Swithenbank girls and for our quick response. She described them as *guardian angels* and hopes they will visit Mrs Cripps again.'

'Interesting that the twins were the ones most fearful of the visit,' said Katy.

' "Where angels fear to tread . . ." ' said Jim with a smile.

Katy and I nodded. We were both familiar with the famous Alexander Pope quote.

'Very apt,' I said.

'What about telling Mrs Swithenbank?' asked Katy.

'Let me talk to her first,' said Jim. 'I'll be cautious when relating the details.'

'Your bullying talk worked,' I said.

Jim looked thoughtful. 'Yes, I suppose it did . . . but not in the way we expected.'

On Friday morning I looked out on a different world. The colours of my life were changing. Russet leaves of autumn had long gone now, to be replaced by a stark monochrome landscape. Snow had fallen in the village, a sprinkling at first like winter confetti but beneath it the frost was hard and unforgiving.

When I arrived at school I stopped and stared at the

children who had arrived early. They were playing a variety of games and there was no limit to their imagination.

'Mornin', Mr Sheffield,' said Big Frank. 'Them skin'eads are at it again.' He was emptying the playground litter bins and held up an empty half-bottle of Captain Morgan Black Label Jamaica Rum. 'Keep findin' 'em from time t'time.'

'Thanks, Frank. I'll mention it to Mr Patterson.'

'Party afternoon,' said Frank.

'Yes, looking forward to it. Catch you later.'

When I walked into the entrance hall Grayson was there. He was carrying a series of posters about the Nativity. 'Good morning, Jack. Last assembly of 1976 coming up.'

I helped him with a couple of cardboard boxes before walking into my classroom and sitting at my desk. A Christmas card was waiting for me. It was from Claire Braithwaite. Next to a picture of a cheerful robin was the message 'Hope you get something nice for Christmas' and I smiled.

Our final assembly before Christmas was always special. Jim thanked all the staff and children for their hard work and read out a letter from Mrs Beecham. It ended with the words: 'Please thank all the angels who sang for us and made the Eternal Peace Residential Home a happier place this Christmas.'

Katy was sitting next to me and Jim gave us both a knowing look before announcing a games afternoon was in store and our Christmas postbox was open for letters to Santa.

Then it was Grayson's turn to recite the familiar story of the birth of Jesus interspersed with a few of our favourite Christmas carols accompanied by Izzy on piano.

We ended as usual with the Lord's Prayer before the children ran outside to play on the frozen playground.

Morning break was busy in the staff-room and the forth-coming Christmas television programmes were discussed. Celestine and Grayson were looking forward to the *Songs of Praise Special*; Audrey said she never missed the Queen's speech; Diane was delighted there was another opportunity to see *Love Story* on Boxing Day while everyone agreed that, with the rest of the country, we would all be watching *The Morecambe and Wise Christmas Show* on Christmas Day with their special guest, Elton John.

Meanwhile, Celestine was looking flustered and said she was concerned about how she would budget for paying her television licence.

'There's a new twenty-five-pence television licence stamp on sale now,' said Audrey. 'Just ask for a savings card and fill it with your stamps. That's what I shall be doing.'

'You're a good friend, Audrey,' said Celestine with feeling.

In the far corner of the staff-room Izzy and Tom were discussing the merits or otherwise of the Sex Pistols. The punk rock band had released a debut single 'Anarchy in the UK' to mixed reviews.

'Brilliant,' said Izzy.

'Different,' said a less-than-convinced Tom.

Meanwhile, Tristan appeared to be in a strange mood once again and was in conversation with Grayson.

'I used to be an Anglican, vicar.'

Grayson was curious. 'Oh yes?'

'But now I'm an Angli-can't.'

'Ah, I see.'

'It's a joke, Mr Huppleby.'

'I guessed it was.'

Katy intervened. 'Take no notice, Tristan can't help being a nerd.'

'*Nerd?*'

'Yes, boringly studious.'

'It's not a word I've come across,' said Grayson.

'You obviously don't watch *Happy Days*,' said Katy with a wry smile.

'No, I can't say I do.'

'It was made popular by a character called Fonzie,' explained Katy.

Our clerical Chair of Governors simply looked bemused.

Tristan got up to leave. 'But only when he used it as a *pejorative*,' he said angrily.

'I was only teasing,' said Katy. 'No hard feelings.'

'Really?'

'Oh, Tristan,' said Audrey. 'Please don't be upset.'

Tristan stopped in his tracks and stared at Audrey. 'Audrey, sometimes you're too saintly for your own good.'

'I'm just trying to be helpful,' said Audrey.

'Saint Audrey,' said Tristan with sarcasm. He looked at Katy. 'So I'm *boringly studious*, am I?'

'Tristan,' said Katy, 'there's no need to be unkind to Audrey.'

He walked to the door but paused. 'Audrey, you'll be pleased to know there really was a Saint Audrey.'

'I didn't know that,' said Audrey in surprise. 'I'm impressed.'

'I wouldn't be if I were you. She was the seventh-century saint of sore throats,' and he hurried out.

'Oh dear,' said Audrey, suddenly feeling deflated.

'Something is troubling that young man,' murmured Grayson.

School lunch was well received by all the children. A serving of shepherd's pie and peas was followed by a special treat. A large spoonful of strawberry jelly quivered in the bottom of each bowl alongside a bright yellow block of Walls' ice cream.

After finishing their meal in double-quick time, the Swithenbank twins were so eager to get out on to the playground they left open the hall doors.

Mrs Starkey was quick to reproach them. 'Oy! Close them doors. Y'weren't born in a barn.'

'Jesus was, Miss,' retorted Tracey.

'T'vicar said so,' added Stacey and they ran off.

It wasn't often Mrs Starkey was left speechless.

Then it was time for the children's games; the infants had use of the hall for the first half of the afternoon. Rhonda led all the youngest children in the usual favourites including Statues, What Time Is It Mr, Wolf? and Musical Chairs. After break it was the juniors' turn: they packed away their board games and enjoyed an energetic hour of British Bulldog followed by a dancing competition and a disco.

At the end of school I was chatting with the children as they collected their coats and scarves. They were looking forward to their Christmas presents. Gary Cockroft had his heart set on a *Tiger Annual*, Dawn Whitehead had spotted a *Tammy Annual* in the understairs cupboard, while Jeremy Prendergast was confident he would be waking up on Christmas morning with a copy of *The Look and Learn Book 1977*.

As they hurried out into the darkness I reflected on my own childhood and the excitement of waking up on that fifties Christmas morning to a stocking containing a satsuma, a bag of nuts and a three-colour torch. Simple pleasures and special days.

It was late by the time I had tidied my classroom and Jim popped his head round my door. 'Let's have a coffee in my study before we go,' he said.

When I walked in I found he had arranged the two visitor chairs so we were facing each other and we sat down and sipped our coffee.

'Another Christmas, Jack. What are your plans?'

'It will be Christmas Day in Leeds again with my mother and my aunt.'

'Anything else?

'I'm going to a pantomime on New Year's Eve.'

'Oh, yes?'

'Up at North Beck village. A friend is in it and I'm supporting.'

'A friend?' said Jim with a smile. 'You mean the teacher from Bracken you were dancing with last week?'

'Yes, we get on well.'

Jim was never inquisitive and the conversation moved on. 'I wanted to discuss something with you, Jack. It concerns the future or, to be more precise, *your* future.'

I was curious. 'Go on.'

'I appointed you as deputy in 1970 so you will have completed seven years next summer.'

'Yes?' I put down my coffee cup and wondered what was coming next.

'You're a good teacher, Jack. That's obvious. I couldn't have wished for better support.'

'Thanks, Jim. I enjoy teaching at Newbridge.'

'That's clear but it's important you don't get too comfortable.'

'*Comfortable?*'

'It's time to think about the next step. You're still a young man but experienced enough now to take on a new challenge. I don't want to lose you but, then again, it's important I don't stand in your way.'

'So what's the new challenge, Jim?'

'The next logical step is the headship of a small school. Like as not you would keep your teaching, possibly full-time depending on the size of the school.'

'I see. It's crossed my mind but I've never really pursued it.'

'I like to see my staff develop and it's my role to help them and not hold them back. There will be other deputy heads in the pipeline just like you. So don't take this the wrong way. I'm trying to be positive.'

I sat back in my chair and looked at Jim. He was the head but also my friend and I had huge respect for him. Whenever he spoke it made sense and his words had gravitas.

'Well, you've certainly given me something to think about. Perhaps we can discuss it further in the spring term.'

'Let's do that . . . and one more thing . . .'

'Yes?'

He stood up and pulled a box of chocolates out of his top drawer. 'My wife bought these for you and asked me to wrap them but I didn't think you would mind.' He grinned and handed them over, unwrapped. 'Happy Christmas.'

'Thanks, Jim, and please thank Elizabeth. A kind thought.' I stood up and we shook hands. 'I appreciate the advice. Many thanks and all the best for Christmas and the New Year.'

I had a lot on my mind as I walked out to my car and was surprised to see Big Frank pumping up my tyres with a foot pump.

'Couldn't catch the bastard,' he muttered. 'Let down all yer tyres.'

I stood there shocked. 'Did you see who it was?'

'Not a kid, Mr Sheffield. It were a man. Tall an' skinny. Spotted 'im when ah were leavin' t'boiler 'ouse.'

'Thanks, Frank.'

'Looks like someone out there dunt like you.'

I sighed and wondered who it might be.

Chapter Nine

The Lost Art of Pantomime

'Here's your ticket for the pantomime,' said Donna.

It read:

North Beck Amateur Dramatic Society
present their Annual Pantomime
'ALADDIN'
Starring the ever-popular Helen Barraclough
Friday, 31st December at 7.00 p.m.
Ticket: 50 pence

'Fifty pence? Sounds expensive, so it should be good.'

'Don't raise your expectations, Jack.'

'That bad?'

'Worse.' She shook her head in mock despair. 'Well, for a start, Aladdin is not that smart and keeps forgetting his lines.'

'Not promising then.'

'And wait 'til you see Princess Jasmine.'

'Ah well . . . what about Sherri?'

'I'll sound biased now but she's probably the best actor we've got and she's only thirteen.'

'What part did you say she was playing?'

'Princess Jasmine's maidservant.'

'Hence the kimono you mentioned.'

'Yes. My mother bought me a new sewing machine last Christmas, so it came in handy.'

'And are you still looking after props?'

'Sadly, yes. It's a bit hectic. I'm working with a guy called Victor, who is lovely, but he's also looking after the curtains plus the off-stage sound effects.'

'Could I help?'

She considered this for a moment. 'Actually . . . I don't see why not. An extra pair of hands would be useful.'

I handed back the ticket. 'So I guess I won't need this as I'm now officially a member of the backstage staff.'

She put the ticket back in her handbag. 'You might live to regret this, Jack.'

'Not at all. What could possibly go wrong?'

She raised her eyebrows.

'Oh well,' I said. 'I guess it's for a good cause.'

'Yes, to repair the church clock. It's been half past nine for the last two years.'

'So correct twice a day.'

Donna sighed. 'Time for another coffee, Jack.'

'And maybe a toasted teacake before the shopping.'

She smiled. 'So romance is not dead after all.'

I stood at the counter and looked back at this beautiful woman as she took a small leather book from her handbag.

She was growing her blonde hair again and tucked it behind her ears as she scribbled notes. I enjoyed being in her company: it was relaxed, convivial and it felt, well . . . just right.

It was 11.00 a.m. on Monday, 20 December and we were back in the coffee shop in Leeds city centre where we had met in early September. She had driven in with Sherri and Georgie and the two girls had left to do their own teenage shopping in Leeds market. For my part I had checked my tyres very carefully before leaving home and hadn't mentioned the incident to Donna. It remained a mystery . . . and a concern.

Our first stop was Lewis's, the famous department store on the Headrow. Opened in 1932, it was the jewel in the retail crown of this great Yorkshire city.

The shop was busy with Christmas shoppers and I tagged along behind Donna, who seemed to know exactly where to go. We began on the ground floor where I had absolutely no interest in the perfumery department. Conversely, Donna spent considerable time studying the vast range of different scents. Shopping for me was always a brisk, no-nonsense activity, particularly at Christmas . . . buy it, wrap it, deliver it.

Having said that I had no idea what to buy for Donna so I followed her around and appreciated the wonderful decorations while considering the options. Finally, after an eternity trying to comprehend the various styles in the women's fashion department, we moved on and I snapped up gifts for my mother. This year's inflation rate had been over 16 per cent and prices seemed higher but I managed to buy a Morphy Richards Pop-Up Toaster for £11.95 and a Goblin Teasmade at £32.95.

'Nice to wake up to,' I said.

Donna gave me a mischievous grin and I guessed what she was thinking.

Weighed down by our bags we returned to her car and filled the boot with her shopping.

'I've arranged to catch up with Sherri and Georgie on the town hall steps at two o'clock, so what do you want to do?'

'I've still got a bit more shopping to do and this is a good opportunity. So why don't we leave it for now and meet up again in The Cock & Bottle on Christmas Eve.' Izzy had asked staff and friends to come along to hear her performance and there had been a good response.

'Sounds good. See you then.' She kissed me on the cheek and I watched her walk away.

Back in Lewis's the Christmas number one was playing. For a change it was a soothing song as Johnny Mathis sang 'When a Child Is Born'. Twenty minutes later I was walking down Briggate with what I thought would be the perfect gift for Donna. A young lady called Cheryl on the perfume counter had recommended Max Factor Blasé but I wasn't keen on the name so played safe with a bottle of Yves Saint Laurent Opium Eau de Toilette. She even gift-wrapped it for me. Then, as an afterthought, I took a chance on some Harmony Setting Lotion. I had no idea what it was for but the bottle looked attractive.

On the way back to my car I called in at the supermarket to buy a couple of pork pies for my evening meal. At the checkout an announcement blared out, 'Could someone come right away please for butchery?'

'Sounds a bit drastic,' I said but the lady on the till didn't respond. She was probably wondering why she got all the failed comedians.

That evening, back in Bradley village, I settled down in front of the television and a roaring log fire with my pork pie supper, a bag of takeaway chips from the pub and a bottle of Worthington's Pale Ale.

When I went to bed Donna was in my thoughts.

It was lunchtime on Christmas Eve and, in The Cock & Bottle, I joined a few of the staff sitting next to the fireplace. Donna had telephoned to say she would be delayed but would definitely be there after dropping off Sherri at her mother's. There were presents to deliver. I sat at a table with Jim and his wife. He had opened a bar tab and the staff were making good use of it.

Neville was there with his friend David, who raised his glass of wine and said, 'Don't forget, Jack. The invitation is there to come along to our Philately Society meetings.'

I smiled in acknowledgement but my mind was elsewhere. Izzy had arrived and sat down close to me. She put her hand on my shoulder. 'Thanks for coming, Jack. I hoped you would be able to make it.'

I looked around. 'You've got lots of support.'

'Yes, a good turnout. We're building up a bit of a following with the locals so it's going well.' Katy was standing at the bar with Mike Foster and Tom Deighton and she gave us a wave. 'That reminds me: Katy and I are having a party on New Year's Eve. Can you come? Should be fun.'

'I'm helping out at Donna's pantomime in her village hall. Not sure what I'll be doing after that.'

'Well, think about what you would *like* to do.' Izzy was never anything but forthright.

'Let's see how things go. Anyway, I'm looking forward to your singing.'

She moved a little closer. 'Have you any requests?'

I thought back to my sixties record collection. 'Well, I always enjoyed Joan Baez and Donovan and, of course, the Beatles.'

There was a tiny raised temporary stage at the far end of the bar and her two friends were tuning up. 'I know just the one,' she said. Then she stood up and squeezed through the crowd.

There was huge applause when Izzy stood on the stage. She looked great in her knitted crop top and flared jeans and her voice was warm. My mind drifted and I wondered what might have happened if Donna had not come back into my life.

She announced the first song. 'This is for a special friend, Donovan's "Catch the Wind".' She strummed her guitar and smiled as she sang about being in the warm hold of my loving mind.

Suddenly Donna was sitting next to me. 'Hi, sorry to be late. Sherri always helps my mum with the Christmas tree.'

'Great you could make it. What would you like to drink?'

She pulled off her scarf. Her cheeks were glowing. 'Just a lime and lemonade please.'

When I had ordered I looked back from the bar. Donna

was in animated conversation with Elizabeth Patterson. For a moment they both looked up at me and I gave a wave of acknowledgement.

Katy tapped me on the shoulder. 'Hi, Jack. What are you doing for Christmas?'

'At my parents' in Leeds.'

She grinned. 'Same here . . . but in Hornsea. Usual couple of days. Too much to eat, party games and Morecambe and Wise with an eggnog.'

'Sounds familiar except it's Guinness. My mother swears by it.'

Back in my seat, I handed Donna her drink, which she sipped gratefully. 'Thanks, I needed this. It's been busy.'

We listened to the music while Izzy sang the beautiful theme song from *Mahogany*, Diana Ross's 'Do You Know Where You're Going To'. As a rousing finale everyone in the pub joined in the chorus of 'Black Velvet Band' after which Jim served up a well-earned gin and tonic for Izzy.

I turned to Donna. 'It looked like you had run a marathon when you arrived.'

'Yes, felt a bit like that. You know what it's like when you're rushing – things get in the way.'

'Why, what happened?'

'Probably just kids, although our village is usually quiet and peaceful. Some idiot took the milk from the caddy outside my front door and then tied up the garden gate with baling twine. Took me ten minutes to get out to the car.'

'Oh dear, sorry to hear that. Anyway, you're here now. What about Sherri?'

'She's fine. Loves her nan, who spoils her rotten. She's

bought her a little Sony tape recorder so she can play her cassettes. Looks really good. She'll spend hours with it in her room no doubt. I've just bought her clothes. Boring but practical.'

'By the way, Katy and Izzy are having a party on New Year's Eve. I'm invited but I told them I was involved in your panto.'

'You could go on afterwards.'

'Not without you.'

'That's sweet, Jack, but I'll be at home with Sherri.'

'I was hoping to see in the New Year with you.'

'That might be possible. Let's see how we feel after *Aladdin*. I'm sure we'll both need a drink by then.'

Eventually we circulated around the pub and it finished up with all the women sitting by the fireplace and all the men propping up the bar discussing Leeds United's First Division holiday fixtures against Manchester City, Sunderland and Arsenal.

There were hugs and festive greetings as we left.

'Will I see you tonight, Jack, at Midnight Mass?' asked Jim.

'Yes, I promised Grayson.'

'That's good. See you later then.'

I walked with Donna back to her car. I had a duffel bag over my shoulder and from it I took a shoebox wrapped in Christmas paper with a surfeit of Sellotape. Inside were the gifts from Lewis's. 'Happy Christmas, Donna.'

'And here's yours, Jack.' It was beautifully wrapped in shiny green paper with a red ribbon.

'Thanks. This is a nice surprise.'

She smiled and we kissed. 'Enjoy your Christmas, Jack.'

'You too. See you on New Year's Eve.'

As I drove home Slade's now familiar 'Merry Christmas Everybody' was blasting out on the radio but, once again, I felt the sadness of parting.

It was Midnight Mass and whirling snowflakes drifted against the ancient walls of St Luke's in Newbridge. As always, it brought home to me the true meaning of Christmas.

Jim was there with his wife, Elizabeth, along with Audrey and Celestine, and I sat in the pew behind them. By 11.30 p.m. the church bells stopped ringing and the oak door was closed. The church was filled with villagers from all walks of life and quiet gradually descended on the congregation like a warm blanket. Around us the windowsills had been decorated with glossy green holly, bright with red berries, and tall candles cast a flickering light.

The organ was playing softly and a solo voice sang the first verse of 'Once in Royal David's City'. The choir entered, each member carrying a candle. It was good to be part of another Yorkshire Christmas.

The next morning I was up early and I packed my car for my traditional Christmas visit to my mother's home in Leeds. She lived with her sister, May. Like two peas in a pod, they chattered all day in their broad Glaswegian accents.

Sadly, my father had died in 1972, having never fully recovered from his days in the navy during the war. He was one of the survivors after the sinking of HMS *Prince of Wales* in the South China Sea in 1941 and was never the same again. The young, fit, happy man who left to fight in 1939 was a shell of his former self when he returned home. As my mother often said, 'Trauma is a terrible thing.'

It was a familiar routine with a huge Christmas dinner and a few simple gifts. My mother had bought me a pair of leather driving gloves and a bottle of Old Spice. Donna had also bought me an identical bottle of Old Spice so I guessed it would be a new fragrant me in 1977. Meanwhile, Aunt May presented me with what she considered to be gifts that were both practical and sensible. I thanked her for my Elastoplast First Aid Kit at £1.99 and a tyre pressure gauge from Halford's at sixty pence. She had not removed the price tags. In light of recent events it struck me that the tyre pressure gauge was well timed.

When I left on Boxing Day I was presented with a tin containing a dozen mince pies, then showered with hugs and kisses. Proudly wearing my new driving gloves I drove straight to Grassington and Upper Wharfedale Rugby Club.

The Boxing Day fixture against local rivals Harrogate was a close-fought game with Wharfedale winning thanks to a brilliant last-gasp try from our captain Michael Harrison, a former England schoolboys centre. This festive fixture was always a special event and celebrations went on long into the night. A television was flickering away in the corner and, after the sports results, there was a news item that reminded us we had said a final farewell to some of the luminaries of our time including L. S. Lowry and Benjamin Britten.

Snow was falling again as I drove home past the Christmas lights on Skipton High Street and on to the peace of Bradley village.

At lunchtime on New Year's Eve I met Donna in Sally's Tea Rooms in North Beck High Street. Sherri was already in the village hall rehearsing a dance routine.

'Jack, I'll introduce you to Helen Barraclough when we go in. She's the prima donna of the local am-drams. Always gives herself the leading role and has done, apparently, for the past twenty years.'

'So what part is she playing?'

'The princess.'

'I thought that usually went to a young girl.'

'Yes, Jack, but this is Helen's show.'

'I see.'

'The guy in the far corner is her husband.' A portly man in his fifties was enjoying a large helping of apple pie and custard. 'That's Bernard Barraclough.'

'So what part does he play?'

'None. He avoids the panto like the plague. Says he's sick to the back teeth with it and it spoils Christmas every year.'

'So no support.'

'Only financial. He pays for everything.'

'A wealthy man then. Clearly not a teacher.'

'He's done well for himself. He owns the chain of Rub-a-Dub-Dub Car Washes in West Yorkshire. Started with a hose pipe, bucket and sponge and worked his way up from there.'

'A local entrepreneur, then?'

'Definitely. So Helen leads a life of leisure and the amdrams are the focal point of her life.'

We enjoyed our tea and crumpets and set off for the village hall where we were met by the larger-than-life Helen.

'Jack,' said Donna. 'This is Helen, our artistic director and principal actor.' It was a well-rehearsed line.

A stocky lady in her forties and with an enormous bosom stood before me.

'Oh, how delightful to meet you,' said the effusive Helen. She kissed me on both cheeks with all the decorum of a sink plunger. 'Donna has been such a help with the multifarious props and her daughter is an exquisite dancer.' She looked me up and down. 'Have you thespian tendencies? Next year it's *Beauty and the Beast* and you've definitely got the height and the broad shoulders.'

I felt like saying I didn't think I was pretty enough but Donna gave me that familiar *behave yourself* look.

While Donna went to talk to Sherri I met the lugubrious Victor, the props manager, yet another portly man in his fifties. 'Now then, are you Donna's teacher friend?'

'Yes, I'm Jack. Pleased to meet you. I said I would help with the props.'

'Well, yer very welcome, Jack.' We shook hands. 'I'm Victor Barraclough. M'brother, Bernard, is married to *She-Who-Must-Be-Obeyed*.'

'You mean Helen?'

'Yes, 'fraid so.'

'You don't sound too happy about that.'

He sighed deeply. 'Ah don't mind tellin' you. It's local knowledge anyway. Ah pity m'brother.'

'Really?'

'Yes, 'e's a martyr f'staying wi' 'er.'

'Oh dear, I'm sorry to hear that.' I tried to sound sympathetic but was beginning to understand why. 'So, what's the problem with Helen?'

He clearly saw me as a sympathetic friend, so he checked left and right, and spoke in a low voice. 'Well, let's put it this way . . . wi' a face like a wet weekend she's definitely no 'Elen of Troy.'

'Why is that?'

He grinned. 'Well, if she was, that King Menelaus would've stood on t'cliff top an' waved 'er goodbye wi' a smile on 'is face. He would 'ave said t'that Prince Paris o' Troy, yer welcome to 'er, mate.' He was on a roll now. 'All them lads in 'is thousand ships could 'ave gone fishin', an' 'e would've sacrificed 'is favourite goat to thank that goddess Aphrodite for arrangin' it.'

I was impressed with his knowledge of Greek legend but even more so with the description of his sister-in-law.

'So what's our job?'

'Props, Jack.' He held up a sheet of paper. 'We follow t'list and give 'em stuff they need.'

'Sounds straightforward,' I said.

I couldn't have been more wrong.

The dress rehearsal didn't go well and I could see that Donna's assessment of the main characters was accurate.

Norman Plumb, the local coalman's son, was clearly miscast as Aladdin. The prompter was kept busy reminding him of his next line to which he kept replying, 'Y'what?'

Helen Barraclough was a particularly unconvincing

Princess Jasmine. Her opening number, Marmalade's 'Falling Apart at the Seams', was not the best choice as she was dressed like a trussed turkey: bursting out of a kimono that was also falling apart at the seams.

The casting of the local undertaker, Benson Frith, as Widow Twankey was clearly a mistake. Benson was renowned for his sombre manner and sad countenance, perfect for his profession but not for a pantomime dame. His jokes were weak and delivered with all the aplomb of a cold funeral in February. Also his Dance of the Seven Tea Towels would have been better left in the kitchen cupboard.

Fred Peddle, the local butcher, as Abanazer, the wicked wizard, was probably the best of the main characters, although I guessed that waving a meat cleaver instead of a wand would be off-putting for those in the front row.

Sherri, meanwhile, was word perfect and danced beautifully with a group of other teenage girls. At the end, a red-faced Helen was not in the best of moods but still managed Churchillian resolve. 'Break a leg, everybody. It will be perfect this evening.'

By 7.00 p.m. the North Beck village hall was full to bursting. This was clearly one of the highlights of the year for the locals.

Even so, there was some grumbling at the door regarding the fifty-pence entrance fee as, in past years, the quality of the performance had left much to be desired. Apparently last year's power cut had caused a particular furore. Helen, in her outsize Goldilocks outfit, had been singing Mud's number one 'Lonely This Christmas'. It proved an apt choice as, by the end of the song, she was the only one left. Even the Three Bears had decided to forgo their porridge and vacate to the pub next door for a candlelit pint.

The lights dimmed and Victor pulled the cord to open the curtains to reveal Aladdin pulling up his bright red tights while his mother stirred the contents of a posser tub. The narrator, Beatrice Critchley, the local chiropodist, picked up her microphone, blew into it loudly and set the scene. 'In a land far far away, Aladdin and his mother are struggling to make ends meet. However, Aladdin dreams of becoming a prince and rich beyond his wildest dreams . . . but that would require MAGIC!'

'Cymbals, Victor,' whispered Donna.

Victor was still tying up the curtain rope. There was no time to waste. Donna grabbed the pair of cymbals and crashed them together. A startled Victor let go of the curtain rope and it descended again. Immediately, the audience clapped, presuming that was the end of scene one.

'Curtain, Victor,' said Donna with a little more urgency.

I couldn't help because I was holding a wooden sign that read 'The Street of a Thousand Scrubbers'. It had broken during the dress rehearsal and I had to hide at the side of the stage and hold it at arm's length.

Happily, things improved when Sherri and the ensemble, in brightly coloured Chinese costumes and pushing a cardboard rickshaw, performed a balletic interpretation of Cole Porter's 'Come to the Supermarket (in Old Peking)'.

Everything seemed to be going well until Abanazer asked the audience how to open the cave.

'Open Sesame,' shouted the front row.

Aladdin stepped inside and, remarkably, remembered his line. 'Look, a lad in,' he said. Then he jumped out of the cave, 'And a lad out!'

However, no one laughed.

The narrator spoke again in a voice of doom: 'Aladdin is trapped in the cave for eternity by a magic spell,' and the lights dimmed. I had placed a small trampoline at the side of the stage in preparation for the dramatic entry of the Genie.

Donna and I turned expectantly to Victor.

'I've lost it!' he said.

'Lost what?' said Donna.

'The lamp.' He raised his voice. 'The bloody lamp! It's gone!'

'We need it *now*,' said Donna.

Jerry Blenkinsop, the local cobbler, looked agitated. He had been practising his high-flying entrance in his bedroom and had ruined the springs on his single bed.

'It'll be that dozy Aladdin,' hissed Victor. 'He doesn't know whether he's coming or going.'

'Close the curtains, Victor . . . quickly!' said Donna.

The curtain lowered and Jerry sat on his trampoline wishing he had used blue make-up on his spindly legs as well as his face and chest while Donna searched frantically for the lamp.

'We'll have to find something else for him to rub,' I said lamely. I looked around. 'How about the kettle?'

'You're joking,' said a disgruntled Aladdin from the darkness of his cave.

'Y'can't use a bleedin' kettle,' muttered the despairing

Genie. I guessed he was going blue in the face but that would have been hard to tell.

Donna shook her head and lifted up the battered stainless steel kettle. 'It's got a spout. Better than nothing.'

It went downhill from that moment on. The audience laughed in derision when Aladdin rubbed the kettle. Meanwhile, the blue and white Genie sprained his ankle and the flying carpet revealed a mouse when it was unrolled. Chaos ensued and Princess Jasmine ran off the stage.

Like a true professional the narrator droned on, determined to complete the final page. By then the audience had departed.

It was late when we walked back to Donna's cottage. Sherri prepared a hot chocolate for us all and we sat by the fire and recounted the events of the evening. It was a happy time and I stayed until Big Ben chimed midnight on the television and the three of us joined hands and sang 'Auld Lang Syne'.

Finally Sherri said goodnight and climbed the stairs to bed.

'I know I can't stay, Donna.'

She sighed and nodded. 'Another time, Jack,' she said quietly and glanced back at the stairs.

I donned my duffel coat and scarf and we went out to the tiny hallway. She opened the door and we looked out on the still land. It was the time of the long nights when darkness ruled the world. The falling snow muted all sounds and, for a moment, a mantle of peace cloaked our world as we stood there holding hands.

Beneath an indigo sky it felt as though we were at a crossroads in our lives. There were decisions to be made and there was caution in her voice as she looked up at me. 'I don't want to take it too fast, Jack.'

'I understand.'

We kissed, then parted.

Above us the fleeting ghosts of distant clouds drifted by.

I walked away with only the voice of the wind whispering in my ear and wondered what the New Year would bring.

Chapter Ten

Words without Thoughts

It was Monday, 3 January, the first day of the spring term, and when I left home the stillness of winter stretched out before me, a world of silence under a blanket of snow. The road out of the village was a dark river of ice that wound between the frozen hedgerows and the sleeping trees. Wood smoke hung heavy in the morning air as I drove gingerly up Newbridge High Street and into the school car park.

"Appy New Year, Mr Sheffield,' shouted a familiar voice. Big Frank, wrapped up like Nanook of the North, leaned on his snow shovel and gave me a wave. 'Cleared a path right to t'front gate,' he panted.

'Well done, Frank. Many thanks and a Happy New Year to you too.'

"Ard work in this weather but t'kids'll love it.'

'I'm sure they will,' and I trod carefully up the salt-covered steps and into the entrance hall.

Izzy was playing the piano when I walked into the hall.

'Happy New Year,' I said.

She turned and smiled, 'And to you, Jack.' She studied me for a moment. 'So . . . where were you on New Year's Eve?'

'I called in at Donna's and then went home again. How was the party?'

'Brilliant. You missed a treat. Really good crowd. Loud music. Dancing. Usual stuff.'

'Sounds good.'

'It's my birthday on the twenty-first of this month so there's another party in store. You must come to that one.'

'The twenty-first . . . so you're an Aquarius.'

'That's me, Jack. The individualist of the zodiac.'

'Sounds like you know your star signs.'

'I love astrology. So when's your birthday?'

'Not 'til the summer – August.'

She grinned. 'I might have guessed. Leo . . . king of the jungle.'

'Maybe, but not the bossy sort. More a team-playing lion, I hope.'

'So you keep your fiery emotions in check.'

She was teasing me again but it was fun. 'Not always. Anyway, tell me about your birthday.'

'It's on a Friday this year, so you've no excuses. Staff only this time. Hope that's OK.'

She turned back to the piano, pushed her long hair from her face and played the first verse of 'Morning Has Broken' in preparation for our first assembly of 1977.

As I walked back to my classroom I remembered that Donna had an April birthday. I recalled dominant Arien qualities included coming straight to the point. However, thoughts of star signs disappeared quickly when the bell went and thirty children, bursting with news and energy, hurried to their desks.

''Ave you 'ad a good 'oliday, sir?' asked Pauline Ackworth.

'An' did y'get anything nice f'Christmas?' asked Gary Cockroft. 'I got a pogo stick an' a football.'

'And I got a Monopoly set, sir,' said Jeremy. 'We played for hours and I owned a hotel on Mayfair.'

'Wish I did,' I replied.

'I got a Spirograph, sir,' said Dawn Whitehead, 'an' m'brother got a model Evel Knievel stunt bike.'

'That's exciting, Dawn.'

'Not for our Timmy it wasn't, sir. It nearly took 'is eye out!'

'Timmy?'

'Yes, sir, our cat.'

'Oh dear, so how is it now?'

'Fine, sir, m'brother repaired it.'

'Actually, I meant the—'

Fortunately, Susan Verity butted in: 'Willy Wonka was on telly, sir,' and so we moved seamlessly on to *Multi-Coloured Swap Shop* and the new series of *Doctor Who*.

After registers everyone settled down and I looked at their expectant faces. It was an important year for them, their last at Newbridge before moving on to the comprehensive school with its forty-minute lessons, large gymnasium, new friends and teenage acne.

'Boys and girls, after our maths and English this morning we shall be starting a new project in our topic books.

It's about a famous Englishman called Captain Scott who made a journey to the South Pole.'

I had a map of Antarctica, a globe and lots of pictures of the expedition, including a copy of the last entry in his diary.

'We could act it outside in the snow, sir,' said Jeremy Prendergast.

'Can I be Captain Scott, sir?' asked Gary Cockroft.

'Why do boys get all the best parts?' asked Pauline Ackworth defiantly.

'Good point, Pauline.'

Jeremy attracted my attention. 'Sir, doesn't Captain Scott die in his tent?'

'Yes, that's right.'

Pauline raised her hand once again. 'On secon' thoughts, sir, let Gary be Captain Scott.'

Gary stared at her, slightly bemused and not sure whether to be pleased or annoyed.

Jim was on good form in morning assembly. He welcomed back everyone for the new term. 'Let's make it a good one,' he said with a smile.

Izzy accompanied the morning hymns and Grayson led us in prayers. The theme was making sure we were not unkind. 'Think what you say,' he said. 'Sometimes words can be hurtful,' and I reflected on the import of his words.

At morning break I was wrapped up in my old college scarf and duffel coat on playground duty while watching the children making snowmen and throwing snowballs on the school field.

I saw Izzy coming down the entrance steps with a steaming mug of coffee.

She gave me a broad smile from under her bright red bobble hat. 'This is for you, Jack.'

'Thanks, Izzy. I was engrossed talking to the children and didn't pick up a hot drink.'

'That's what Audrey said and Neville's brought in a tin of his scones for afternoon break. He's going to warm them up in the kitchen and serve them with his home-made jam.'

'A treat in store.'

She turned to go back into school. 'Like my party, Jack.'

I sipped the coffee and smiled.

It was lunchtime when I caught up with the rest of the staff. Audrey was serving up tea and Grayson had just completed a Bible story lesson in Rhonda's class.

'Lovely assembly, Grayson,' said Celestine.

'Thanks,' he said. 'Important to start the year on the right foot.'

'An important message,' I said.

'That could be our New Year resolution in the staff-room,' said Rhonda with a grin.

'You mean being careful what we say?' said Katy.

'Yes,' said Grayson, 'nothing unkind.'

'Like not calling me a nerd again,' said Tristan with feeling.

Katy frowned. 'Come on, Tristan. It was said in fun. I did say I was sorry.'

'Let bygones be bygones,' said Grayson.

'Allelujah,' said Tristan.

Celestine looked up concerned. '"Words without thoughts never to heaven go,"' she quoted.

Tristan stood up. 'Shakespeare,' he said. '*Hamlet*, Act Three, Scene Three.' Then he picked up his mug of coffee and walked out.

'I'll have a word,' I said and followed him out into his classroom.

He was sitting at his desk, clearly troubled.

'I love Shakespeare,' I said, 'but your knowledge of his plays is remarkable. How do you do it?'

Tristan looked up, surprised. He was expecting me to take issue with his outburst. 'Well . . . I read. It's my main hobby. I'm working my way through the novels of Charles Dickens at present.'

'Another one of my favourites. I was Main English at college.'

There was a flicker of a smile. 'Same here.'

'You could do me a favour when you have time.'

'What's that?'

'There's a boy in my class, Jeremy, who reminds me of you. A great reader. Perhaps you could talk to him at some time and share some thoughts about books.'

'I know him, Jack. A quiet, studious boy.' He grinned. 'And yes . . . a bit like me.'

'I don't think Katy meant any harm, by the way.'

'I guess not . . . but words can hurt and I don't want to be *different*. I get frustrated. Some of the conversations in the staff-room can be so low level.'

'Perhaps so, but it's their way of relaxing. Simply talking about everyday things can be a release . . . shopping, television, clothes, holidays, baking cakes. The list is

163

endless. Maybe just chip in now and again. That's all I do.'

'OK, Jack . . . and thanks. I'll talk to Katy before the end of school.'

I left him preparing his classroom for an afternoon art lesson. He wrote the title 'Snowflakes Patterns' on the blackboard and then placed a sheet of black sugar paper and a stick of white chalk on each desk.

Back in the staff-room Rhonda and Audrey were sitting next to the single-bar electric heater.

'I'm taking Bryn to the January sales after school,' said Rhonda.

'Have you got something special in mind?' asked Audrey.

Rhonda pulled a paper cutting out of her pocket. 'This is it. A Sunbeam Multi-Cooker.'

'I've heard of those,' said Celestine.

'It does the things an oven can do at half the cost and you can move it into the dining room for serving.'

Audrey took the advertisement and studied it. 'Sounds wonderful.'

Rhonda was on a roll. 'Thermostatic heat control, Teflon coating, saves on electricity and you can wash it in the sink after cooking. What more could you want?'

'Someone to do the washing up,' said Katy, who was sitting nearby with Tom and looking through the new sports-equipment magazine.

'That's Bryn's job,' said Rhonda emphatically.

'Does Bryn know what he's going shopping for?' asked Katy with a smile.

Rhonda shook her head. 'I only tell him what I need him to know, nothing more, nothing less.'

Tom looked up from the magazine. 'So you don't mince your words then, Rhonda.'

'Not with men, I don't,' and she gave him a withering look.

It was afternoon break and Tom Deighton looked out of the staff-room window. 'Bleak out there. Might be no football next weekend if the pitch is frozen.'

Katy nodded. 'Mike said the same.' It was common knowledge among the staff now that Katy and Mike Foster were definitely an *item*.

'He was talking to me about a summer holiday,' said Tom.

'Yes, we're looking for somewhere sunny and cheap.'

Tristan looked up, 'Hey, Katy, in this morning's paper it was advertising eight days in Sicily for sixty-nine pounds.'

'Thanks, Tristan,' said a surprised Katy.

'I'll drop it off on your desk before the end of school.' He glanced across at me and smiled.

Small steps, I thought.

At the end of school Jim called into my classroom. 'Just a quick word, Jack. Audrey has typed out the agenda for this evening's governors' meeting.' He passed over a typed sheet of paper. 'You'll see that Mrs Peacock is now the local-councillor representative.'

'Oh dear,' I said. 'That's not good news.'

Jim sighed. 'It will make it a long meeting.'

'Probably some relief for her husband, I imagine,' I said.

'Yes, the poor man,' said Audrey. 'Gerald is really under

the thumb these days. I heard at the dry cleaner's that he has name tags sewn into his trousers.'

'Doesn't surprise me,' said Jim.

'We shall all have to be careful what we say,' said Audrey.

'Yes. Good point,' said Jim. 'In fact, I was going to say let *me* deal with her. She's sure to raise countless issues under Any Other Business.'

'Are you going to tell Grayson, as he will be chairing it?' I asked.

Jim pursed his lips. 'I don't think so. We'll just hope for the best.' He glanced at the clock. 'Thanks and see you at seven.'

On my way home I pulled up outside Snoddy's Stores.

Michelle was behind the counter listening to her transistor radio. Dr Hook was singing 'A Little Bit More' and she was humming along.

'Hello, Michelle. You're looking happy today.'

The fact that this also implied she rarely looked happy on other days didn't occur to her. 'It's t'fabric shop up the 'Igh Street, Mr Sheffield.'

'What about it?'

'They're sellin' pop socks an' textured tights. They're brilliant.'

'Really?' It sounded as though the owner of this old-fashioned shop had decided there was profit to be had if it appealed to a younger generation with disposable income. Michelle Snoddy was clearly thrilled.

I checked the list in my pocket. My needs were fairly

basic. 'Please could I have some Frosties, a loaf, a tin of beans, a packet of Wagon Wheels and a bottle of Tizer?'

While Michelle tried to work out the total on her calculator I stared at the box of Kellogg's. They had converted all their cereal boxes to metric.

I couldn't imagine leaving behind pounds and ounces, gallons and pints, feet and inches. It was a new world that included pop socks and square crisps and there were moments when I felt it was leaving me behind.

Back in Bradley village I had a hasty meal of beans on toast followed by a Wagon Wheel with a mug of tea before getting changed for the governors' meeting and another drive on the icy roads.

I crunched over the packed snow in the school car park just as Jim pulled up in his new car. He had treated himself to a Chrysler Alpine. The 1976 'Car of the Year' at a little over two thousand pounds was way out of my price range. In any case, I was proud of my Morris Minor. It continued to serve me well even in these conditions.

By six thirty we were seated in the centre of the school hall. Frank had arranged a collection of dining tables in the shape of a long rectangle. Gilbert Snoddy was a long-standing member of the governing body and he gave me a friendly smile. 'Now then, Mr Sheffield. 'Appy New Year.'

Grayson, as chairman, was at one end with Jim to his right and Audrey, as secretary, to his left. The rest of us found the first available seat with the exception of our new local-councillor governor, namely the pedantic Mrs

Clarissa Peacock. She seated herself at the far end of the table facing Grayson. One could almost imagine that it was *she* chairing the meeting.

A formidable presence: when she removed her hat it was noticeable that her hair stayed exactly in place. Clarissa had visited the local hairdresser that afternoon. The severe operation had ended with a rinse of Linco Beer shampoo followed by enough spray to provide her hair with the consistency of a crash helmet.

'Good evening, everybody,' said Grayson, 'and a special welcome to the newest member of our governing body, Mrs Peacock.'

All seemed to go surprisingly well. Jim gave his report on the state of the school, Audrey updated everyone about numbers on roll and I said a few words about our developing curriculum.

The last agenda item concerned 'Fabric of the Building'.

Grayson pressed on: 'Finally we turn to the repair work to the roof of the toilet block. My understanding is it is progressing well.'

'Not so,' muttered a voice.

Everyone looked in the direction of Mrs Peacock.

'I decided to check this myself,' announced Mrs Peacock, 'and I regret to inform you there has been an erectile dysfunction.'

'Pardon?' said Grayson and Jim simultaneously.

'A malfunction of the erection, vicar,' continued Clarissa.

Audrey paused in her shorthand and glanced at Jim, who responded with an imperceptible shake of the head.

'What's t'problem?' asked Gilbert.

'It's plain to see. There's a problem with the trusses, according to Mr Cannon.'

'Frank didn't mention this to me,' said Jim.

'Are you sure you heard correctly?' asked Grayson.

Clarissa was becoming heated. 'Of course I did, vicar, and may I say you have not chosen your words with sufficient care. I'm indignant and my indignance is not to be denied.'

'Come, come, Mrs Peacock,' said Jim, 'no offence was intended and I shall investigate this matter.'

'Is that all?' said Grayson hopefully.

'No,' said Mrs Peacock defiantly.

'What is it you wished to say?' he asked with what he hoped was a neutral expression.

'I'm concerned about the admissions policy. We're bringing in too many children of, well . . . an *African* persuasion, so to speak, and I am confident there is a hooliganistic element.'

Gilbert was struggling to follow. ''Scuse me for interruptin', Mrs Peacock, but what the flippin' 'eck are you on about?'

'I'm saying it won't be long before we are surrounded by ubiquitous foreigners.'

Jim had heard enough. 'I need to remind everyone,' he said quietly, 'that we don't refuse admissions because of creed or colour.'

'Quite so,' said Grayson.

'That can *never* be our policy, Mrs Peacock,' I said firmly.

Jim looked at me and raised his eyebrows.

For Mrs Peacock this was a red rag to a bull. 'I do believe

there are times when Mr Sheffield attempts to destabilize the machinery of effective discourse.'

'Perhaps we simply need to select our choice of words with care,' said Grayson, trying to calm the troubled waters.

It occurred to me that we had come full circle since his morning assembly.

Finally the meeting closed and I followed Mrs Peacock out into the darkness.

'I'm not happy, Mr Sheffield,' she muttered.

'I'm sorry to hear that,' I replied while feeling in my pocket for my car keys.

'The meeting was an unmitigated disaster but that, of course, is my personalistic opinion.'

'I see,' I said hesitantly.

'The Revd Huppleby was merely spouting his usual apathetical politics. In my view his philosophical outbursts exacerbated the disturbance of the meeting.'

I stared at this disconcerting woman. There was a dewdrop at the end of her nose: an unappealing sight. 'Yes, well, must get off,' I said.

'Life has always been painful for me, Mr Sheffield.'

'I'm sorry to hear that.'

She lowered her voice in a conspiratorial manner. 'Yes, I have *irregularities*.'

'Really?'

'Yes, with my coccyx . . . it's not aligned.'

That's not all, I thought.

Grayson had raised the issue of words without thoughts this morning. In Mrs Peacock's case it was also words without meaning.

'Well . . . goodnight, Mrs Peacock,' and I hurried away to the car park.

My home was welcome on this bitterly cold evening and I built up the fire and settled down. Outside snow was falling again and a gusting wind drew the flickering flames up the chimney while the logs crackled and glowed.

I turned on the television and saw that a new programme called *Poldark* had begun. It immediately grabbed my attention. I loved historical drama. The series was set in Cornwall in the 1780s. The main character, Ross, had returned home to inherit a house, two copper mines and to marry someone called Elizabeth. However, he had been reported dead and others had laid claim to his house. It was an intriguing plot.

When it ended I made a mug of tea and put my feet up to read. I was a fan of Tom Sharpe and was enjoying his 1974 novel *Porterhouse Blue*. In it he said that if a little knowledge was a dangerous thing then a lot was lethal. I smiled and thought of Donna. I knew a lot about her now . . . but not everything.

It was late but, on impulse, I rang her.

'It's me.'

'Hi, Jack.' She sounded sleepy.

'Is this a bad time?'

'No, just a busy day. You know what it's like. First day back.'

'How has it gone?'

'Fine. The children loved the snow.'

'I was wondering if you wanted to go to the sales this weekend.'

'Sherri asked the same thing. I was thinking of York for a treat.'

'I could drive you.'

'That might be good . . .'

'So maybe Saturday. What time?'

'To be honest, Jack, I think Sherri would enjoy it with just the two of us.'

'Great, I'll look forward to it.'

'Sorry, I didn't make myself clear. I meant just Sherri and myself.'

'Oh, I see.'

'Hope you understand, but . . .'

'I get it. You don't want to commit.'

There was a long silence. 'Not quite, Jack.'

'So what is it?' I sounded abrupt and regretted it immediately.

'It's complicated.'

'My turn to say sorry. I didn't mean to press you. I guess I won't be going to heaven.'

'Pardon?'

'Sorry, just something the vicar said in assembly this morning.'

'What . . . about going to heaven?'

'More to do with thinking before you speak. My fault. I shouldn't assume.'

'I thought you understood. I told you last week. It's happened so fast. I need time.'

'I do understand.'

'And I have to consider my daughter in all of this.'

'It's your decision and I'm here if you need me.'

I heard her sigh. 'It's just that I've made mistakes with men.'

The penny dropped. 'You mean Sherri's dad, Barty Withinshaw?'

'I'll tell you more about him one day, Jack.'

'Donna ... ring me if you change your mind. Either way I'm here.'

'Thanks, Jack. I had better go.'

'Goodnight, Donna.'

'Bye, Jack.'

There was the buzz of the phone as the call ended and I sat there wishing I had handled the conversation differently. That was the problem with words. They spilled out and you couldn't take them back.

When I walked into my silent bedroom I stared out of the window before closing the curtains. It was the time of the wolf moon, the first full moon of the year, and the land was full of stark shadows.

Chapter Eleven

Turbulent Times

'Sir! Sir! There's a crack in our ceiling!' shouted Jeremy Prendergast. He looked alarmed. It was 9.00 a.m. on Friday, 21 January and an eventful day lay in store.

I had been about to take the register when there was a noise above our heads. The plastered ceiling in our Victorian building was very high. From it four fluorescent lights hung from heavy chains. A crack about two feet long had suddenly appeared, as Jeremy had spotted.

I made a decision. 'Boys and girls, stand up, please.'

There was a rumble of chairs and a few nervous glances up at the ceiling.

'We're going to walk out to the hall. There's no need to rush.'

The children were well behaved and we had rehearsed a fire drill several times in the past. Row by row they walked out and, with a last look at the ceiling, I followed them.

'Gary, knock on Mr Patterson's door and ask him to come into the hall, please.' Gary Cockroft hurried away.

'Now, boys and girls, we're going to do Mr Cannon a big favour and get out the dining tables and chairs earlier than usual and work in the hall this morning.'

The children seemed enthused by this idea. It was different.

Suddenly there was an almighty crash from the class-room. I opened the door and looked back inside. A large chunk of plaster about the size of a coffee table had fallen from the ceiling and landed on the desks in the centre of the room, followed by a cloud of dust. I shut the door quickly.

Jim arrived while the children were arranging tables and chairs and we stood by the classroom door. 'Problem, Jim,' I said quietly. 'We got out just in time. The ceiling is clearly unsafe. I'll teach the children in the hall for the time being.'

He opened the door and looked inside. 'Thank God you vacated in time. I'll check on the rest of the classrooms and tell the staff what's happened. Then I'll ring County Hall. Good job it's a Friday. It gives us the weekend to get it sorted.' As always, Jim was taking it in his stride.

I turned back to the children, who were sitting around five of the dining tables. They were looking up at me expectantly. We had no books, no blackboard, no pens . . . nothing.

'First of all, boys and girls, well done to Jeremy who spotted the problem. Let's give him a clap.'

Jeremy smiled. Fame at last for this quiet bookworm.

'Now I would like Jeremy's group to come with me to the stock cupboard to collect some paper and pencils. While we're gone I want you to discuss how to work out how many days have gone by since you were born.'

'Last year was a leap year, sir,' said Claire Braithwaite.

'So there was an extra day, sir,' said an eager Susan Verity. 'February the twenty-ninth.'

'That's right. Well done, girls.'

'And when it's a leap year it's always the Olympics,' added Susan for good measure, 'and that Nadia Comaneci scored a perfect ten in gymnastics.'

I was always impressed by the knowledge this little girl displayed.

'That's brilliant, Susan. In fact, we could do some gymnastics later today.'

'And score perfect tens,' added Tracey Swithenbank with a grin.

'Can we do it now, sir?' asked her sister.

I smiled, 'Soon, girls . . . after maths and English.'

I glanced at the clock in the hall. It was nine fifteen. *Tough start to the school day,* I thought . . . but there was more to come.

In fact, Friday hadn't begun well at home either. Earlier that morning I had looked out on a cold and hostile world. It had been a frozen dawn and the pale sun in the east had touched the land with icy fingertips. As my Morris Minor had crunched over the frozen snow a nimbus of frozen droplets covered the hedgerows and the heavy mist felt like a cloak of despair. The bleak journey to school had taken much longer than usual and I had been the last to arrive in the car park.

By the time morning assembly came round the children in my class had stacked the tables and chairs at the side of the hall. The rest of the staff knew about my ceiling and had looked at the damage for themselves. Meanwhile,

Izzy was playing a quiet introductory piece on the piano as the children walked in.

'Happy birthday,' I whispered in her ear and she smiled.

As I sat down Jim walked to the front of the hall and silence descended.

'Good morning, boys and girls.'

'Good morning, Mr Patterson,' chorused the children.

'Good morning, everybody.'

Jim explained that my class would be working in the hall so there would be changes to the timetable. He also stressed there was nothing to worry about and the ceiling would soon be repaired.

After Celestine had read an extract from C. S. Lewis's thought-provoking *The Lion, the Witch and the Wardrobe* and Izzy had led us in a rousing rendition of 'All Things Bright and Beautiful', Grayson ended the assembly with the Lord's Prayer. He had completed his weekly Bible story lessons, which had included Neville's class. I realized that some of the children had not entirely comprehended the full meaning of 'Moses and the Ten Commandments', when, at morning break, I saw our local vicar sipping his coffee and frowning at the writing the children had completed. The exercise books were piled on the book-shelf next to him. I picked up one and smiled when I read the spidery writing of Billy Oldroyd. He had writ-ten: 'Moses went up Mount Cyanide to get the Ten Amendments'.

Grayson had written in red ink underneath 'Please check your spellings'.

It struck me that the spellings were, in fact, *perfect*.

*

Through the window I spotted a large white van pulling up outside. On its side a bright blue sign read:

'GET PLASTERED'
L. Crump
No job too small

Mr Crump was an overweight thirty-something with a distinct beer belly and a double chin. I met him in the entrance hall.

'Hello, I'm Jack Sheffield, the deputy head.'

'Ah'm Lenny . . . Lenny Crump. Gorra call this mornin' from County 'All 'bout yer ceiling.'

'Thank you for coming so promptly, Mr Crump. It's my classroom you need to see.'

When we walked in he stared up, folded his arms and shook his head. 'Big job,' he declared. ''Igh ceilin'.'

'When can you do it?' I asked.

He sucked air through his teeth in the time-honoured fashion of tradesmen through the ages. 'Mebbe Thursday.'

'Any chance of sooner? I'm having to teach the children in the dining hall. It's causing a lot of disruption.'

It was at this moment that Audrey appeared after serving coffee to the staff. 'Hello, Lenny. I saw your van. How is your mother?' Audrey turned to me. 'Betty is a lovely lady. Makes wonderful sausage rolls for the church fête every year.'

'She's fine, thanks, Miss Fazackerly.'

'I'm so pleased you're here.' Audrey smiled up at me. 'Lenny is a wonderful plasterer.' She gave Lenny a beatific smile. 'So when can you come in to help us, Lenny?'

On this occasion Lenny *blew* air through pursed lips

and stared up as if seeking divine guidance. 'Ah could come t'morrow mornin'.'

'That's excellent, Lenny, and do give your mother my best wishes.'

Audrey gave me a wink as she walked away while Lenny took out his notebook and tape measure and we returned to my classroom.

Once again it struck me that a good secretary like Audrey was worth her weight in gold.

After a warming school dinner of boiled beef, potatoes and cabbage followed by cornflake tart and custard, I walked into the staff-room where the usual diverse mix of conversation was going on.

Tom Deighton was wishing he could afford one of the new Ford Fiestas that were about to go on sale. Meanwhile, Celestine was telling Audrey that lots of mature ladies were using Oil of Ulay to keep them young. Audrey had smiled politely but secretly believed a weekend with James Hunt would be a better solution.

I decided to leave them to it and seek out Katy in her classroom.

Izzy was with her making a list while Katy was at her desk counting the kitty money from her purse. All the staff had chipped in with a contribution towards this evening's party.

'How's it going?' I asked. 'Need any help?'

'Thanks, Jack,' said Katy. 'We need to pick up some bottles of wine on the way home.'

'I made a list,' said Izzy. 'A dozen bottles of wine including Beaujolais, St Emilion and Liebfraumilch.'

'And a bottle of Blue Nun for Rhonda,' said Katy.

Izzy added it to the list. 'What about beer?'

'I've got a big can of Watney's,' I said, 'and Jim said he would bring a crate of Pale Ale.'

Katy sat back in her chair. 'There's a lot to do in the cottage, Izzy. Food and nibbles plus a bit of a tidy-up.' There was the merest hint of concern in her voice.

'How about I do the shopping for you?' I said.

Katy nodded. 'That would be a big help. They have cheap wine at the new Tesco in Milltown.'

'I've not been there.'

'It's really easy, Jack,' said Izzy, passing over the list. 'You can't miss it. Big car park, quick service.'

'Fine, I'll go on my way home. See you later.'

At the end of school I was preparing to leave when Big Frank called in to empty my waste-paper basket.

''Ello, Mr Sheffield.'

'Hello, Frank. End of another week.'

'Yes, it'll be cold on them terraces t'morrow at Oakwell.' Frank was a big fan of Barnsley Football Club.

'Who are you playing?'

'Brentford.' He grinned. 'Soft southerners. We'll give 'em a good northern welcome.'

'I'm sure you will.'

He leaned on his broom. There was obviously something else on his mind. 'Found another one o' these in that bin near to t'gate.' He looked left and right and whispered, 'Bloody kids.' From the pocket of his overalls he pulled out another empty half-bottle of Captain Morgan Black Label Jamaica Rum.

'Any ideas?' I asked.

'Ah'll check wi' Gilbert when ah call in for m'fags. 'E might know. Thing is 'e allus goes round the 'ouses first afore 'e gets to t'point. It's like watching paint dry.'

I smiled. I knew what he meant. 'Thanks, Frank. Let me know how it goes.'

It was half an hour later and the supermarket car park was covered in fresh snow.

I looked up in surprise at the huge store. Supermarket shopping was new to me. I had always bought everything I needed from the high street shops in Newbridge or at home in Bradley.

I recalled Donna proclaiming, 'This is the future, Jack. Get used to it.'

There was sheet ice under the snow and I almost slipped as I walked towards the entrance. A line of trolleys was outside and I collected one, inevitably with squeaky wheels. It was making such a din I paused in the doorway and decided to change it for one that didn't sound like fingernails scratching on a blackboard. It was then a sudden pandemonium broke out.

'STOP, THIEF!' was the loud cry.

'STOP, THIEF!' came a second shout.

I turned to look as a skinny, balding man in a baggy anorak ran towards me and crashed into my trolley. He toppled over it and crashed down on to the tiled floor. The trolley ripped my trousers, grazed my knees and sent me rolling into a tall pyramid display of special offer Alpen cereal. Boxes tumbled down and burst beneath me as my forehead hit the wooden base.

The shoplifter was still clutching his six-pack of Long Life beer when two huge teenagers in blue store uniforms leaped over me and grabbed him. I blinked. They were identical and I guessed I was seeing double. After lifting him like a rag doll, they frog-marched him back into the shop and passed him on to the security guard.

I sat up, dazed and disorientated in a cloud of rolled oats, wholegrain wheat flakes and crunchy hazelnuts. The identical pair reappeared before me and they were smiling.

"Ello, sir. D'you remember us?' said the one with his hair parted on the left.

'Ah'm Ronnie an' 'e's Reggie,' added the one with his hair parted on the right.

'You were our teacher at 'Eather View.'

'We work 'ere now, sir.'

'Ah'm on fish,' said Ronnie.

'An' ah'm on meat,' added Reggie.

They helped me to my feet and patted the crushed muesli from my shoulders. Realization dawned. I remembered Ronnie and Reggie Atha as eleven-year-olds back in 1970. Now they were slightly taller than me and built like professional wrestlers. Incongruously, their mother had been a big fan of the Kray twins, the sixties London gangsters . . . hence the names.

'Hello again, boys. Good to see you and thanks for your help. It was a bit of a shock. This is my first visit to the supermarket. I hope it's not always like this.'

'No, sir,' said Ronnie.

'You were jus' unlucky, sir,' added Reggie.

It occurred to me that, with their hair parted on

opposite sides, when they looked in a mirror they would see their identical twin.

Ronnie seemed to be the leader and looked at his brother. 'You go an' tell Spotty Derek t'tek over on fish while ah 'elp Mr Sheffield.'

Reggie nodded. 'See y'later, sir, an' if y'want a nice chop jus' come t'me.'

'Thanks, Reggie.' I looked up at Ronnie. 'I'm pleased you got a job with your brother.'

'Ah allus look out for m'brother, sir.' He lowered his voice. ''E's a bit on t'slow side but 'onest as t'day is long.'

'It's good that you help each other, Ronnie.' I had recovered now. 'Look, I'll be fine. I'm just here to collect a few things for a staff party.'

'OK, sir, an' if y'come again, mebbe on a Sat'day, we 'ave a break at 'alf ten.'

'I'll do that.'

I shook his hand. He had a grip like a vice. When he walked away I recalled the eager young boys they had been long ago and how I had wondered what would become of them.

Back in my bungalow I took a shower and repaired the damage to my bruised head. There was a cut above my left eye and I covered it with a plaster. The image in the mirror resembled a prizefighter. A change of clothing helped and it was a moderately respectable version of myself that finally arrived in Skipton outside Katy's cottage. I collected the box of wine bottles and the can of beer from the boot and staggered across the pavement through the snow.

It was Katy who answered. 'Hi, Jack, thanks for this.' She grabbed the can of beer and ushered me inside. 'Put the box in the kitchen and hang up your coat.' In the light of the hallway she saw my face. 'What happened to you?'

'I slipped in the supermarket. A shoplifter bumped into me.'

'A shoplifter?'

'Yes, don't worry. He was caught by a couple of my old pupils from Heather View. They work there.'

'Small world.'

'Yes, it was a surprise. They're bigger than me now.'

'By the way, are you playing rugby tomorrow? Because that's how you usually look *after* the game!'

I grinned. 'It might frighten the opposition.'

'Anyway, grab a beer, sit down by the fire and relax. The others should be here soon. We're almost ready. Izzy's upstairs getting changed.' She looked down at her track-suit bottoms. 'Which is what I need to do before Mike arrives.'

'Oh, I thought Izzy said it was staff only.'

'Well, Mike was keen and Tom asked if he could bring his girlfriend.'

Izzy suddenly appeared, coming down the stairs. She looked stunning in a figure-hugging black dress. 'Jack, you made it.'

'Happy birthday once again . . . and you look great.'

'Thanks . . . Whatever happened to you?'

'Long story.'

'Well, we've got all night.' She led me into their cosy lounge. Her guitar was leaning against an upright piano in the corner and a table had been pushed under the window and filled with sandwiches, crisps and sausage rolls. 'Shall I get you a drink?'

'A beer, please,' and she glided into the kitchen.

I had told Donna the party was staff only but it appeared that was no longer the case and I wondered what she was doing in her cottage in North Beck.

Soon the cottage was filled with the members of staff, eager to enjoy a relaxing evening together. Neville turned up with a tin of home-made savoury snacks and Audrey had brought one of her fruit cakes. Izzy had made a modest birthday cake, namely a Victoria sponge, filled with jam, covered in pink icing and topped with a ring of tiny candles.

Celestine played 'Happy Birthday' on the piano and we all sang along. Izzy blew out the candles as Rhonda shouted, 'Make a wish,' and I wondered what it might be as she closed her eyes and smiled.

Jim was standing alongside me enjoying a tankard of Pale Ale. 'Remember these nights, Jack,' he said quietly. 'Good for staff morale and team building.'

'You sound as if you're still on duty,' I said.

'I guess I always am. You'll know for yourself one day when you become a head. Life changes in subtle ways.'

I watched him as he circled the room making sure he spoke with everyone and listening to their latest news.

It was around ten o'clock when Izzy picked up her guitar and we sang along to a few Joan Baez and Bob Dylan favourites. Neville appeared to be acting as waiter while Mike and Tom looked after the impromptu bar. Katy, in a lightweight trouser suit, simply looked relaxed as she lounged on the sofa with a glass of cider in the company of a slightly inebriated Tristan. He was telling her why Prime Minister Jim Callaghan was the answer to all our problems. I noticed Frank was looking at him with some concern.

When I walked into the kitchen I found Izzy slicing up the birthday cake and Audrey stacking the slices on a large plate. 'I'll take these around,' she said.

'Another drink, Jack?' asked Izzy.

'No, thanks, I've got a tricky drive home.'

'You don't have to go. I think Mike is staying over.'

The offer hung in the air. I didn't reply.

It was then I heard the telephone ringing.

Katy came into the kitchen. 'Jack, it's for you.'

The telephone was on the small table in the hall and I picked up the receiver. 'Hello.'

'It's me.'

'Oh . . . hi, Donna. Are you OK?'

'Hope you don't mind me ringing.'

'Of course not.'

'I had Katy's number because of netball and you mentioned the staff party.' There was a pause. 'Jack . . . I need your help.'

'What is it? You sound upset.'

'I've just been out to my car and someone has slashed the front tyres.'

'Oh no. That's terrible.'

'It's just that I feel . . .'

'Look' – I glanced at my watch – 'I can be with you by eleven. Make sure the door is locked and the windows are shut. Have you called the police?'

'No.'

'What about Sherri?'

'She's fine. In bed.'

'Don't worry. I'm on my way.'

I grabbed my coat and scarf from the hallway and hurried back into the lounge. Katy was chatting with Tom and looked concerned as I pulled on my duffel coat. 'Leaving already?'

'Sorry, Katy. Problem at Donna's.'

'Anything I can do?'

'No, but thanks anyway. I'll have a quick word with Izzy.'

She was heating up some sausage rolls in the kitchen.

'Izzy, I'm so sorry but I have to leave. Donna has just telephoned. She needs some help.'

She looked disappointed, removed her oven gloves and gave me a hug. 'Thanks anyway for coming. I hope you get it sorted.'

'It's been a great party. Happy birthday.'

She stretched up and kissed me on the cheek. 'Please come back if you can.'

'I'll try but, in all honesty, I think it might be difficult.'

Minutes later I was scraping ice from my windscreen and blowing on my key to heat up the door lock. A malevolent wind blew ice crystals in my face while, above me, ragged clouds raced across a spectral sky. The journey to Donna's was hazardous and I had to resist the temptation to speed. As I arrived in North Beck village dormant trees shivered beyond the frozen hedgerows. I pulled up in front of her Mini Clubman Estate. The two front tyres had been slashed to ribbons.

I rattled the door knocker.

'Who is it?'

'Donna, it's me.'

The door opened and I stepped inside. Her face was flushed and her eyes were red with recent tears.

'Thanks for coming. I didn't know what to do.'

I took off my duffel coat and scarf and hung them on a peg in the hallway.

'Let's have a hot drink and you can tell me about it.'

I added a couple of logs to the dying embers of the fire and soon she came back with two mugs of hot chocolate.

'Is Sherri OK?'

'Yes, asleep upstairs. She knows nothing about this.'

I held her hand and there was only the ticking of the clock and the crackle of burning logs. I had never seen her so frightened. 'Tell me,' I said gently.

She put down her hot drink and clasped her hands. 'It was such a shock. I went out to get some books from my car and noticed the front near tyre was flat. Then I saw that both the front tyres had been slashed . . . many times. It scared me.'

'I understand. Probably local drunks or hooligans. The police will sort it.'

There was silence again as she shook her head. 'No police, Jack.'

'Why not?'

'It could be something else.' She stood up quickly, walked towards the fireplace and knelt on the hearth rug to stare into the flames. 'It's happened before.'

'When?'

'Ten years ago. The same things. Milk bottles. Garden gate. Car tyres.'

'I'm not following.'

She turned to face me. 'It's not hooligans, Jack . . . it's Barty.'

'Why do you think that?'

'He did this before. I never told anyone and I've never wanted to share it with Sherri.'

'Share what?'

'When we parted he went off with another woman. I got over that and, to be honest, I was relieved.'

'Why?'

'He had a temper, Jack. He was strange . . . almost unhinged. Happy one day, violent the next. I never told anyone.'

'So why do you think he's responsible? Surely this is long in the past now. When did you last see him?'

'Probably ten years ago. Sherri must have been about three and I was living at my mother's. He was waiting outside the hairdresser's where I worked.'

'And what happened?'

'He wanted to get back together and I told him to stay away. I had begun to earn a decent wage hairdressing and occasional bar work. I'd bought a second-hand car. A week later the tyres had been slashed.'

'But why would he come back now?'

'Because he said he would.' She bowed her head. 'One day . . . and, in his mind, I'm probably his only option.'

'I can understand your concern but it might not be what you think.'

'How so?'

189

'My tyres were let down a while back. The caretaker thought it was local skinheads causing trouble. It seems to be happening more and more these days. So you could tell the police without mentioning Barty if you wish, although I think you should. In the meantime, just be extra vigilant with security and see how it goes.'

Donna looked relieved. 'You might be right.'

I held her hand. 'I could stay if you wish.'

'Not with Sherri here, Jack, but thanks anyway. I'll be fine now. Sorry to have upset your evening.'

I got up to leave. 'If you're sure you're OK, I'll go now, but ring if you need me.'

She gave a tired smile and we walked into the hallway and faced each other.

'Thanks, Jack. Safe journey.'

I kissed her. She responded and for a moment we held each other.

'Goodnight, Donna. Get some rest.'

It was midnight as I drove home through the darkness. I turned on the car radio for company. David Soul was singing the new number one, 'Don't Give Up On Us'.

It had been a long day . . . a turbulent day and I thought of Donna and wondered about her past life.

Chapter Twelve

A Turning World

'Jack, have you given any more thought about headships?'

I had been so engrossed in my work I had forgotten our conversation at the end of last term. 'Sorry, Jim. To be honest I haven't.'

It was 8.30 a.m. on Friday, 4 February and Jim and I had arranged a meeting before school to discuss the need to develop our reading scheme. We had settled on investing in the Ginn Reading 360, a series of graded books, and Jim asked me to lead a staff meeting to discuss it further. As I got up to leave his next remark came as a surprise.

'Take this with you.' It was a copy of this week's *Times Educational Supplement*. 'I spotted a couple of headships that may interest you.'

'Thanks. Where are they?'

'There's one just over the border in Lancashire.' He smiled. 'As a Yorkshireman I guessed it may not appeal.'

'I'll take a look anyway.'

'And there's another north of York. The head is retiring in the summer.'

'Sounds good.'

'Definitely should be of interest.'

'I appreciate your support, Jim.'

'That's what I'm here for.'

'I know you're doing what you think is best for me . . . but I'm really happy here.'

'No pressure, Jack. It's for you to decide but it could be the next step for you. In the meantime, let's get this new reading scheme up and running.'

I paused in the doorway. 'And, by the way, the *Look and Read* television programme is going down well. Izzy will be in the staff-room at ten o'clock for twenty minutes with a group of readers from my class and Katy's.'

'Good to hear and pleased Izzy is helping out apart from her music.'

I folded the paper, walked back to my classroom and stood by the window. It was a view I knew well: the playground, the High Street and a snowscape that stretched out to the far horizon. It had been dark when I drove to school and there had been a fresh fall of snow during the night. Now a rim of molten gold crested the far-off hills and a pallid light raced across the land. There was a special radiance to the day as the low, slanting sunlight lit up the mist and bathed the frozen earth.

On this bright and bitterly cold morning the children played happily and I reflected that I had seen them grow up as each year went by. A generation of five-year-olds were now the eleven-year-olds in my class, ready for the next stage in their lives. In this turning world the carousel of children came and went, arrived and moved on, while I remained here, a fixed point in life and time. I looked down at the newspaper in my hand.

Perhaps it was time to move on.

Shortly before ten o'clock Izzy called into my classroom. 'Time for your reading group, please,' she said with a smile.

She had pushed our mobile television on its huge rubber castors into the staff-room as the hall was in use for Rhonda's physical education lesson. The group had become a regular weekly event that had proved very popular for both the children and Izzy, who enjoyed teaching something other than music.

Eight children stood up and walked out, each carrying their English notebook and a Berol pen. Izzy had her teacher's brochure giving the background to Richard Carpenter's story *The King's Dragon*, along with follow-up activities.

'Thanks, Mr Sheffield,' she said with a smile. 'I'll have them back by twenty-five past.'

With the reduced numbers of pupils remaining I used the time to hear readers and note the progress of each child in my reading record folder. Five minutes before morning break Izzy returned with six of the children. Gary Cockroft and Danny Bishop had stayed behind to make sure the room was left in a tidy state.

In the school office Audrey glanced up at the clock. She was typing an important letter but it was ten twenty-five and time to prepare the staff-room for morning coffee.

When she walked in Gary and Danny had pushed the television set out into the entrance hall and were putting the chairs back in place.

'Hello, boys. Thank you for doing a good job.' She quickly lined up the coffee mugs, put a plate of biscuits on the worktop and then turned to fill up the kettle at the sink.

The boys hurried out and returned to the classroom.

I was first to arrive in the staff-room at morning break and Audrey was preparing the mugs of coffee. 'Hello, Jack. Did you get the message about Grayson?'

'That he wouldn't be teaching my class today? Yes, thanks. Where is he, by the way?'

'In York. A big meeting of the clergy. It's an annual event and he never misses it.'

'What's it about?'

'It's the "Hunger in the Third World" symposium.'

'Sounds important.'

Audrey gave a cautious smile. 'Yes, but the best thing is it's a seven-course lunch.'

'Ah, I see.'

She studied me for a moment and saw I was deep in thought. Then she smiled and passed over a mug of coffee. 'Come on, Jack. Live dangerously. Have a custard cream.'

Audrey always knew how to lift the spirits.

Then I looked at the plate of biscuits. There were no custard creams. 'Are we on short rations, Audrey?'

Audrey stared at the plate. 'But I filled it a few moments ago.' She looked at the open door. 'Unless it was those boys,' she murmured quietly. 'But surely not . . .'

Suddenly Celestine walked in. 'Good morning, Audrey.'

'Good morning, Celestine. You seem to be in a chirpy mood.'

She smiled and held up her *Woman's Weekly*. 'Ten pence well spent.'

'And why is that?' asked Audrey as she spooned Nescafé from a large tin.

'My Aries star sign is interesting. It says it's an eventful phase for personal relationships, the start of new beginnings and fresh opportunities.'

'That's encouraging news,' said Audrey, unconvinced but ever the supporter.

Audrey would have preferred the ten pence to go in the church collection but loyalty to her friend always came first. It was well known that Celestine was a keen disciple of Madame Francesca's star signs.

The pan of milk had boiled and Audrey was carefully topping off each mug. 'Anything else of interest?' she asked.

'Well, there's a Fiona Sloan outfit here. It's a flared skirt with a chevron pattern and matching blouse.'

'That's interesting, how much?'

'A little expensive at forty-six pounds but quality comes at a price.'

'Of course.'

'And I must say, Audrey, it would be absolutely perfect for you.'

'Really? Why's that?'

'Well . . . it's for the *fuller* figure.'

Audrey concentrated on pouring the milk and was pleased she was a Christian and not at that moment telling Celestine exactly what she thought of Fiona Sloan and her overpriced garments.

I wanted to prepare my next lesson concerning Cities of Europe and had a large map to pin on the noticeboard so I drank my coffee quickly and walked back to my classroom.

To my surprise Danny Bishop was in the book corner sitting on the carpet and eating a biscuit. 'Danny, what are you doing in class? You should be on the playground.'

He jumped up in alarm. 'Sorry, sir, ah were jus' readin'.'

His old grey jumper was covered in biscuit crumbs and there were three custard creams on the shelf beside him. I recalled Audrey's puzzlement when she realized there were none on the biscuit plate in the staff-room.

It wasn't difficult to work out what had happened. I sat down on one of the low chairs. 'Danny, where did you get those biscuits?'

'Dunno, sir.' His cheeks were red. He had seemed a good boy during the time I had known him, if perhaps a little listless on arriving at school. His clothes were old, patched and threadbare in places.

I spoke quietly: 'I won't be angry if you tell me.'

He was silent and stared down at his scuffed boots.

'I know you were with Gary helping to tidy the staff-room after the television programme. That's right, isn't it?'

'Yes, sir.'

'So I trusted you to do a good job because I know you are a good boy.'

He nodded. 'Thank you, sir.'

'I also know you are an honest boy.'

'Ah try, sir.'

'So you must tell me the truth now. Did you take those custard creams from the plate in the staff-room?'

He pursed his lips and stared out of the window. Then he looked back at me, 'Yes, ah did . . . an' ah'm sorry.'

'You know stealing is wrong, don't you?'

'Yes, sir.'

'So why did you do it?'

"Cause ah were 'ungry, sir.'

'Hungry?'

'Yes, sir, 'cause ah don't get no breakfast, jus' m'school dinner an' sometimes summat t'eat at night. M'mam sez there's no money.'

'Where is your mother now, Danny?'

'She's at 'ome, sir, wi' m'sisters.'

I recalled Mrs Bishop arriving at school pushing a pram and holding a toddler by the hand when she came to register Danny.

'Danny, listen to me carefully. You're not in trouble this time but you must not do this again. Do you understand?'

'Yes, sir.'

'Now, go out to play.' I saw him look at the custard creams. 'Eat those first and make sure there's no crumbs on the carpet.'

I shall never forget seeing the relief on his face.

At twelve o'clock the bell rang for lunchtime. The Cities of Europe project had gone well and it was good to see Danny taking part. I called into Jim's office.

'Excuse me, Jim, but I need to go out for about half an hour. I should be back for second sitting. I'm a bit concerned about the new boy in my class, Danny Bishop. Thought I would call in and check with his mother.'

'Yes, I know the boy. Mother was a bit distressed, I recall, when she enrolled him. Father had left home. Let me know if I can help.'

I collected my duffel coat and old college scarf and stepped out into a white world of frozen snow. My breath steamed in front of me as I walked past Frank's house and on to the Union Street council estate. These were the poorest houses in Newbridge and we had to make extra efforts to support these families.

When I knocked on the door of number nine I could hear a child crying inside. The door opened and a haggard face appeared round the door. I guessed we were about the same age but the lines on Doris Bishop's face showed that she had clearly had a hard life.

'Oh, Mr Sheffield. Is our Danny all right?'

'He's fine, Mrs Bishop, and working hard. If this is a good time, I just needed a quick word.'

'Y'better come in. Ah jus' need t'give little un 'er bottle.'

I followed her into one of the most sparsely furnished houses I had ever seen and we sat at the kitchen table. Three-year-old Maddy was sitting on the floor playing with some plastic bricks and three-month-old Rose began to suck furiously on a bottle of milk.

'Mrs Bishop, Danny is a good boy but when he arrives at school he's hungry.'

She sighed. 'Ah know. 'E could eat f'England could my Danny but there's no money after ah've paid rent. Ah get nowt from 'is father. But 'e does get a school dinner which ah 'ave t'pay for an' ah do m'best t'put food on t'table at night. It's 'ard, Mr Sheffield.'

'Mrs Bishop, did the secretary mention free dinners to you when you brought Danny to school?'

'She did but ah've never accepted charity.'

'It's not charity. It's your *right*. You're entitled.'

'But 'ow would 'e feel? Free dinner kids stood out like a sore thumb at 'is las' school. Ah don't want that.'

'I'm sorry to hear that but Newbridge is different. We don't separate free dinner children from the others.'

'Ah 'ear what yer sayin' but ah don't want Danny t'be shown up. It were fine when 'is dad were bringin' in a wage but that's not 'appenin' now.'

I sat back and looked down at the little girl on the floor and the babe in her arms. 'Mrs Bishop. Let me tell you something. *I* was a free dinner boy.'

'You . . . an' yer a teacher?'

'That's right. I was brought up on the Gipton Estate in Leeds and my mother didn't have enough money to feed me either.'

She was clearly surprised. 'Gipton? Ah know it.'

'So there's no need to feel embarrassed.'

'But when t'secretary mentioned it there were a form t'fill in an' ah'm not good at writing.'

'I can do that for you and then you would have a little more spare money. You would be able to give Danny a bowl of cereal or some toast before he leaves for school.'

I could see she was coming round to the idea. 'Well, thank you. It's been a bit 'ectic since we moved in. Ah've left 'im a bit t'get on 'imself while ah see to t'little uns.'

'Right then. It's settled. I'll arrange it and I won't mention this conversation to Danny.'

'Thank you kindly, Mr Sheffield.' There was a tear in her eye as I left.

It was clear that Danny had enjoyed his afternoon. With a warming school dinner inside him he had been active in our PE lesson in the hall and was attentive during our class story time, *The Voyage of the Dawn Treader* by C. S. Lewis.

Danny and Gary were keen to get their coats when the bell went at 3.45 p.m.

'Me an' Danny are off to our 'ouse, sir, to watch *Crackerjack,*' said Gary.

'Well, enjoy it, boys and, Danny, make sure your mother knows where you are.'

He gave me a sheepish grin. 'Yes, ah will, sir,' and they ran off into the darkness.

I was still preoccupied with the events concerning Danny Bishop when I pulled up outside Snoddy's Stores. The High Street was almost empty and no one seemed to be attracted by the huge sign in the window advertising 'Half-Price Offers'. Even the bell above the door sounded muted as I walked in.

Gilbert was standing by his new frozen-food cabinet and staring at the contents. He was clearly unhappy.

'Wonderful new addition to your shop, Gilbert.'

He tossed in a box of fish fingers and closed the lid. 'It's to 'elp me compete.'

'Compete?'

'Wi' that supermarket in Milltown. M'customers are going there now.'

'But you give personal service. That must count for a lot.'

'Yes, but they can sell stuff cheaper. If it goes on like this ah'll be out o' business. It's been m'life 'as this shop, man an' boy. Long 'ours. Built it up from nowt.' He glanced across at his daughter. 'Ah thought my Michelle might tek over from me but she's not interested.'

His daughter was sitting in the corner of the store eating a chunky Yorkie Bar and reading the first issue of *Blue Jeans*, a magazine that had hit the shelves two weeks ago. Apparently it had been advertised as 'the great new pop and love-story paper for girls' and teenagers were loving it. She had been thrilled because the magazine cost only twelve pence and included a free denim-look carrier bag that she was sure she would use one day.

He walked behind the counter, 'So . . . what's it to be, Mr Sheffield?'

I glanced at my list. 'Please can I have a tin of Slice 'n Fry Corned Beef, a sliced loaf, a packet of Jammie Dodgers, a jar of Maxwell House and a bottle of Quosh?'

'Comin' up.'

'And an Arctic Roll from your frozen-food selection, please.'

''Elp yerself, Mr Sheffield.'

He packed everything in my shopping bag.

'This looks interesting.' There was a wire basket on the counter.

'All 'alf price. If stuff gets damaged ah still need t'sell it.'

There were some bent tins of Heinz spaghetti, a few over-ripe bananas, a couple of broken Double Decker chocolate bars and, incongruously, a garlic crusher at seventy-five pence.

I wasn't attracted to any of them but picked up one of the battered tins to add to my purchases. Then I paid, the till went *ker-ching* and he gave me my change.

'Times are changin',' he called after me, 'an' ah'm bein' left be'ind.'

Out on the pavement I looked back at Gilbert's brightly lit shop. The march of the supermarkets would one day call time on his empire.

As I drove off it occurred to me that, like Gilbert, if I waited too long the world would overtake me and *I* would be the one who was left behind.

I was preparing my evening meal when the phone rang. It was Norman Tyndale, Chairman of Upper Wharfedale Rugby Club.

'Jack, bit of news for you.'

'Yes?'

'We want you to be pack leader for the rest of the season.'

'That's a surprise.'

'Paul Duckworth has a long-standing injury. Although that's not a good choice of words as the poor sod can't stand up. A farming accident by all accounts.'

'We'll be sad to lose him.'

'So we've got Big Cyril from the second team to play prop tomorrow.'

'Good choice.'

'Definitely. Eats nails, spits rust. Y'don't mess with Cyril.'

'Well, thanks for letting me know. Much appreciated.'

'And don't forget it's a one o'clock kick-off so we can watch the Ireland–England game on the telly in the club-house afterwards.'

'I'll be there in good time. Looking forward to it.'

'Thanks, Jack. I knew we could rely on you. You're our most experienced forward and you've still got a few years left in you.'

'Thanks, Norman.'

'See you tomorrow,' and the line went dead.

This was unexpected. I had clearly moved up in the pecking order of my rugby world.

During my evening meal I recalled my conversation with Jim and spread out the *Times Educational Supplement* on the kitchen table. As I sifted through the advertised posts I came across the Lancashire headship that Jim had mentioned. It was certainly of interest and sounded a good school. However, it was the one to the north of York that caught my eye. This was definitely the more appeal-ing of the two. The advertisement read:

Headteacher required for Ragley-on-the-Forest C. of E. Primary School, near York, from September 1977, following the retirement of Mr J. Pruett. Application forms are avail-able from County Hall, Northallerton.

Closing date: 21 February 1977.

It occurred to me I would have to get a move on if I intended to apply. I took out my map of Yorkshire and located the village of Ragley. It was near the market town of Easington and at the foot of the beautiful Hambleton Hills. There was no doubt it was an attractive prospect.

Later, I built up the log fire and settled down to watch James Bolam in *When the Boat Comes In*. As always it was good entertainment. It had just finished when the phone rang.

'Hi, Jack.'

'Hi, Donna. Nice surprise.'

'I was thinking about you playing rugby tomorrow, Jack. I thought I would bring Sherri and Georgie up to Wharfedale. I'm sure they would enjoy it.'

'That's great news. Do you want me to pick you up?'

'No, thanks. My car is fixed now so no problem.'

'It's an early kick-off at one o'clock because of the international match on the television. So what are you doing afterwards?'

'I could make us a meal.'

'Us?'

'Yes. Just the two of us. I'll be taking the girls to Georgie's house straight after the game. They're having another sleepover.'

'Fine, see you tomorrow. Goodnight.'

'Goodnight, Jack.'

When I closed my bedroom curtains the shadow of a midnight owl flitted across the virgin snow. Outside the land was still.

Once in bed I decided to relax with some of the verses of my favourite poet, T. S. Eliot. I had always found his

Four Quartets to be the most evocative writing. I smiled when I read once again the first poem in the series, 'Burnt Norton'. In it he spoke of a still point in a turning world where there remained a sense of stillness and peace.

It seemed to sum up the moment I had reached in my life.

Chapter Thirteen

Sticks and Stones

It was Tuesday, 1 March and the beginning of an episode in my life I shall never forget. The day had begun well with hope of a season that was turning. The distant land was bleak and windswept but beneath the earth new life was stirring and the dark days were receding. A hint of spring was in the air and it was with a feeling of expectation that I drove towards Newbridge.

Big Frank was hurrying out of the boiler house when I arrived. 'Mornin', Mr Sheffield, can't stop.'

'Good morning, Frank. Not like you to be rushing off.'

He paused and grinned. 'It's m'wife's birthday. Ah need t'get a card an' a present sharpish from Gilbert's.'

'Wish her a happy birthday from me. How is she?'

'She's fine. Jus' gorra new job.'

'Oh yes, what does she do?'

'She's a stunner is my Pauline,' said Big Frank proudly.

'Good to hear . . . but what's her job?'

Frank looked puzzled. 'Ah've jus' told yer. She's a stunner . . . works in an abattoir.'

The penny dropped. 'Ah, I see.'

When I walked into the entrance hall Neville was coming out of the stock cupboard with an armful of sugar paper. He was in an animated mood and smiled. 'Morning, Jack. Don't forget it's my turn for the Philately Society meeting tonight. Starts at seven. You don't need to bring anything. There will be plenty of refreshments.'

'Thanks. Looking forward to it. How many will be there?'

'Usually around a dozen. Now the snow has cleared we should get a good attendance.'

'I'm afraid I no longer have a stamp album.'

'Don't worry, they're a friendly bunch and, you never know, you may start collecting again,' and he walked away whistling to himself.

At morning break Prince Charles was in the news.

'Did you see Charlie Boy has a new girlfriend?' said Katy.

'Who's that?' asked Celestine.

Katy looked at her newspaper. 'Well, it seems his latest girlfriend, Davina Sheffield, has got fed up with him. He has a new interest: namely Fiona Watson.'

'Never heard of her,' said Tom after picking up his mug of coffee and a milk chocolate digestive.

'Apparently Fiona's a twenty-three-year-old beauty queen who has modelled for *Penthouse* magazine.'

'So an ideal future queen,' said Tom with heavy sarcasm.

'Well, he's only a young man and he does need to have some social life,' said Audrey, our ardent royalist. 'It must be difficult being in the limelight all the time.'

'The Queen won't be pleased,' said Rhonda.

'Will she ever?' said Tom. 'Goodness knows who he will choose eventually.'

'Whoever it is,' said Katy, 'I pity her.'

'Changing the subject,' said Audrey, 'did anyone see Frank Sinatra on the news last night?'

'Wonderful singer,' said Celestine.

'Almost as good as Tom Jones,' said Rhonda.

Audrey pressed on. 'He's performing at the Royal Albert Hall tonight in front of Princess Margaret.'

'Maybe she'll be with her young lover, Roddy Llewellyn,' said Katy. 'Another royal we have to pay for who does us no good.'

Audrey sighed. 'More coffee, anyone?'

I had just finished my lunch and Mrs Starkey was on form once again. She was berating Billy Gubbins.

'Come on, eat y'crusts an' yer'll get curly 'air.'

'But ah don't want curly 'air, Miss.'

'I want never gets!' shouted Mrs Starkey.

As I walked into the entrance hall with Izzy she looked up at me with a smile. 'Whoever came up with a description of women as the "fair sex" had clearly never met Mrs Starkey.'

'Very true.'

It was at this moment that Jim leaned out of his office

and beckoned me inside. These meetings had become regular events when we could share news.

As usual, he came straight to the point. 'So you didn't follow up those headships I mentioned.'

'Gave it plenty of thought, Jim, but the time wasn't right. Other things going on in my life.'

There was a moment's pause, almost as if he knew that I was thinking of Donna.

'OK, Jack, but keep it in mind.' There was a letter on his desk and he passed it over. 'In the meantime, have a look at this. I know it's a long way off but the local council have been in touch asking us how we can support the Silver Jubilee celebrations in the village.'

I scanned the letter. 'I remember now . . . the seventh of June.'

'Yes, it's a Tuesday. The Monday is the Spring Bank Holiday. We'll no doubt be involved in a street party on the High Street. We're back on Monday the eleventh of April after the Easter break so I suggest we organize a staff meeting during that week so we're well prepared.'

'There will be a few with conflicting interests who may want to be involved in their own local party.'

Jim gave a wry smile. 'Not least the Republicans on the staff.'

'You mean Katy.'

'Yes, and perhaps one or two others, so we shall have to deal with it sensitively and respect their views.'

'I understand,' I said and returned the letter to his desk.

'OK, Jack. Thanks for your time. I'll get Audrey to put a date in the diary for the staff meeting.' I stood up to leave. 'Just one more thing. How's Tristan these days?'

'Fine, I think. He's doing some terrific work in his class. The desert island stories by his class really need displaying in the entrance hall.'

'Good idea. See to that. We must celebrate his achievements. It's just that there are occasional days when he seems . . . well, preoccupied.'

It was dark when I arrived outside Neville's quaint cottage on the outskirts of Milltown. It was a quiet, secluded cul-de-sac. The small front garden was carefully landscaped and the neat porch was brightly lit and welcoming.

I rang the doorbell and David Lovelock answered. 'Come on in, Jack. So pleased you could make it. Neville's in the kitchen. Hang up your coat and come and join us.'

'I know Neville said don't bother to bring anything but here's a contribution.' I passed over a Tupperware box of iced buns and a couple of bottles of Pale Ale.

'Thanks, I'll add them to the feast,' and I followed him into an immaculate kitchen. So different to mine.

Dramatic French impressionist reproductions filled the walls, and herbs – parsley, sage and thyme – were being grown in ceramic pots on the windowsill. Neville was putting the finishing touches to a tray of drop scones he had just removed from the oven. He looked very smart in a bright yellow shirt and multi-coloured waistcoat.

'Good evening, Neville. This looks magnificent.'

He gave me a shy look of appreciation. 'Thanks, Jack. I always try to put on a bit of a spread for the members.'

David patted Neville on the shoulder. 'This is their favourite venue, Jack.' He gestured towards the refreshments. 'You can see why. He's been slaving away for the past couple of nights.'

A snowy white cloth covered a large pine table and on it was displayed a veritable cornucopia of tasty treats. Vintage lace doilies covered fine china plates on which were arranged a huge selection of chicken vol-au-vents, prawn *bouchées*, apple turnovers, Eccles cakes, French cream twists, egg and ham patties and a magnificent veal and ham pie.

'Fancy a drink, Jack?' asked David. He gestured towards a huge glass bowl. 'There's my fruity vodka party punch. Got a kick like a mule.'

'If you don't mind, a beer would be good, please.'

'Coming up, but you don't know what you're missing.'

I was sipping a cool tankard of Yorkshire beer when Neville ushered me into the lounge. On the oak sideboard the members had displayed their stamp albums to which Neville had added a *Stanley Gibbons Checklist of the Stamps of Great Britain* along with his very own *Ace Golden Eagle Stamp Album* complete with maps.

Most of the members had arrived. It was an eclectic group from all walks of life, as I soon discovered.

'Jack, let me introduce you to Cecily,' said Neville.

A slim lady in a tight black dress with a plunging neckline stood before me. She had a pale face and wore bright red lipstick. Her long fingernails were painted crimson and she ran them through her frizzy, greying hair.

'Pleased to meet you, Cecily.'

She smiled. 'Oh, how lovely, a new member and such a handsome one.'

'Actually, I'm not a member, simply one of Neville's teaching colleagues.'

'So, another teacher. I'm sure you will keep me in my place.'

I smiled politely.

'Would you care for a cigarette?'

'No, thank you, I don't smoke.'

'One of my many vices, I'm afraid.' She produced a packet of Slim Kings from her handbag, took one out and lit it with an extravagant gesture. 'I love their quality and length.' She held up the cigarette and blew smoke over my shoulder. 'You ought to try one. They calm the nerves beautifully.'

'Maybe another time.'

Neville decided to rescue me. 'I'm just letting Jack meet a few of the members.'

'I'm here if you need me, Jack,' said Cecily and this time blew smoke in my direction.

He tugged my sleeve and ushered me towards the fireplace. On the mantelpiece next to a tiny vase of dwarf narcissi was a photograph of the teenage Neville in his school uniform looking slightly sheepish on the Champs-Élysées. 'And this is Joy, our librarian friend.'

A short, bespectacled twenty-something looked up at me. Her face was creased with worry.

'Hello, Joy. How are you?'

She stared with a haunted expression. 'Hello, Jack. Not too good, I'm afraid.'

'Sorry to hear that.'

'I'm concerned about Mars.'

'Are you?'

'Yes. The Viking One spacecraft sent back pictures last year and I'm now convinced there's life there.'

'Really?'

'Definitely. There's lots of evidence to show that during the ancient Noachian time period the liquid on the surface would have been habitable for microorganisms.'

A neutral response seemed appropriate. 'Can't say I've ever considered it.'

'You need to, Jack. I suffer from insomnia now, considering the implications of our dying planet. A new society on Mars is our only hope.'

It struck me as I moved on to meet other members that Joy did not exude the qualities of her name.

Although I was in the midst of this wide-ranging album of philatelists, I finally met someone with whom I had an affinity. Douglas, a sixty-year-old taxidermist and once a pessimist, was now full of *joie de vivre*.

'Philately has changed my life,' he declared as he took me to see his stamp album.

'Has it?'

'Oh yes, you see I can leave *death* behind me.'

'That's good to hear.'

'It's given me a new window on the world with an insight into politics, geography and the history of nations. I absolutely love it.'

'That's wonderful, Douglas.'

He opened his album. 'You must see my Magyar collection.'

'Love to.'

'And this week I'm in absolute heaven. I've just added a threepenny Sierra Leone stamp.'

Definitely a step up from death, I thought.

For the next few minutes we travelled Douglas's world of stamps to the West Indies with diversions to Cyprus and North Borneo. It was interesting to see the head of the Queen on many of them, a reminder of the extent of the British Empire.

I enjoyed the evening flitting from one conversation to another and Neville was the perfect host.

Then it happened. It was a simple act that lasted mere seconds.

I was the last to leave and, after saying goodbye and collecting my coat, I remembered my Tupperware box and walked back to the kitchen.

The door was ajar and David and Neville were both at the sink. Neville was speaking softly to David and very tenderly caressing the back of his hand with his thumb. It was a simple gesture but it meant so much. It was in that instant I understood. Neville and David were more than friends.

'Hi, sorry to burst back in. Just collecting my cake box.'

David recovered quickly. 'Help yourself, Jack.'

Neville just stood there aghast.

'Goodnight and thanks again.' I made a swift exit.

As I reached my car, suddenly David appeared, distraught and out of breath. 'Jack, please don't say anything. Our lives would be hell if this came out.'

'Of course, David. I'm Neville's friend and would never do anything that may cause him harm.'

He took a deep breath. 'It started simply enough. Neville was another philatelist just like me. At the outset we simply shared a love of stamp collecting. It developed from there.'

'I understand. Please don't worry and thanks again for the evening. I really enjoyed it.'

'Well, perhaps you might come again.'

'Thank you, I'm sure I shall.'

As I drove home, I turned on the radio. Julie Covington was singing 'Don't Cry for me Argentina': a wonderful record, but my mind was elsewhere.

That evening I thought of Neville. It occurred to me that life must be difficult for both Neville and David in today's society. Homophobia was still rife. I remembered John Hurt portraying the homosexual icon Quentin Crisp, in *The Naked Civil Servant*, a groundbreaking film on Thames Television. The reaction had been one of contrasting emotions and headlines. Last year, Jeremy Thorpe had finally resigned as leader of the Liberal Party after being accused of indulging in 'homosexual acts', while British Home Stores had sacked an openly gay trainee. Meanwhile, the London Gay Teenage Group had been established, the first gay youth group in the world, and a journey to eliminate prejudice and intolerance had begun.

I recalled that ten years ago there had been an Act of Parliament that decriminalized homosexual acts in private between two men so long as both had attained the age of twenty-one. Times were changing but attitudes often remained the same.

When I finally turned out the light I determined that tomorrow I would speak with Neville.

*

On Wednesday morning it was clear that Neville had the same idea. He was waiting for me in the car park and his face was pale. 'Jack, please can I have a private word?'

'Of course. Let's go into my classroom.'

He was silent until we sat down at my desk.

'I know you saw me, Jack.'

'I did but please don't be concerned.'

'You don't understand. For me it was the final straw.'

'Surely not.'

'I can't go on like this any more.'

'Neville, please don't worry.'

He put his head in his hands. 'In my world I always presume I will be offered pity or contempt.' There were tears in his eyes. 'I feel as though I've lived in a world of night and shadow for too long.'

'Neville, society is moving on.'

'If you were me you would think differently.'

'Life is full of *ifs*.'

'If . . . if only.' He shook his head. 'I'm not talking about the Rudyard Kipling poem, Jack. "If you can keep your head . . ." '

I realized that for Neville 'if' was merely a condition or a supposition, a grammatical anomaly. Sadly, his life had been full of ifs and buts.

'But surely this is just *sticks and stones*.'

'Yes, but in this case the words really *do* hurt . . . and they could hurt us all.' He looked down at the desktop. 'So it's time to draw a line under it. There have been whispers, not least from Grayson.'

'The vicar? Surely not. What did he have to say?'

'Not to me personally. To Audrey. She knows and is a dear and loyal friend.'

'That's good to hear.'

'She said he had heard rumours and started quoting Leviticus.'

'Go on.'

' "You shall not lie with a male as with a woman." '

'I'm sad to hear he may have that opinion. I'm sure you could find an alternative quotation.' Deep down I found the vicar's views abhorrent; it made me even more aware of the struggles of disadvantaged groups in our society.

'Perhaps . . . but it's too late for that now.'

'What do you mean?'

'I was a fool thinking I could keep it quiet for ever.' He sighed deeply. 'It's like being on the edge of a cliff. I can't go back and I can't go forwards. So I'm going to see Jim at the end of school today.'

He got up and walked to the door.

'But what do you intend to say to him?'

He lowered his head. Defeated. 'I'm going to resign.'

It had been a difficult day but the needs of the children were all-consuming: hearing readers, marking maths books, English exercises involving adjectives and adverbs. I finally met up with Neville again in the entrance hall at afternoon break. He was carrying a mug of tea and looked tense.

'Neville, can I get you to change your mind? We could discuss it privately before you see Jim.'

'No, Jack. Thanks anyway. I know you mean well but

my mind is made up. Anyway, you must excuse me, I'm on playground duty.'

When I walked into the staff-room Audrey was pouring tea from a large pot. I was the first to arrive.

'Hello, Jack, here's your tea.' She handed it over. 'Black with a slice of lemon. Just as you like it,' she added with a smile.

'Thank you, Audrey.'

She looked up and saw the concern on my face. 'What is it?'

'I've been speaking to Neville.'

She studied me for a moment. 'Yes, he mentioned to me today that you knew.'

'I'm pleased you have been there to support him.'

'Don't worry,' she said quietly. 'I learned long ago to be a keeper of secrets.'

The door opened and Katy, Tom and Tristan walked in discussing our new reading scheme. Audrey gave me a knowing look and continued to pour the tea.

At the end of school I walked into Neville's classroom. He was saying goodnight to the last of the children in his class.

'Your reading is really coming on, Joe,' he said to an eager Joe Poskitt. 'Take this book home and read it to your mum or dad to show them how you have improved.'

'Thanks, sir.' The little boy clutched his new book entitled *At the Zoo* and hurried out to collect his coat and scarf from the cloakroom.

When the classroom was empty Neville sat down in his

chair. 'Jim said he would see me at four o'clock. He doesn't know what it's about.'

'I see. In that case I would like to come in with you.'

'That's kind, Jack, but there's no need.'

'I want to be there . . . to support you.'

'Very well but my mind is made up.'

I helped him tidy his book corner until he glanced at his wristwatch. 'Time to go,' he said quietly.

Neville tapped on Jim's door and we walked in.

'Oh, hello, Jack. I was just expecting Neville.'

'I'm simply here to offer some support.'

He glanced up at Neville and realized quickly there was something large at stake here. 'You had better sit down.'

Neville took a deep breath. 'Thank you for taking the time to see me. I have something for you. I wrote it at lunchtime.' He placed a sealed envelope on Jim's blotting pad.

Jim left it there. 'What can I do to help, Neville? There's clearly something on your mind.'

There was silence while Neville found the words. 'It's a letter of resignation, Jim. I really am so sorry. You've been a terrific colleague and I've loved my work here at New- bridge but, sadly, there's no alternative. I'll stay until the end of the academic year, if you wish, for the sake of the children in my class. However, I shall understand if you wish me to leave sooner than that.'

It was interesting to watch Jim's response. He was calm and picked up the letter and put it to one side so it no longer dominated the centre of his desk. 'I'll ask Audrey to make us a hot drink. She's still busy in her office. Would you like a coffee? I'm certainly ready for one.' He got up and walked towards the door.

'Yes, please,' I said.

'Thank you,' said Neville.

Audrey was at her desk when Jim entered her office.

'Audrey, would you be so kind as to bring three coffees into my office? Then when you've done that please leave your door open and if anyone wants to see me say I'm very busy.'

Audrey immediately recognized the gravity of the situation. 'Certainly. I'll bring some biscuits as well and I'll be here for a while yet. I've got some filing to finish off.'

An unspoken look passed between them.

Back at his desk Jim studied Neville's gaunt expression and said quietly, 'I'm here to help. After the coffee has arrived you can tell me what is on your mind.'

Audrey came in with a tray of coffee and biscuits and placed it on Jim's desk. When she had left and closed the door Jim passed round the hot drinks. Then he sat back and sipped his coffee. 'Now, Neville. What is it you wish to say?'

There was a long silence until Neville finally spoke. 'I've met someone that I care for.'

'Go on,' said Jim.

'It's a man.'

'So what is the problem?'

'This could cause great embarrassment to the school. So I have no alternative but to resign.'

'And why is that?'

Neville gave a level stare. 'Jim . . . I'm gay.'

Jim was silent for a moment. 'Neville, I know that. In fact, I've known for a long time . . . but this is your *private* life.'

'I wasn't aware you knew. Audrey knows and now Jack.'

Jim nodded. 'So I'm still waiting for you to tell me what the problem is.'

Neville clasped his hands on his lap and looked down. 'Our Chair of Governors has been expressing concerns.'

'Oh, has he?'

'He mentioned to Audrey there had been some rumours flying around.'

That elicited a reaction from Jim. 'I'll have a word with Grayson,' he said firmly.

Neville looked up. 'But he may insist on my resignation.'

Jim shook his head. 'If he does I'll tell him mine will follow immediately.'

Neville was shocked. 'Oh dear.'

Jim looked across at me. 'What have you got to say, Jack?'

I chose my words carefully. 'Neville is one of the finest teachers I have ever met. He is a trusted and hard-working colleague. I'm proud to call him my friend.'

'I agree,' said Jim.

There were tears in Neville's eyes. 'Thank you,' he said. 'But this could cause you difficulties.'

Jim repeated a quotation he had used in the past when we had met problems. ' "Anyone can hold the helm when the sea is calm." '

Neville nodded and managed a weak smile. 'I

recognize the quotation, Jim. Publilius Syrus, a Latin writer and a wonderful wordsmith.'

'That's right. Well said.' He stood up and walked around the desk. Then he shook his hand. 'Neville, come and talk to me again whenever you need to.'

'Thank you, Jim. I'm very grateful.'

I opened the office door. 'I'll walk with Neville to his car.'

Jim held up the sealed letter. 'Neville, I'll dispose of this, shall I?'

When I drove home the current number one was on the radio. Leo Sayer was singing 'When I Need You' and I reflected that the words meant different things to different people.

Chapter Fourteen

Brighton Rock

It was Friday, 25 March, the last day of term, and the two-week Easter holiday beckoned. On the journey into Newbridge the hedgerows were bursting into life and the yellow petals of forsythia were bright in the morning sun. After the recent frosts the willow with its fluffy, tactile flower buds gave a message of new life. In the distant fields young lambs were taking their first tentative steps and the sky was pale blue. Spring had arrived and the long dark days of winter were forgotten.

I pulled up outside Snoddy's Stores on the High Street. In the window was a large poster that read:

Newbridge PTA
Invite you to 'TWIST & SHOUT'
A sixties dance evening in the school hall
Friday, 25th March 1977
Tickets £1 including refreshments

The bell above the door rang cheerfully when I walked in. Gilbert was out replenishing his stock so Michelle was behind the counter. As usual she appeared uninterested as she leaned back in her chair and listened to her transistor radio. The new number one, 'Chanson D'Amour' by the Manhattan Transfer, was on full volume.

'Good morning, Michelle.'

She turned down the volume. 'Mornin', Mr Sheffield.'

I noticed she was wearing a tartan wristband. 'What's that for?'

'Bay City Rollers.'

I vaguely recalled the teenage group from Edinburgh in half-mast baggy trousers from a couple of years ago.

'So are you a fan?'

'O' course. Ever since "Shang-a-Lang" an' "Bye Bye Baby". Ah love 'em all but m'favourite is Woody.'

'That's good to hear,' I said with what I hoped was a sincere expression.

'What's it t'be?'

'Just a jar of Bird's Instant Coffee, please. I've got a 5p token.'

'Ah don't do tokens. M'dad does 'em.'

'Never mind. I'll take it anyway.'

I paid and Michelle turned up the volume once again. I left her dreaming that one day she could sell a jar of coffee to Woody, her tartan-clad friend, instead of a quirky teacher in a sports coat with leather patches on the elbows and wearing Buddy Holly spectacles.

*

Izzy was in the entrance hall when I walked into school. She was staring at the PTA poster on the noticeboard. 'Hi, Jack. Looking forward to the dance?'

'Yes, should be fun with a few memories of great songs. I was at a Beatles concert in Leeds back in '63 and they sang "Twist and Shout".'

'I saw them as well. It was in '63 at the Birmingham Hippodrome. I was fourteen and screamed my head off. Crazy times.'

'I guess you've got an outfit.'

Izzy gave me that infectious smile. 'Yes, I've gone for hippie gear: long floaty dress, headband, flowers in my hair. Sixty-seven, summer of love and all that. Can't wait. What about you?'

'Not sure, still thinking.'

'The others are getting into the spirit of it. Tom's going as a Hells Angel, Tristan's pinched his elder brother's old Mod outfit and Katy has got some hot pants and really high boots. She looks amazing.' Izzy looked at her wristwatch. 'Anyway, must rush. I'm playing in the vicar's assembly this morning.'

As she headed for the school hall I reflected on the sombre meeting that had taken place between Jim and Grayson. Our Chair of Governors had been left in no doubt about the value of Neville to our school. I heard from Audrey that Grayson had left Jim's office ashen-faced.

That apart, it had been a busy last few weeks and the staff were ready to let their hair down or, in Audrey's case, just the opposite. She had decided on a fiercely back-combed Helen Shapiro beehive creation that would make her look six inches taller.

*

At morning break we were relaxing in the staff-room when Izzy stood up. 'Excuse me, everybody, but I have an announcement.'

The hubbub ceased and we all looked at her.

'Would anyone like to go to Brighton? My friend Harriet lives there. She was at college with me and said bring a few friends if you wish. Big house, rich parents. They're on the Italian Riviera at present.'

'All right for some,' mumbled Rhonda.

'When are you going?' asked Tom.

'I'm going tomorrow with Katy but we've got the house for five nights – until Thursday. So back here for Easter.'

'Mike is taking me and Izzy,' said Katy, 'so there's room for one more.'

'I'm keen,' said Tom.

'What about your girlfriend . . . the nurse?' asked Izzy.

'That's over.'

'Sorry to hear that,' said Audrey.

Katy smiled. 'Mike said she got fed up watching *Match of the Day* on Saturday nights.'

Diane saved Tom's blushes. 'I would love to go if only to visit the Body Shop but I'm going to Scarborough with my boyfriend.'

'The Body Shop?' asked Tom. 'What's that?'

'Oh, it's wonderful!' said Diane effusively. 'I read all about it. Opened last year by a woman called Anita Roddick. I would love to meet her. She's showing the world that business can be a force for good and only uses ethically sourced ingredients.'

'Sounds good,' I said, 'but what exactly is it? What does she sell?'

Izzy smiled. 'Beauty products, Jack.'

'Oh, I see. Well . . . I'm not really into that sort of thing.'

'We worked that one out long ago,' said Audrey with a grin.

Tom was curious. 'Di, why is this shop so special?'

Diane was on a roll. 'It matches *my* philosophy,' she said with a look of fierce determination, 'and it should be our vision for the future. You see, there's no animal testing.'

'That's good,' said Neville. 'Some of the experiments are dreadful.'

'And I've heard they recycle bottles and packaging,' said Audrey.

Diane was enthused. It was one of her favourite subjects. 'This is what's needed to help the planet and why I support Anita Roddick's vision.'

I nodded. 'Well I'm for all of that.'

'And she's one hundred per cent vegetarian,' said Izzy with a smile in my direction.

'Oh dear.' I shook my head. 'I like steak and chips.'

'And meat pies,' added Tom for good measure.

'I know you do,' said Izzy. 'No one is expecting you to become a vegetarian overnight.'

'That's a relief,' I said.

The bell went for the end of break and we all trooped back through the hall.

Izzy was beside me. 'Jack, there's lots to do in Brighton. Have a think and I'll check with you again tonight. Come for a couple of days if you like, then it won't interfere with your rugby.'

She gave me a mischievous smile and walked into

the hall for a *Singing Together* radio broadcast with Tom's class.

During lunchtime I was on the same table as Danny Bishop. He was one of the free dinner children now and it had made such a difference to Mrs Bishop. I had returned to see her while Audrey had made sure all the necessary forms were completed.

Danny was tucking into his meal of toad in the hole covered in piping hot onion gravy. Not having to pay for his dinner meant coming to school each day with cereal and toast inside him and the occasional bowl of porridge. This had given Danny the energy he needed to complete his morning's work. It was good to see the transformation in this keen little boy. When Mrs Starkey asked if anyone wanted seconds, he was the first to raise his hand.

After lunch in the staff-room Katy was reading her *Daily Mirror*. 'I see Maggie's had another drubbing,' she said triumphantly. It was common knowledge that Prime Minister Jim Callaghan had been giving Margaret Thatcher a difficult time.

'What's happened?' asked Celestine.

'She's been advised to get rid of her scriptwriters and make it up herself in future,' added Katy.

'Probably wise,' said Audrey. 'Since that Lib–Lab pact she's bound to struggle.'

'Definitely,' said Katy. 'Although she says she's not bitter about the Liberals.'

'And if you believe that you'll believe anything,' said Tristan. 'The thing is you can't underestimate her. She's a force of nature and might even be Prime Minister one day.'

Katy laughed. 'And pigs might fly, Tristan.'

'I agree with Tristan,' said Audrey. 'It would be good for a woman to run the country for a change.'

'My thoughts exactly,' said Celestine.

'Pity she's not Welsh,' added Rhonda. 'Then even *I* might vote for her.'

Katy read on. 'It says that Callaghan and Maggie are like master and apprentice.'

'She won't always be an apprentice,' murmured Tristan and returned to his *Teacher's Reading 360 Manual*.

At the end of school I helped Frank and a few members of the PTA to arrange tables around the hall with space for dancing in the centre. It seemed that everyone had rallied round. The notable exception was Clarissa Peacock. The pompous Chair of the PTA had not been a supporter of an event she considered to be an evening of drink and debauchery. However, her husband, Gerald, had stepped in to suggest a weekend in Canterbury and a visit to the cathedral. Clarissa had agreed immediately and everyone breathed a sigh of relief. Another absentee was Donna as Sherri was performing in a production at The Ridge.

By five o'clock I was back home when the phone rang. It was Donna.

'Hi, Jack. Just to let you know I'm taking my mother and Sherri to Whitby for a holiday. It will be good for both of them, particularly my mother: fresh air and a break from hairdressing.'

'When are you going?'

'Tomorrow. I found a lovely B and B for four nights. Back on Wednesday.'

This was a surprise but I tried to be positive. 'It will be good for you as well. Whitby is a great place: Captain Cook, the abbey and some of the best fish and chips in Yorkshire.'

'You've definitely missed your way, Jack. You should work for the tourist board. Anyway, what are your plans?'

'Some of the staff are going to Brighton tomorrow. I've been invited to go along. It's a friend of Izzy who apparently has well-off parents.'

'Sounds fun. Are you going?'

'I wasn't sure.'

'You ought to go. Then both of us will have a seaside break.'

'Maybe . . . so shall I ring nearer Easter?'

'Yes, do that.'

It was 6.30 p.m. when I arrived at school and parked alongside a collection of cars that had changed Britain's roads. Next to my Morris Minor Traveller was a Hillman Avenger and a Vauxhall Viva flanking the bedrock of suburban Britain, an Austin 1100.

My so-called sixties outfit was a last-minute decision. I had been considering going as a Beatle but then I heard Roy Orbison singing 'Only the Lonely' on the radio and I recalled he wore spectacles just like mine. With some difficulty I soaked my long hair and combed it into a quiff. From the back of my wardrobe I found an old sixties navy suit from an era before flares along with a white shirt and black tie. Convinced I was the perfect Roy Orbison looka-like I walked into school.

The school hall was a hive of activity. Tristan and Tom, as a Mod and a Rocker, were facing each other and smiling. Tristan had removed his baggy khaki parka covered in badges to reveal a smart Italian suit with tapered trousers, a white polo shirt, Union Jack waistcoat and incongruous white bowling shoes. Tom had gone for a Marlon Brando *On the Waterfront* look with a studded leather jacket, white silk scarf, scruffy jeans and heavy boots. Although a non smoker, Tom had a cigarette lodged behind one ear. They were certainly a contrasting pair.

'Perfect,' I said as I walked up to them. 'I guess your Lambretta and motorbike are parked outside. Takes me back to the clash between Mods and Rockers on Brighton seafront.'

'I've decided to go to Brighton,' said Tom. 'How about you?'

'Haven't decided.'

'I can't,' said Tristan. 'I'm spending some time with my family.'

'Anyway,' said Tom. 'Great Buddy Holly outfit.'

'"Raining in my Heart" was my favourite,' said Tristan.

'Actually, it's—'

Suddenly our conversation was drowned out by our DJ for the evening.

Big Frank had helped Donald Cleghorn, or 'DJ Donny' as he was known in Newbridge, to set up his limited range of technical equipment. It consisted of three electric light bulbs, red, amber and green, attached to a length of plywood painted black. It was reminiscent of a road safety test with a musical accompaniment. Donny had decided to use the school's record player and speakers as they were far superior to his own. However, Donny came cheap. As Jim had explained: in return for a crate of Guinness, what more could you expect?

Donny was testing the microphone. 'Evenin', pop pickers, it's Disco Donny here welcomin' you to t'PTA dance night wi' that big 'it from 1963, Dave Clark Five singin' "Glad All Over" an' that's 'ow ah'm feelin' right now.'

Neville, wearing a striped shirt in an attempt to look like a member of the Beach Boys, was staring at him in disbelief and praying Donny took care of his pride and joy – namely our audio system.

Katy passed by carrying a tray of food from the kitchen. 'Hi, Jack, have a sandwich.' With her long legs, knee-high boots, crimson hot pants and a white blouse, she looked amazing.

'Hi, Katy. Great outfit.'

'Don't you just love the sixties,' she said. 'Imagine walking down Carnaby Street dressed like this.' She stepped back and studied me for a moment. 'Pretty good, Jack . . . I still love Buddy Holly.' Then she hurried away to prepare an arrangement of pork pies and ham sandwiches.

Jim appeared and tapped me on the shoulder. 'Jack, can you spare a moment?' He smiled at my outfit. 'Well done for entering into the spirit of it. Looks as though it will be a good night.'

We walked into his study and sat down. He glanced down at his suit and tie. 'You'll gather I've not been home yet. A few things cropped up. Paperwork mainly but I took a call from Greg Maddison, the head of Sun Hill Primary, shortly after you left. It was about Izzy.'

'Sun Hill? I know she works there occasionally.'

'Yes. Greg was keen not to step on my toes – it was a courtesy call, off the record, but I thought I would share it with you.'

'What did he have to say?'

'He mentioned that Izzy was like a breath of fresh air.'

'No surprises there then.'

He smiled. 'She's certainly dynamic. It was the fact that she's stepped in occasionally to do some supply teaching for him when staff have been on a course. Apparently she loved it and he's impressed.'

'Yes, she's a born teacher.'

'The point is he knows we're her main employer with three days a week and he doesn't want to cause any friction.'

'Why would that be the case?'

'His numbers have gone up with all the new building in the village. County Hall have informed him he can increase his staffing next September. So he's keen to offer her a full-time post.'

'I see. She would be an asset to his school, especially with the music she can offer.'

'I've no idea whether this is what she wants. He was keen to clear it with me first before having a chat with her about how she perceived her future. Obviously, I said I appreciated the call and I'll wait to hear more.'

'Thanks for sharing this. It would be sad to see her go.'

He held up a few sheets of paper. 'So if Izzy goes we shall need a replacement. I'll have to contact the local authority to check out available peripatetic music teachers.' Then he pushed the pile of paper to one side. 'Anyway, let's join the party and have a drink and some of Neville's delicious food.'

When we returned to the hall, Donny was blasting out 'She Loves You' by the Beatles and Audrey, along with a few other ladies of the PTA with equally backcombed hair, were dancing in a circle around their handbags.

Tom served us with two glasses of Guinness and Jim raised his glass. 'Cheers, Buddy Holly,' he said with a grin and wandered off to talk to Celestine and Diane.

I spent time at the side of the hall chatting with Neville. He mentioned that David Lovelock was now spending weekends with him; it was good to see him so relaxed. Meanwhile, the music of the sixties echoed around the hall. Donny played Mary Hopkin's 'Those Were the Days', Cilla Black's 'Anyone Who Had a Heart' and the Seekers singing 'I'll Never Find Another You'. When I moved on to collect another drink, Rhonda was dancing to Tom Jones and the 'Green Green Grass of Home'. All the staff were there and it was at times like this when we mixed alongside the parents that the real spirit of the school shone through.

Izzy was by my side when Donny put Roy Orbison's 'Oh, Pretty Woman' on the turntable. 'That was supposed to be me,' I said.

'I thought it might be,' said Izzy graciously. 'Although you've got a hint of Freddie and the Dreamers.'

We sat together at a table and she took a postcard out of her shoulder bag.

'Just thinking of Brighton, Jack. This is the address. It's right on the seafront. Wonderful home with an amazing roof terrace. We've had a few terrific parties up there.'

'Thanks.'

We talked about life and school and she mentioned she had done some supply teaching at Sun Hill and really enjoyed it. I didn't mention my conversation with Jim.

It was ten o'clock and the Monkees were singing 'I'm a Believer' when Jim had a word in Donny's ear.

'OK, ev'rybody,' shouted an inebriated Donny. 'Couple more t'finish wi', kickin' off wi' t'Fab Four an' "Twist an' Shout".'

Izzy grabbed my arm and pulled me to the centre of the floor. Soon I was doing a passable interpretation of the Twist, elbows pumping, knees bent, while Izzy seemed effortless in her movement.

'An' now, all you guys an' gals out there. It's t'las' record. 'Ave a smooch if y'fancy. Dim them lights an' let's go out wi' Elvis an' 'is sixty-one tear-jerker, "Are Y'Lonesome Tonight".'

Big Frank dimmed the lights; Izzy looked up at me and smiled. I held her close as we moved slowly round the floor.

'So, have you decided about Brighton?'

'Not sure.'

'I think you would enjoy it.'

'Rugby training is on Wednesday night.'

'There's more to life than rugby, Jack. But you could just come down for a couple of nights.'

It was hard to resist this enigmatic woman. I made a decision. 'OK . . . I'll be there on Monday.'

On Monday morning I packed an overnight bag and set off for the south coast.

It was a six-hour journey and mid-afternoon when I

arrived in Brighton and parked on Marine Parade. I climbed out of my driver's seat, stretched my stiff limbs and walked across the road to the wide promenade. The sharp salty air was refreshing while, above my head, the sound of seagulls filled the skies.

I leaned on the rail above the shingle beach and remembered being here as a student many years ago on a weekend visit with members of my English group. I had expected a mix of fish and chips, candyfloss and clairvoyants but it wasn't like that. I had read Graham Greene's *Brighton Rock* and seen the film with Richard Attenborough playing the violent gang leader Pinkie Brown. Walking the streets and stepping on to the pier had brought it to life for me. The previous year three thousand youths had descended on the town and Mods had fought Rockers on the seafront. I realized, though, that Brighton was different now.

Behind me was an elegant row of five-storey Regency homes. I knew Harriet's parents owned the one at the end of the terrace and I looked up. A figure was waving from one of the windows. It was Izzy and she was smiling.

Harriet was the first to greet me. She stubbed out her sweet-smelling roll-up cigarette and gave me a hug. In her outrageous pink flares and baggy long waistcoat with Bohemian-style cross-stitch patterns she certainly looked striking.

Tom, Mike and Katy had gone for a walk on the promenade so it was just Harriet and Izzy who fussed around me, showing me my room on the third floor and finishing up on the roof terrace with a beer and a cheese sandwich. The view out over the sea was spectacular.

*

That evening the six of us sat in one of Harriet's favourite pubs drinking local beer and enjoying a prawn salad with a jacket potato. I was pleased to be here. School seemed a world away and the conversation was lively with Harriet as the perfect host. That night after a long day I slept well and woke to the smell of fried eggs and chatter from the kitchen. Harriet and Izzy were busy preparing breakfast.

Mid-morning the following day we all went out to explore Brighton. There was a cool sea breeze and we wrapped up warm.

'Roy Orbison was singing here at the beginning of the month,' said Harriet as we stood looking up at the Brighton Dome. 'He has such a wonderful voice.'

I smiled, thinking back to the PTA dance.

'And Twiggy is here next week.'

'I thought she was a fashion model,' said Tom.

'No, she sings as well,' said Izzy. 'She had a record out last year, "Here I Go Again".'

'Must have missed that one,' said Mike with a grin.

'Shame you lot aren't here next week,' said Harriet. 'I've got tickets for the Poly. One of my favourite groups is performing.'

'Who's that?'

'The Throbbing Gristle.'

'Really?' I said. 'Strange name.'

'Some of the group members have quite individual names as well,' said Harriet. 'There's Genesis P-Orridge and Cosey Fanni Tutti to name but two.'

It was good to wander around the town. Brighton's Marina was under construction and the skateboarders were out in force around Churchill Square. We went to the Polysound record shop on Gardner Street and flicked through dozens of vinyl records. Harriet bought Manfred Mann's Earth Band album, *The Roaring Silence*. '"Blinded by the Light" is just brilliant,' she said.

It was after another pub meal that we split up. The women wanted to go to the Body Shop and the men decided to find a pub and talk about football.

While we were discussing the merits of Brighton and Hove Albion, the three women had arrived at 22 Kensington Gardens and were staring in the window of the Body Shop.

'So, Harriet,' said Katy. 'What do you think of Tom?'

'I like him,' said Harriet without hesitation. 'Tall, dark and handsome.'

'The only thing is,' said Katy, 'his girlfriends don't seem to last more than a couple of weeks.'

Harriet grinned. 'I was thinking more of a couple of nights.'

The three of them shared a knowing smile.

'So, don't you fancy Jack?' asked Izzy. 'He's sweet.'

'I suppose if you were looking for a steady boyfriend he would be ideal,' said Harriet. 'I'm after a bit more excitement.'

'You haven't seen him play rugby,' said Katy. 'He's scary when he tackles.'

'I'd rather tackle Tom. More my type. So, girls . . . my favourite shop. Let's go in.'

After an age of discussion they came out with Patchouli oil, Bergamot and White Musk perfume and then wandered round a few boutiques.

Later we all met up again on the promenade for fish and chips eaten out of newspaper and a visit to an off-licence to stock up with drink and crisps for the evening.

It was a carefree evening up on the roof terrace again, chatting until the early hours and oblivious of the chilly wind and scudding clouds.

On Wednesday morning Izzy and I prepared a warming breakfast of porridge and honey followed by toast and marmalade. There was no sign of the others so we set out to walk along the wide promenade.

'Glad you came?'

'Yes, a welcome break. I love this place. So different to home.'

Two young men were walking towards us. They wore torn jackets, black leather trousers with zips in unusual places, studded belts and brothel-creeper boots.

'Definitely *different*, Jack. I'm guessing you're not into Punk.'

Their dirty T-shirts sported the words 'ANARCHY' and 'CHAOS' and the taller of the two had a shaved head and a badge that read 'Bored Teenager'.

'This is the new movement. There's many like this now, wandering the streets and in the clubs.'

I looked over my shoulder as they disappeared into one of the side streets. 'I wonder why he's bored.'

'Weren't you ever bored as a teenager?'

'No. I was too busy playing sport, delivering papers, doing schoolwork, running errands.'

She gave me a knowing look but then suddenly stopped. 'Hey, look what's here.' It was a stall selling Brighton rock.

'It's ages since I've eaten rock. I can still hear my mother saying it rots your teeth but she would buy me one anyway and say it was a treat.'

'Happy memories.'

Her eyes were bright. 'Shall we?'

'Yes, why not?'

'I'll pay,' she said.

The plump man in a white coat and straw hat held up two sticks. 'Here you are, darling. One for the beautiful lady and one for yer lucky boyfriend.'

He gave me a wink as we walked away.

'Wishful thinking,' she said with a grin.

We paused. It was time to return. 'Let's walk back on the beach,' she said and passed over one of the sticks of rock.

'I'll save mine for later,' I said.

'Me too,' she said and stared at the rock before putting it in her pocket. 'Clever, isn't it, how they get the writing in the middle.' She took my arm as we walked down the steps. 'I guess that's what I like about you. You're like the rock. You don't change.'

'Not sure what you mean.'

'When you get to the end of the stick of rock it still says *Brighton* through the centre. It doesn't alter halfway.'

The pebbles crunched beneath our feet and the wind was in our face.

'Maybe that's my problem. Work, rugby, reading and not much else.'

She held my arm a little tighter. 'You're a lovely man, Jack, but you don't seem to let your hair down very often. Teaching seems to consume your life.'

'I guess it's because I love my work.'

'But is it enough?'

I was deep in thought as the vast seascape stretched out beside us and dancing spray flecked the tips of the waves. Above us, a canopy of ragged cirrus clouds drifted on a brisk wind. For a few minutes it was just the two of us on a faraway beach, each with our own thoughts . . . together in Brighton.

Soon it was time to leave. There were hugs from Harriet and a kiss from Izzy. 'Thanks for coming, Jack,' she said quietly, 'and a safe journey home.'

As I headed north out of the town on the A23 towards London, on the radio Simon and Garfunkel were singing 'The Sound of Silence'.

I was back in Bradley by four o'clock so I had time before rugby practice to prepare a hasty snack and unpack. It was then I noticed it . . . a bright red stick of rock.

I was smiling at the memory when the phone rang.

It was Donna and she sounded distressed.

'Hi, Donna. Is everything all right?'

'Not really. We've had a lovely time and got back at lunchtime. Everything seemed fine but I've just been out to the car and the gate was tied up again.'

'What? Kids?'

'Not this time, Jack. It's more serious. This time it's barbed wire.'

'Oh no! That's dreadful. You must report it to the police.'

'Yes, I will.'

'Shall I come over?'

There was a pause. 'Yes, please. I would appreciate that.'
'Leave the barbed wire. I'll see to it.'
'Thanks. I'm beginning to get worried about Sherri.'
'I can understand that.'
'I don't think you do, Jack.'
'Why is that?'
'I've just got a bad feeling about all of this.'

Chapter Fifteen

A Bad Penny

It was Monday, 11 April, the first day of the summer term, and I was awake early. Light spilled over the horizon from the edge of the world and the morning sun was mellow as dawn crept across the land. It was with a feeling of expectation that I dressed quickly and left early for school.

As I drove out of Bradley village I noticed how the season was moving on. Almond trees were in blossom and, in the eaves of the cottages on the High Street, swallows had returned to their nesting places. Outside The Eagle pub was a large earthenware plant trough with a glorious array of tulips, a barrage of colour: red, orange and purple. It lifted the spirits and, as I approached Newbridge, I hummed along to ABBA's latest number one, 'Knowing Me, Knowing You' . . . and thought of Donna.

She had seemed more relaxed by the end of the two-week break. The vandalism to her gate had been reported to the police but nothing had come of it and there had been no incidents since. Our relationship had developed and we were spending more time together. Sherri had accepted me as her mother's 'friend' and I felt at peace with my world as I drove into the school car park.

Meanwhile, outside Donna's cottage in North Beck, the morning air carried the soft scent of wallflowers as she and Sherri drove out of the village. Both were full of anticipation for the new term and what lay ahead.

They were unaware they were being watched.

When I walked to the school entrance a familiar figure greeted me. 'Welcome back, Mr Sheffield,' shouted Big Frank from across the playground.

'Morning, Frank. How are you?'

'Fair t'middlin'.' He seemed to be limping more than I recalled as he approached me and leaned on his broom. Clearly there was something of interest to impart. 'Good news,' he said. His eyes were bright with excitement.

'What's that?'

'World Championship snooker 'as come to t'Crucible in Sheffield. Starts t'day.'

'Yes, I read about it.'

'Ah play down at t'workin' men's club Thursday nights. Gorra thirty-three break once.'

'That's great, Frank. I read in the *Radio Times* that the matches will be on television. You'll enjoy that.'

Frank gave a deep sigh. 'No good t'me.'

'Why not?'

'Ah've gorra black an' white telly. Can't tell a blue from a brown.'

'I suppose not.'

'Ah'll probably go round t'Nobby's 'ouse t'watch 'igh-lights. 'E's jus' got a bran'-new *colour* telly.'

I guess he would have, I thought.

Frank turned to go into the boiler house; then he paused. 'Ah did 'ave some good news at beginnin' of the 'oliday.'

'What was that?'

'My Pauline put a few quid on Red Rum in t'Gran' National.'

'That's good news.'

'She were over t'moon. Mind you, she said Red Rum reminded 'er o' me when ah first took 'er dancin'.'

'Why's that?'

'She said we'd both got two left feet!' He wandered off, chuckling to himself.

Jim was outside his office door as I walked in. 'Good morning, Jack. Can you come in for a moment?'

He closed the door after me and I saw Grayson sitting in one of the visitors' chairs. Our local vicar stood up, resplendent in a smart suit and clerical collar. 'Good morning, Jack. We're blessed. Another new term and fine weather.'

'It is indeed,' I said and we shook hands.

Jim gestured to me to sit down. 'Jack, Grayson and I were just following up a conversation about Neville.'

'Oh yes.' I noticed there was caution in his words.

'We've agreed that Neville's personal circumstances are not likely to change.'

Grayson gave a benevolent smile. 'We believe in miracles but we don't depend on them.'

'Quite,' said Jim a little testily.

' "Stolen waters are sweet," ' quoted Grayson, ' "and bread eaten in secret is pleasant." '

Jim sat back in his chair. 'Grayson . . . I'm familiar with the Book of Proverbs.'

'I thought you might be,' added Grayson with feeling.

Jim turned to me. 'The simple message is that we have confirmed Neville is a valuable member of staff and the discussions we had last term won't be raised as an agenda item at the next governors' meeting.'

'I'm pleased to hear that,' I said. 'It's important we move on from the prejudices of previous times.'

Grayson frowned. I could see he was searching for an apt response but none was forthcoming.

'Meanwhile, on to a more immediate issue,' said Jim, changing the subject. 'Harry Stubbs and his wife are calling in after school. As two of the most senior residents of the village, they've volunteered to coordinate the Silver Jubilee street party. I was hoping both of you might be able to attend.'

'Yes, I'll be there,' I said.

Grayson shook his head. 'Sorry. I'm about to leave for an ecumenical meeting in York but I'll go along with whatever you decide.'

'Fine,' said Jim. 'Thanks, Grayson, for your time and I'll report back to you later.'

I followed Grayson into the entrance hall but he did not say anything. With his head down he walked quickly to the main door and hurried out.

During morning break Rhonda was reading Katy's *Daily Mirror* and an article entitled 'One of the most explosive showbiz stories of the decade'. It gave chapter and verse of Tom Jones and his affair with Marjorie Wallace. Back in 1973, after the nineteen-year-old American had been crowned Miss World, she had attracted the attention of both Tom Jones and Engelbert Humperdinck. It was Tom who had won her affections.

'Shocking,' muttered Rhonda. 'And him a married man.'

'Who's that?' asked Celestine.

'No one you know,' said Rhonda. She replaced the newspaper quickly on to the coffee table and covered it with a catalogue for maths equipment. The Welsh crooner was her hero and she didn't want to sully his name in conversation with her colleagues. Fortunately Audrey interjected with a timely query.

'I'm still getting used to metric measures,' said Audrey. 'I wanted some new curtains and they're selling fabric in metres and centimetres instead of feet and inches.'

'I can help,' said Celestine. 'I've got a tape measure with metric on one side. I can get you one if you like.'

'That's kind,' said Audrey.

Izzy was sitting next to me flicking through the pages of her *Okki-tokki-unga* song book. She was checking the guitar chords for 'Nicky, knacky, knocky, noo'.

'Thanks for Brighton,' I said. 'Great experience.'

She gave me that infectious smile once again. 'I knew you would like it. We ought to do it again some time.'

The offer hung in the air like a tempting treat as I sipped my coffee.

At lunchtime I was sharing a table with Izzy and six children from Katy's class. Mrs Starkey was on the warpath again. Billy Gubbins was sitting next to his friend Gary Cockroft on a nearby table, eating fish pie, carrots and evil-smelling cabbage.

Mrs Starkey looked down ominously at the bristle-haired boy. 'Mek sure y'be'ave yerself today.'

'Ah will, Miss,' said Billy without hesitation.

Mrs Starkey gave him a look that would have made most ten-year-old boys tremble but Billy was unmoved. 'So remember, Billy, y'do as ah say, not as ah do.'

It was an aphorism I had not heard for a while.

Izzy smiled at me from across the table. 'Nothing like a warm welcome to school dinners,' she whispered.

'What does that mean, Miss?'

'It means what it says,' said Mrs Starkey. She turned her attention to Gary, who was staring forlornly at a portion of cabbage that had the appearance of rotting seaweed.

'An', Gary Cockroft, eat y'cabbage. That goes f'you as well, Billy Gubbins.' She folded her arms and stared down at the two boys. 'Ah've told you a thousand times.'

'But ah've not 'ad a thousand dinners,' protested Billy. Maths was one of his specialities.

'It'll all end in tears if y'talk t'me like that.'

'Boys don't cry, Miss. At least they don't in Barnsley. M'mam sez so.'

'Oh, does she?'

'She does, Miss.'

'SHE! SHE!' shouted Mrs Starkey. 'Who's she? Cat's mother?'

Billy didn't even flinch. 'We've gorra cat, Miss.'

'Ah don't care if you've got *three* cats.'

'No, only one. Miss. An' can ah 'ave a spoon t'finish off m'fish pie, please?'

'What did yer las' slave die of?'

'Gary told me it were all right to 'ave a spoon, Miss.'

'If someone asked you t'jump off a cliff would y'do it?'

'No, Miss, but ah would if they gave me a spoon.'

Mrs Starkey's face underwent a transformation. She stared down at this pugnacious South Yorkshire boy with his cheeky face and an answer for everything ... and smiled.

As she walked to the next table she recalled that was exactly what she had been like forty years ago. *Credit where credit's due,* she thought.

The representatives of the Newbridge Social Committee arrived as the bell went for the end of the school day. Harry Stubbs, a short, bespectacled man in a grey three-piece suit, walked in with his wife, Ena. She was dressed in a thick tweed skirt and jacket and at five feet nine inches she towered over her husband. In the village it was well known that it was *she* who wore the trousers in her household. With the demeanour of a bulldog that had swallowed a wasp she sat down and directed Harry to be seated next to her.

I followed them in and sat down in my turn.

'Thank you for coming,' said Jim. 'I've invited Mr Sheffield to share in our discussions and, of course, we're here to do all we can to support the village and to make the Silver Jubilee celebrations a success.'

'Thank you kindly, Mr Patterson,' said Ena, 'an' t'you as well, Mr Sheffield. Ah've written down all m'plans.'

'That's good,' said Jim. 'Can we see them please?'

Ena turned to Harry. 'Let's 'ave t'list, please, luv.'

Harry looked surprised. 'Ah 'aven't got it.' Grey hair stretched across his balding pate in a Bobby Charlton comb-over and he patted the strands nervously.

'Ah told you *pacifically* t'bring m'list.'

'Ah don't recall, luv.'

'Y'put it on t'kitchen table afore we left. It were there, plain as t'nose on yer face.'

Jim raised his eyes and looked at me. I knew what he was thinking. Harry's bulbous nose was far from 'plain'. A regular in The Black Horse, Harry always finished off with a whisky chaser after his usual four pints of Tetley's Bitter. In consequence, a web of veins formed purple tracks across his ruddy cheeks and gathered round his spectacular proboscis. Deep in thought, he stroked his nose with a nicotine-stained finger. 'Sorry luv, yer right.'

'Anyway, at least one of us can remember what were on it,' declared Ena triumphantly. She took a deep breath. 'Women's Institute are providing cakes an' sandwiches; Scout troop are putting up trestle tables; village 'all c'mmittee are running t'bar; Gilbert is providin' ice cream; Girl Guides are mekkin' jelly by the cartload; Salvation Army Brass Band will be playin' music an' t'PTA are servin' tea an' 'ome-made lemonade.'

'And what would you like us to do?' asked Jim.

Ena was on a roll. 'We thought t'kiddies could mek paper 'ats, table decorations an' buntin'.'

'Fine, we'll do all of that,' said Jim, 'and if you need anything else please ask.'

'There was summat.'

'Oh yes?'

'Ah were talking t'Miss Fazackerly an' she mentioned 'bout Mr Wagstaff doin' a bit o' cookin' wi' 'is class an' ah thought mebbe t'kiddies could 'ave a bakin' competition.'

'A good idea,' said Jim. 'I'll check with Mr Wagstaff and see what we can do. Was there anything else you can think of?'

'Only what ah read in t'paper 'bout pickpockets.'

Jim shook his head. 'I've not heard about that.'

'They're comin' over from Germany an' France an' Italy by all accounts. Gangs o' thieves to pick pockets in t'crowds at Jubilee time.'

'I'm sure the local police will keep us safe, Mrs Stubbs.'

'Let's 'ope so. Ah don't want no foreigner puttin' 'is 'and in my purse.'

Not if he values his fingers, I thought but said nothing.

'What did y'jus' say?' asked Harry.

Ena grabbed him by the arm. 'C'mon, y'soft ha'porth.' She stood up and gave him a withering look. As they walked out she muttered, "E's deaf as well as daft.'

I closed the door behind them. 'Short but sweet, Jim.'

'Yes, Ena doesn't waste her breath.' He scribbled on his notepad. 'Well, at least we know what we're doing towards the big day. Perhaps you can check with Neville about the baking?'

'Yes, fine.' I got up to leave. 'Thanks, Jim . . . So, is there anything else? I wanted to display the children's Easter writing and paintings before I leave.'

'No, nothing else . . . except, what did you decide about the headship applications?'

'No decisions, Jim. There're other considerations at present.'

He nodded cautiously. He couldn't know for sure, but I guessed he was thinking that Donna might be one of them.

Audrey often worked late and she tapped on the door and walked in. 'Sorry to disturb you but there's a call for Jack . . . sounded urgent.'

'Excuse me, Jim.'

I hurried next door and picked up the receiver. 'Hello.'

'Jack, it's me.'

'Hi, Donna.'

'Can you call in? Something's happened.'

'What is it?'

'I'd rather explain when you're here.'

I glanced at the office clock. 'I'll be there in half an hour.'

Donna was standing by the front door when I arrived. I opened the garden gate and hurried down the cobbled path past the border of wallflowers. 'Thanks for coming so quickly, Jack. I'm sorry to drag you here straight from school.'

We went inside and sat in the lounge. 'Tell me what's happened.'

Donna clenched her hands together and glanced at the door to the kitchen. It was closed. She spoke quietly. 'I collected Sherri from school. She had a drama meeting for a summer production, so we were later than usual. When we walked in there was something different. The photos on the hall table didn't look quite as I had left them. A few minutes later Sherri came out of her room and came downstairs. She was smiling and said thanks for the surprise.'

'And what was that?'

Donna stood up and opened the kitchen door. Sherri was doing her homework. 'Jack's here. We're just having a chat. Are you OK?'

'Yes, Mum,' came the reply. 'French grammar. It's fine.'

Donna closed the door, picked up a photograph from the mantelpiece and sat down beside me. She held it up for me to see and continued in a low voice. 'Sherri was holding this. It was one taken long ago when Barty and I were in Leeds. She had found it on her pillow and presumed I had left it there because she occasionally asks about her father.' Donna clasped her hands and breathed out slowly. 'You see what this means. It's Barty. He's back and he's been in the house.'

She was trembling and I held her hand. 'We need to contact the police.'

'I know I should but I'm worried about Sherri. She doesn't know the truth about him and now he's turned up again like a bad penny.'

'How did he get in? You obviously locked up.'

'There are only two keys, I have one and Sherri has the other in case she ever gets home before me. The first thing I did was to check the windows round the back. There's one that we must have left slightly open. It's bolted shut now.'

'Just to be on the safe side, let me check all the windows. Tomorrow I could buy some hardware and fix extra security.'

She gave an imperceptible nod. 'I would appreciate that.'

'If the police come they would probably talk to your neighbours to see if they saw anything suspicious.'

'I guess they would but if I escalate this it could affect Sherri. She would have to know what a terrible man her father is and I don't want that for her.'

I squeezed her hand gently. 'Donna . . . you must see what this is. He just wants to control you.'

I saw the tension in her face. It was as if a catharsis had taken place. This man had sown terror and had re-appeared to reap a long-awaited harvest.

'Shall I stay tonight? I could sleep on the couch.'

'No, Jack.' She glanced at the kitchen door. 'Thanks anyway. Sherri still sees you as a friend, nothing more at present.'

I changed tack. 'Have you eaten?'

She shook her head.

'Then let me get a fish and chips supper. The shop was open as I drove past. Sherri would think it was a treat.'

There was relief on her face. 'Yes, thanks. Let's do that. I don't feel like cooking.'

I got up. 'Lock the door behind me and put the kettle on.'

The hot food was a good idea and Sherri was in good spirits, enjoying the unexpected supper and chattering about the forthcoming drama production, being picked for the rounders team and whether ABBA's Agnetha, Anni-Frid, Björn and Benny were bigger than the Beatles.

Later we were drinking coffee in the lounge when Donna looked at Sherri. 'Did you finish your homework?'

'Yes, Mum.' She looked at the clock on the mantelpiece. It was almost nine o'clock. 'So, can I watch *Charlie's Angels*?'

Donna gave a gentle smile. 'Yes, but then straight to bed.'

'Thanks, Mum.'

'I'll have a chat with Jack before he leaves.'

I stood up. 'Goodnight, Sherri.'

'G'night,' she murmured, staring at the screen. The three beautiful crimebusters were about to begin another adventure in the latest designer clothes and without ever smudging their perfect make-up.

'She wants hair like Farrah Fawcett,' said Donna as we walked back into the kitchen.

'Don't we all,' I said.

It was the first time she had smiled since I arrived. 'I'm grateful to you for coming, Jack. It really helped.'

We sat down again at the table and talked. As we did the tension slowly left her face. It was late when I collected my coat from the hallway. We stood there outside her door facing each other, a tableau frozen in time. Then she lifted her face to let the light breeze caress her skin.

'Goodnight, Donna. Ring me any time.'

'I shall . . . and thank you.' She reached up and kissed me gently on the cheek and walked back inside. I heard her lock the door.

As I drove home I thought of Barty. It was clear that, for Donna, he was a dark, brooding presence who had stolen some of the light of her life. This was a troubled man seeking a strange sort of vengeance.

On the outskirts of North Beck, Barty Withinshaw had parked his van in a layby as he watched the cars drift out of the village. When my distinctive Morris Minor Traveller passed by his eyes narrowed. Then he leaned back, lit up a cigarette and smiled.

It was back in 1963 that he had met Donna, then a bright, seventeen-year-old schoolgirl. He had been a twenty-year-old window cleaner with few prospects. However, with his leather jacket, tight jeans and winkle-picker shoes he exuded a great deal of false charm. Slender and sinewy and with shoulder-length brown hair, he considered himself something of a *catch*. But when he realized Donna was pregnant he had jumped on his Lambretta and moved to Halifax with yet another girlfriend in tow.

Looking back, he realized Donna was the only one he had ever really loved. Ten years ago he had arrived at her door in an attempt to rekindle the relationship. She had rejected him and told him to stay out of her life. He had stayed in Milltown for a while, playing childish tricks on her until she threatened him with the police.

Years had passed and, with a series of failed relationships behind him, his behaviour had progressed from irrational to violent. It was then he had decided that Donna must pay for the hurt he believed she had caused him. For Barty the ashes of resentment were burning again. He had managed to convince himself that he had been treated harshly by Donna. It was convenient . . . she was his best option.

He knew he had always been *different*, an individual, one of a kind, the joker in the pack, but the future began now and it would soon be time to make a move. He lit up another Silk Cut King Size and drove away.

It was midnight and Donna stared out through a crack in her bedroom curtains. Her eyes were unforgiving. On this dark night when the moon was cold she prayed this man would vanish from their lives. She imagined he was out there somewhere in the twilight, a vulpine shadow in the gloom. She recalled the fury in his thin, sardonic face when they had last parted, long ago, and the brimstone in his words.

Now he had returned and she had to protect her daughter.

She walked silently on to the landing and heard Sherri's gentle breathing. When she returned to her bedroom she walked with supple grace, an elegant woman with a fierce determination. She was a mother who had grown in understanding and she knew what she must do.

Chapter Sixteen

Broken Dreams

Cock-a-doodle-doo! Cock-a-doodle-doo!

My bedside clock read 4.56 a.m. 'Bloody rooster!' I muttered.

It was Friday, 20 May and Rocky the Rooster had woken me up yet again and disturbed my pleasant dreams.

I clambered out of bed and opened the window. The air was warm and a reluctant light had begun to spread over the sleeping land. Beyond the hawthorn hedgerows, cattle were grazing contentedly in the open pasture land and in the far corner of a distant field was Amos Bolinbroke's allotment and chicken run.

His latest acquisition was a rooster with striking plumage, a long flowing tail and bright pointed feathers on its neck. The barman in The Eagle had told me the rooster's name was Rocky and he had an internal clock that anticipated sunrise. Apparently his crowing was a signal to other roosters that, if they trespassed, there would be a fight. I decided to have a word with Amos, the village odd-job man, to see if there was a way of silencing Rocky . . . without the use of a shotgun!

It was a sunlit morning as I drove out of Bradley village. The pink petals of cherry trees scattered like countryside confetti across the High Street and, beyond the shimmering fields of green unripe barley, purple heather streaked the distant Pennine Hills. On my car radio Deniece Williams was singing 'Free' as I drove towards Newbridge and I thought of Donna and the subtle changes in our relationship.

Her house had been made more secure and I had fitted window locks. She had contacted the police, who said they would try to keep a watch on her cottage. There had been no further attempts by Barty to invade her life but it was clear she was both troubled and nervous.

I was looking forward to seeing her this evening. Sherri was staying over with her friend Georgie so Donna and I had arranged to have a meal together. It had been my idea to go somewhere special so I had booked a table at The Old Swan in the picturesque village of Gargrave. It was a traditional sixteenth-century coaching inn and I thought we would enjoy a relaxing evening there.

When I arrived at school Frank was emptying the litter bins. 'Mornin', Mr Sheffield,' he called out. He was holding another empty bottle.

'Morning, Frank. You've found another.'

'Yes. If y'leave it wi' me ah can sort it.'

'So you know who it is?'

'Mebbe.'

'Is it one of the local teenagers?'

He tapped the side of his nose. 'No names . . . no pack drill, Mr Sheffield,' and he wandered off to collect litter from the other bins.

I was leading morning assembly and my theme was the Green Cross Code. We had received a free leaflet from County Hall entitled 'A Lesson for Life' and the children in my class demonstrated how to cross the road safely. The Swithenbank twins featured in a drama they had devised, illustrating the dangers of crossing between parked cars, running on the pavement and dodging traffic. They were growing up fast. Tracey and Stacey were taller now than Celestine and Audrey and both played for the district netball team.

It was at times like this that I reflected the top juniors were ready to move on. Next week Katy and I had arranged to take them to The Ridge for the first of their visits to their new secondary school. The hall was full of attentive children and, in the middle row, the top infants sat cross-legged with toothless smiles as they enjoyed the assembly. Most of them had lost their 'baby teeth' as Rhonda called them.

Grayson was at the side of the hall, waiting to lead morning prayers. He sat there patient, cautious and inscrutable but when he spoke his words had gravitas and came from the heart. As always he displayed a clarity of mind and a sharp perception but there was no doubt our conversations had become a little strained of late. His outdated views regarding relationships and, particularly, his coolness towards Neville had created a rift between us.

*

At morning break Katy was flicking through the television page of her newspaper. 'David Frost is interviewing Richard Nixon tonight. Should make interesting viewing.'

The disgraced President had finally decided to break his silence after leaving the White House in 1974.

'He could have ended the war in Vietnam sooner,' said Izzy. 'When he came to office sixty Americans were dying there every day.'

'Such a dreadful waste of young lives,' said Audrey sadly.

'I'm surprised he dare show his face,' said Rhonda firmly.

'What a world we live in,' said Celestine, 'and they still haven't caught that Yorkshire Ripper. Makes you frightened to walk the streets.'

'Four victims now,' said Tom. 'Wants stringing up.'

At that moment Neville walked in carrying a magnificent fruit cake. 'New recipe, all of you, do try a slice,' he announced.

Death and violence were suddenly put to one side as we tucked in and Neville, completely unaware of the previous conversation, turned to more immediate matters. 'Now, be honest, everyone, have I used too much mixed spice?'

At lunchtime I spotted a smart new Vauxhall Chevette in the car park and a tall slim woman emerged in a navy business suit that was the height of fashion. Her long ponytail bounced behind her and she carried a black executive briefcase.

I met her in the entrance hall.

'Good afternoon. Can I help?'

She smiled. 'Mr Patterson is expecting me. I'm Tricia Howarth, the new Primary Adviser.'

'Pleased to meet you. I'm Jack Sheffield, the deputy head. Welcome to Newbridge.' I tapped on Jim's door and walked in. 'The new Primary Adviser is here.'

He stood up quickly. 'Pleased to meet you, Ms Howarth. Thank you for taking time to call in. You must be very busy.' They shook hands. 'Do take a seat. Would you like a coffee?'

'Yes, please.'

'Jack, could you ask Audrey for some coffee and biscuits?'

I smiled as I walked out. Only important visitors were offered biscuits.

It was after a ham salad lunch that Jim emerged with our new adviser. Both looked relaxed. It had clearly been a positive meeting.

Jim beckoned me over. 'Jack, could you give Ms Howarth a tour of the school?'

'Certainly.'

We began in the infant department and Ms Howarth seemed very much at home in the various classrooms. She made good contact with everyone she met and promised support where required, particularly in extending our new reading scheme. I was impressed. We finished up in my room.

'Excellent displays,' she said, looking around at the children's work. We had been doing a project on the Industrial Revolution, including a visit to the local mill. 'This takes me back to my school,' she added rather wistfully.

I studied her more closely. She was a lithe, smooth-skinned forty-something, a very attractive woman.

'Do you miss it?' I asked. 'I think I would. I love my teaching, particularly top juniors.'

She smiled. 'Yes, I do, to be honest, but this job has new challenges and it gives me the chance to share good practice and help children in that way.'

I could see she was enthused with her new post and the opportunities it offered. She looked at her wristwatch. 'Thank you for your time but I have another school to visit.'

'I'll take you back to the office.'

We stood up and she studied me for a moment. 'Mr Patterson mentioned he thought you were ready for a school of your own.'

'Perhaps one day,' I said, 'but I'm happy here.'

'Well, think about it and I'll help if I can. That's what I did after my deputy headship, a lovely village school up in North Yorkshire.'

'Yes, Jim and I did look at a few headships up there.'

'One has just been readvertised. Might be worth checking out. Ragley Church of England: the head is retiring in the summer.'

The name of the school rang a bell. 'Well . . . thanks for your interest, Ms Howarth.'

She smiled. 'Happy to help.'

At the end of school Frank was emptying the classroom waste baskets; he knocked on Tristan's door and walked in. "Ello, Mr Lampwick.' He shut the door behind him.

Tristan was mounting a selection of beautiful watercolour paintings and poems. 'Hello, Frank.'

Frank emptied the waste paper into a black bag and leaned on one of the desks. 'Can ah 'ave a word?'

Tristan looked puzzled. This was unusual. 'Of course.'

'From m'upstairs window at 'ome ah can see t'playground.'

'Yes?'

Frank took out of his overall pocket an empty bottle of Captain Morgan Black Label Jamaica Rum.

Tristan sat down abruptly. His face went white. 'Oh no.'

'So we need t'talk.'

Tristan slumped at his desk and put his head in his hands. 'If this gets out I'm finished.'

'Ah know. That's why ah'm 'ere. 'Ow long 'as it been goin' on?'

'A long time,' he muttered quietly. 'It calms me down.'

'Is that all?'

Tristan took a deep breath. 'To be honest . . . I need it . . . most days.'

'That's 'ow ah were when ah came back from m'National Service.'

'Really?'

Frank nodded. 'Ah were like you. Ah needed it . . . ev'ry day.'

'What did you do?'

'Ah 'ad a friend. 'E realized what were wrong. We went to a meeting . . . Alco'olics Anonymous.'

Tristan looked down at his hands. He was shaking.

'So ah've decided to 'elp you jus' like my mate 'elped me. 'Ave a think an' we'll talk again nex' week. An' this is jus' between us. You're a good teacher, Mr Lampwick. It'd be a shame f'school t'lose you.'

Tristan stood up and they shook hands, 'Thanks, Frank.'

When he sat down again it felt as though a weight had been lifted from his shoulders.

I was in Jim's office at the end of the school day.

'Excellent new adviser, Jack. Just what we needed. Thanks for giving her the guided tour.'

'The rest of the staff certainly appreciated her.'

Jim nodded. 'She has *credibility* and that counts for a lot. Her appointment was well deserved. She was head of an inner-city school, a village school and she was a deputy head just like you.'

I gestured towards the copy of the *Times Educational Supplement* on his desk. 'She mentioned that headship in North Yorkshire had been readvertised.'

He passed it over. 'Take this, Jack. Have a look over the weekend.'

Back in my classroom I put it in my satchel.

When I arrived home I decided to sort out the problem of Rocky the rooster and set off across the fields. Old Amos was sitting outside his shed on his allotment. In his seventies and an old-fashioned Yorkshire sage, he was a popular figure in the village. He was chatting with a tall young man who was packing some spinach leaves and a few lettuces into a brown paper bag.

'Now then, Mr Sheffield, 'ow's tha doin'?'

'Fine, thank you, Mr Bolinbroke.'

'This is young Jamie Webb. New in t'village.'

'Pleased to meet you, Jamie.'

''Ello, sir.' We shook hands.

"Elps me wi' odd jobs an' at weekends we deliver veg t'them that needs it.' He looked up at Jamie. 'So tek that lot t'Mrs Bamford an' then come back f'some for yer Mam.'

Harry hurried away and Amos puffed thoughtfully on his pipe. 'Lovely young lad. Shame 'e 'ad bad luck.'

'What was that?'

'Sit thissen down, 'ave a cuppa an' ah'll tell thee.'

The kettle on his Primus stove was steaming and I sat down on a wooden chair. He served me a tin mug of strong tea and I listened to his tale.

'Jamie were eleven back in 1970. Lived in Bradford. 'E were one o' t'best footballers in England. Man United wanted 'im. So did Spurs. But Don Revie spoke to 'is mam an' dad an 'e chose Leeds United. They all agreed t'wait 'til 'e were fifteen. Then, on t'day 'e were gonna sign, 'is parents' car broke down so they said come back t'morrow. That afternoon 'e were asked t'play for t'local pub team. Poor lad broke his leg. F'some reason 'e 'ad wrong treatment so 'e couldn't run any more like 'e used to.' Amos sat back and tamped the tobacco in his briar pipe. "Is dream were shattered. Then 'e moved 'ere. 'E 'elps me now wi' gard'nin', fencin', barn doors, all sorts.'

'Oh dear. What a sad tale.'

'An' y'know t'bes' thing?'

'What's that?'

"E never complains 'bout nowt.'

'I see.'

'Not a single complaint. That sez a lot.'

'It certainly does.' I was beginning to waver.

'Anyway, did tha come f'summat special or were thee jus' passin'?'

266

'Just passing.' I supped the last of my tea and stood up. 'Good luck with your gardening, Mr Bolinbroke. It looks wonderful.'

'Come back some time f'some peas, Mr Sheffield. Ah'll 'ave plenty.'

'Thank you, I shall.'

I glanced at the tall wire netting enclosure where chickens were pecking seeds and the rooster strutted around.

Amos smiled. 'My Rocky's a good lad as well.' He sucked again on his pipe and then gave a deep, throaty chuckle. ''E's another what never complains.'

I collected Donna from her cottage and smiled. She looked stunning in a flower-print summer dress and was carrying a lilac shawl.

'The weekend begins,' I said, 'and you look lovely.'

'Thanks, Jack,' she said simply.

The sun had enhanced her complexion and bleached her blonde hair a little lighter. There was the familiar hint of Yves Saint Laurent and it was a good feeling to have this beautiful woman by my side. I hoped the evening would give her a chance to relax.

Four miles from Skipton on the A65 we drove into the quaint, beautiful village of Gargrave. On the edge of the Yorkshire Dales, it comprised a cluster of Victorian buildings made of Yorkshire stone. The Old Swan was welcoming and we sat at our reserved table and ordered a glass of wine while we studied the menu.

'So, how was school this week?' I asked.

'Busy. We had a meeting at lunchtime to discuss the Jubilee.'

'What are you doing?'

'I'm torn, really. There's a street party in North Beck and one outside my school. I'm working out how to get to both. What about you?'

'I'll be in Newbridge. There's a lot planned for a huge party on the High Street.'

Our conversation ebbed and flowed, generally about school, as we enjoyed a main course of lamb cutlets followed by apple pie and ice cream. It was when the coffee arrived that Donna fixed me with that familiar direct stare.

'Jack, there's something important I have to share with you.'

I sipped my coffee and looked up enquiringly.

'I've given this a lot of thought and made a decision.'

'Yes?'

'Last weekend I had a long discussion with my mother. She will be selling her home in Milltown.'

'So where will she live?'

'With me and Sherri.'

I was silent. This was unexpected.

'Jack . . . I have to look to the future. With what my mother makes from the sale along with my savings we could buy a new home. Also, I could get a mortgage now. It would mean security for us all.'

This had come as a surprise and it didn't appear that I was part of her plans.

'So . . . where will you be looking to live?'

'I don't know at the moment but I do know that I need a fresh start and a new life away from here . . . and away from *him*.'

I was lost for words.

'I'm sorry, Jack, but this is what I must do.'

I stared into her blue eyes and recognized the utter determination in this woman. 'But how do you know this is for the best?'

She gave an enigmatic smile. 'Women always know, Jack . . . always.'

I sat back and sighed. This seemed so final.

It was nine o'clock and the sun was setting. We drank our coffee and, in the midst of the restaurant conversation, there was silence between us. Then I stared out of the window at the purple sky and realized my hopes for a bright future with Donna had gone.

Finally we stood up to leave. I draped her shawl around her shoulders and recalled the softness of her skin.

'I really am sorry, Jack,' she said quietly.

'So am I . . . but you can't run for ever.'

'As long as my child's safety is compromised, I will never stop running.' She gave a deep sigh. 'Old sins cast long shadows.'

It was a saying I recalled my mother using long ago and on this dark night I understood its meaning. When we drove back to Donna's cottage it was clear I wouldn't be invited in. She squeezed my hand, kissed me and stepped out of the car. When she walked into her cottage she didn't look back.

Once inside, Donna checked the windows, turned out the lights and went upstairs to bed. Before she closed her bedroom curtains she stared out at the dark world beyond. She stood there for what seemed an age. For many nights now she had imagined Barty standing there against the furnace heat of a setting sun and, in her troubled dreams, he had appeared as a vision from hell. Ten years ago she had recoiled at his appearance at her door. There was nothing appealing about him any more. As the years went by Barty had become a sinner in a cesspit of lies and now he was back.

Decisions had been made and a new journey awaited. The shattered fragility of previous times had been replaced with an iron stoicism. Life seemed to have become a battleground and she knew it was time to move on.

It was midnight when I, too, found myself staring out of my bedroom window. Clouds scudded across the vast firmament and moonlight flickered through the swaying branches of the high elms.

I thought back to Jamie Webb. For that fine young man it had been a life of shattered hopes. The bright road to a promised land had ended up in a cul-de-sac of shadows and, as Old Amos had said, he never complained. I admired his fortitude and wondered if I could overcome the setback I had just experienced in the same way.

Sleep was elusive during a night of scattered thoughts and broken dreams.

On Saturday morning at 4.55 a.m. I stirred as shafts of light flickered across my ceiling. It was sunrise and Rocky the Rooster had woken me again. I got up and peered through the window. A thin bright line of dawn crested the distant hills, a linear halo of hope for a new day. I slipped on my dressing gown, walked into the kitchen and made a mug of black tea.

I looked in my satchel and took out the *Times Educational Supplement*. Then I sat down at my old pine table and turned the pages to the new headships. The advertised post for the headteacher of Ragley Church of England Primary School in North Yorkshire was there once again.

Chapter Seventeen

Mixed Celebrations

A morning of sun and showers greeted me when I drove into the school car park on Tuesday, 7 June. It was Silver Jubilee Day, a public holiday, and the villagers of New-bridge were determined to enjoy themselves regardless of the weather. The High Street had been blocked off so I took a circuitous route around the back streets to reach the school car park.

Big Frank was there to greet me. ''Ave a look at this, Mr Sheffield. A sight f'sore eyes.'

We walked to the school gate and saw a high street completely empty of parked cars. It looked wider somehow.

'This is 'ow it was when ah were a kid,' said Frank wist-fully. 'No cars, jus' t'coal wagon and t'milk cart an' nowt much else.'

Many of the villagers had made an early start and a long line of trestle tables covered in red, white and blue crêpe paper had been set up down the centre of the street.

Bunting stretched across the road and the upstairs windows were a sea of Union Jacks.

'It looks wonderful, Frank. A special day.'

'Anyway . . . ah've gorra stage t'set up wi' Nobby. 'E's jus' picked up some microphones an' a speaker big as a fridge.' He wandered off before I could ask him where Nobby Poskitt might have *picked up* this high-tech equipment.

Jim and Neville were walking across the playground, both looking relaxed and informal in open-necked shirts and lightweight summer jackets.

'Morning, Jack,' said Jim. 'Good timing. Neville needs a hand to set up the table for the children's baking competition.'

'Morning. Yes, here to help.'

'There're lots of entries, Jack,' said Neville. 'Mums and children have been delivering them all morning. I've got them in my classroom.'

'Fine, lead the way,' I said.

Tom and Katy appeared, carrying one of the dining tables, and we spent the next half-hour walking back and forth from school. Audrey and Celestine had pushed the television set into the hall and we caught glimpses of the events as they unfolded in London.

'There's Princess Margaret,' said Audrey.

'And Princess Anne and Captain Mark Phillips,' said Celestine as the first carriage procession went by.

It was a dramatic scene in London where thousands had braved the rain and camped out in the Mall and Trafalgar Square to catch sight of the Royal Family's procession to St Paul's. The reporter said that more than one million were expected to line the route.

Audrey and Celestine were covering a table with a snowy white cloth when Neville and I arrived carrying the children's baking entries. It was a wonderful display and Neville wrote each child's name on a card ready for the judge. Then Audrey protected everything with the staff-room's collection of tea towels.

'There,' said Audrey. 'It's ready.'

'Thank you, everybody,' said Neville.

It was then that Celestine arrived to make an announcement. 'Audrey, come quick. The Queen is dressed in pink and she looks a picture,' and our two fervent royalists hurried back to the television in the school hall.

'Quite a sight, Jack,' said Jim as more locals arrived in the High Street. 'Looks like Gilbert's making the most of it.'

Gilbert Snoddy, never one to miss an opportunity, had set up a table outside his store selling festive souvenirs. They included tins of chocolate, bottles of beer and jigsaw puzzles.

'And he's not the only one. Look what's just appeared.'

At the far end of the street a number of stalls had been set up by local entrepreneurs hoping to use the occasion to drum up business. They included Charlie Backhouse, the tree surgeon, and his two sons under a banner that read: 'TREE WISE MEN'. Next to them was Mavis Proop in her black coat and pince-nez spectacles. She was sitting behind a table on which was pinned the sign 'MOODY & DYE, FUNERAL DIRECTORS'. Mavis was not happy being in close proximity to Butch the bulldog and his owner Derek Cresswell on the next stall. Derek was sharing a can of beer with Butch while advertising 'THE DOGFATHER KENNELS'.

'Yes, they're all here,' said Jim. 'Definitely a day to remember.'

'And the press too.'

Eugene Pickles, the local reporter from the *Newbridge Chronicle*, was there with his camera and notebook chatting with the locals. He approached us. "Scuse me, Mr Patterson. Any chance of a photo of you with some of the kids an' a quick quote?'

Jim smiled. 'Of course,' and he wandered off to be immediately surrounded by eager pupils.

Soon the children were being ushered to their places for their party tea and Katy and I were standing side by side and smiling at the antics of those we knew in our classes. They were excited and nearly all of them were in their best clothes and wearing cardboard hats and carrying flags.

Jeremy Prendergast was beside us and looked forlornly at the festive scene.

'What is it, Jeremy?' asked Katy. 'You look sad.'

'Hello, Miss. I'm fine, thank you. It's just I wish I had a hat as well.'

Katy had spent seven pence on her *Daily Mirror* and she rummaged in her shoulder bag and passed over the newspaper. 'Here you are, Jeremy. I bet a clever boy like you can make a pirate hat.'

His eyes lit up. 'Thank you, Miss,' and he hurried off to work on his creation.

'Katy, if you don't mind me saying ... I'm surprised you're here.'

She looked thoughtful. 'Yes, nearly didn't, but it's for

school, not the royals. Funnily enough, I quite admire the Queen, it's just all the hangers-on that make me furious.'

'Anyway, good to see you.'

'And the kids are loving their party tea.'

'I guess Mike is doing the same at Bracken.'

'Yes . . . and Donna will be there.'

'I expect she will.'

Suddenly the Swithenbank twins arrived out of breath. ''Ello, sir, 'ello, Miss,' they chorused.

They had dressed somewhat incongruously for the occasion. They were wearing plastic tiaras and identical Flamenco dresses that we later discovered were left over from a dance competition.

'Hello, girls,' I said. 'You're just in time for the party.' The ladies of the Women's Institute were serving crab-paste sandwiches and Garibaldi biscuits followed by jelly and ice cream.

'I like the outfits,' said Katy.

'Thanks, Miss,' said Stacey.

'We've come as Spanish dancers,' said Tracey.

'We like t'be diff'rent,' said Stacey.

'An' we saw t'Queen light a bonfire las' night,' said Tracey. 'It were on telly.'

'There's loads of 'em, sir,' said Stacey with enthusiasm.

'All over t'country,' added her sister for good measure.

Yesterday the Queen had lit the first in a chain of bonfires around the nation.

'Well, enjoy your day, girls,' I said.

'We will, sir,' said Stacey, 'an' we've entered Mr Wagstaff's baking competition.'

'That's good,' said Katy. 'What have you made?'

'Jam tarts, Miss,' said Tracey. 'We've still got two left.'

'Just two?' I asked.

'We ate the rest, sir,' said Stacey.

'An' they were lovely,' said Tracey as they ran off.

'Hi, you two.' It was Izzy with red, white and blue ribbons in her hair. 'Have you told him my news?' She was smiling.

Katy shook her head. 'No, I didn't want to spoil the surprise.'

'Clearly something exciting by the look of you.'

'I've been offered a full-time job from September and I've said yes.'

'That's wonderful. You must be pleased.'

'The thing is, Jack, it's not here.'

I feigned surprise. 'Oh, I'm sad to hear that. So where is it?'

'Sun Hill Primary. I've done a bit of occasional supply teaching on top of my music in the school and the head seemed impressed. He's a nice guy, a bit like Jim only older. It's a lovely school and the kids are great.'

'Sounds perfect for you.'

'Mixed feelings to be leaving Newbridge so soon.'

'Short but sweet.'

'Me . . . or my time here?'

'Both.'

She squeezed my hand. 'I'm sorry we won't be working together, Jack.'

'Me too.'

'I need to tell Jim that I'll have to hand in my notice at the end of this month.'

'You could tell him now,' I said. 'He's over there talking to the parents.'

'I'll come with you,' said Katy.

'By the way, Jack,' said Izzy. 'Is Donna coming?'

'No.'

'Come on,' said Katy and she took Izzy by the arm and ushered her away.

It crossed my mind that at the beginning of the school year there had been the possibility of two women in my life. Now it appeared there were none.

Big Frank and Tristan were sitting side by side on the steps of the war memorial. They were both eating a sandwich and chatting like old friends.

'I appreciate what you've done, Frank.'

'Allus pleased to 'elp.'

'I've not had a drink since we first went.'

'It's workin' then.'

Frank had driven Tristan to Alcoholics Anonymous in Leeds each week.

'I know I have to sort out my own problems. Drink was just numbing them, not dealing with them. By going to the meetings I was given compassion from other addicts. I need that.'

Frank studied the intense face of the young man beside him. 'When did it start?'

Tristan clasped his hands together and lowered his head. 'When my dad died. He was in a car accident. I was fifteen.'

'Ah'm sorry. Must've been 'ard.'

'My mum went off the rails. Never the same again. She started drinking. Then I did. I go home to be with her when I can.'

Across the street the Salvation Army Brass Band began to tune up with discordant sounds. The conductor in his immaculate uniform stood up, tapped his baton, and the strains of 'Jerusalem' filled the air.

'Can't beat a brass band,' said Frank.

'I love music,' said Tristan. 'Play it all the time at home.'

They sat there munching their sandwiches and enjoying the tunes. The older villagers joined in with a rendition of the Vera Lynn classic 'We'll Meet Again', while Frank went to collect two mugs of tea and two fruit scones from the Women's Institute stall.

When he sat down again he looked at Tristan and said quietly, 'Ah'm right proud o' you.'

Tristan was surprised. He looked up at this huge craggy Yorkshireman. 'Thanks, Frank.'

The band began to play 'Abide with Me' as tiny tots sat on their mother's knee and children crawled under the tables. Men raised bottles of beer outside Snoddy's Stores and sang along.

'Ah never 'ad a son,' said Frank. 'But if ah 'ad . . . then ah'd 'ave liked 'im t'be jus' like you.'

After speaking about her new teaching post with a very understanding Jim, Izzy persuaded Katy to walk down the High Street to visit something that had caught her eye.

Gipsy Esmeralda, or Freda Pickersgill as she was known on the electoral register, was a colourful local figure who had parked her caravan in a cul-de-sac behind the fabric shop. She was selling coffee made from the roots of dandelions. The sign on her table read: 'Esmeralda Coffee. Four times more vitamin C than lettuce and more iron than spinach.'

She was doing a roaring trade and if you crossed her palm with silver she would gaze into her crystal ball and tell your fortune.

'Go on then,' said Katy. 'See what your future holds.'

A few minutes later, when Izzy emerged from the darkness of the caravan, Katy asked, 'Well, what did she say?'

'Guess?'

'Has to be a tall, dark stranger.'

'Correct . . . except she didn't say *stranger*.'

Outside the Women's Institute tent, I was sitting with Jim enjoying tea and corned beef sandwiches when Jim nodded towards Frank and Tristan. 'Have you noticed that Tristan is a lot more positive these days?'

'He's definitely looking more relaxed.'

'Yes, I think Frank has taken him under his wing.'

Jim sipped his tea and studied the two of them. 'That's encouraging. Frank is a good man.' He glanced at his watch. 'Almost time for the baking result, Jack.'

In the school hall Audrey had been joined by Rhonda, Diane and Celestine. Audrey had spent twelve pence on a souvenir issue of the *Radio Times* and knew when to watch the royal events throughout the day. It was shortly before half past two and time to listen to the Queen's speech to the Commonwealth.

As always, Her Majesty spoke clearly and with authority. 'These twenty-five years have seen much change for Britain. By virtue of tolerance and understanding, the Empire has evolved into a Commonwealth of thirty-six independent nations spanning the five continents.'

'Uplifting,' said Diane.

'Perfect,' murmured Celestine.

'She's an inspiration,' said Audrey.

'Just like Shirley Bassey,' said Rhonda.

The Queen continued with optimism. 'A Jubilee is also a time to look forward! We should certainly do this with determination and I believe we can also do so with hope.'

'I agree,' said Audrey. 'That's what we all need, a bit of good news and thinking kindly of others.'

'By the way,' said Celestine. 'Where's the vicar?'

'At another street party,' said Audrey.

'I thought he would be judging Neville's baking competition,' said Diane.

'No, he's not,' said Audrey with feeling and reflecting that *thinking kindly of others* only went so far.

'I think it's Mrs High and Mighty,' said Rhonda. She was not a fan of Clarissa Peacock.

'Shall we go outside again?' said Diane.

'Good idea,' said Audrey. 'We've seen the best bits from London.'

Fortunately Audrey was unaware that not everyone in the capital was supporting the Queen's special day. The anarchic band the Sex Pistols had decided to process in a different way by sailing down the Thames while playing their controversial 'God Save the Queen' before being arrested.

The sun had come out and, under a colourful marquee, the small stage was the focal point of the celebrations. In front was a large table on which was displayed the children's baking entries. They ranged from some dubious fairy cakes by

Susan Verity to Gary Cockroft's fruit scones, which would have tested the teeth of a saltwater crocodile. Pauline Ackworth's shortbread looked deceptively appetizing as did the pair of jam tarts by the Swithenbank twins along with Billy Gubbins's surprisingly sophisticated lattice mince tart, but it would need a discerning palate to determine the winner. That task went to the Chair of our PTA and local councillor Clarissa Peacock, who was dressed, appropriately, like her namesake in a blue and green high-neck summer dress and a hat of iridescent feathers. I was standing with Katy at the front of the crowd of teachers, parents and children.

Ena Stubbs mounted the stage, blew into the microphone and began to speak. 'Ladies an' gentlemen, boys an' girls, ah 'ave pleasure in askin' our local councillor, Mrs Clarissa Peacock, to announce t'result of t'kiddies' bakin' competition.'

There was polite applause as Clarissa approached the microphone.

'Thank you, Mrs Stubbs, and it is an esteemed honour to announce the winning entry from this veritable plethora of delectable delights.'

Katy leaned over to me and whispered, 'She's off on one again.'

Mrs Peacock gestured towards the table in front of her. 'I am of course grateful to Mr Wagstaff for his efforts while being cognisant of my responsibilities and can announce the anticipated result.'

Neville blushed profusely while Big Frank muttered, 'Gerron wi' it,' to Gilbert Snoddy from across the street.

'The winner is both apropos and timely as on this auspicious occasion it is not a member of the fair sex.'

'Did she say *sex*?' asked Mrs Sylvia Ackworth from outside the entrance to The Black Horse. She had dyed her hair red, white and blue and was wearing a tight blue mini skirt.

'She did, Sylvia,' said Mrs Marie Whitehead while the phrase *mutton dressed as lamb* crossed her mind.

Clarissa was building up to a grand finale. 'It is in fact a young boy of the male gender who is the champion.' Clarissa picked up a tin plate on which was a huge mince lattice tart, minus a large slice. 'I have sampled all the entries but for his most pretentious and tasty creation, the winner is . . . Master William Gubbins.'

There was a surprised gasp from the group of mothers who had slaved alongside their daughters to produce perfect results from their *Be-Ro Home Recipes* book. A puzzled Billy Gubbins had understood nothing the lady with the Chief Sitting Bull headdress had said apart from his name being called out.

He approached the stage, received the tiny tin cup to thunderous applause, then picked up his mince tart and stepped off the stage.

'Well done, Billy,' I said.

'Congratulations,' said Katy. 'You're the champion.'

'Would y'like a piece, Miss?'

'That's kind, Billy, but you should share it with your mum and dad.'

'No, Miss, they said they wouldn't touch it wi' a barge pole but our Geoffrey liked it.'

'I didn't know you had a brother,' said Katy.

'Ah 'aven't, Miss. Geoffrey's our Yorkshire terrier. M'dad supports Barnsley at football an' Yorkshire at cricket. 'Is 'ero

is Geoff Boycott. Allus calls 'im *Sir* Geoffrey. So that's what
'e called our dog. 'E's smashin' but smells summat rotten.'

'Are you saying it was your *dog* that liked your mince
tart, Billy?' asked Katy with a frown.

'Yes, Miss, but 'e only licked it a few times after m'pastry
fell on t'floor.'

'Oh dear,' I said. The winning entry was looking less
appetizing by the second.

'Floor were mucky, sir, but ah picked out most o' t'bits
that were stickin' to it. So, do y'fancy a bit?'

Katy gave me a knowing look. 'Not just now, Billy, but
thanks anyway.'

The boy hurried away and, as an afterthought,
approached Mrs Peacock, who had descended from the
stage. 'Would y'like another slice, Miss?'

Clarissa had missed her lunch and was hungry. 'Yes,
please, William. That's very thoughtful.' She cut another
large slice, placed it on a paper plate, picked up a fork and
began to eat. 'It's the texture that attracted me,' said Clarissa, staring hard at the dark bits that flecked the surface.
'I'm presuming you used chopped raisins as well.'

'Mebbe, Miss,' he replied cautiously. He had just remembered the mouse droppings on the kitchen floor that his
mother had told him to sweep up.

As the afternoon progressed the children went home and
just a few parents were left sitting outside the two pubs
and enjoying a drink and some welcome peace. After
helping to clear up and return the tables to the school hall
I said goodnight to Jim and walked out of school with
Audrey. Our school secretary was looking forward to

settling down with a nightcap and watching another Audrey, of the Hepburn variety, in *My Fair Lady*.

As I drove home I thought of Donna and wondered what decisions she had made during the last few weeks. We had barely spoken since our meal together in The Old Swan. Back in Bradley village I was surrounded by signs of high summer. Butterflies hovered above the buddleia bushes and the scent of roses hung in the air. By the time I had reached my front door I still hadn't thought of an excuse to ring Donna, but, unexpectedly, the perfect opportunity was there waiting for me.

A large manila envelope was lying on the mat. I picked it up, opened it and sat at the kitchen table. The letter had a North Yorkshire County Council crest. It read:

County Hall,
Northallerton

Dear Mr Sheffield,
You are invited to attend for interview for the post of headteacher of Ragley-on-the-Forest Church of England Primary School on Friday, 24th June at 2.00 p.m.

Jim was the only one who knew of my application. It was time to share it with Donna.

'Hi, it's me.'

'Oh, hello, Jack. I've just got in. A hectic day. How did your party go?'

'Fine, thanks, but I'm just ringing with some news.'

'Yes?'

'I've got a headship interview.'

'That's good. Where is it?'

'North Yorkshire, one of the village schools. The head is retiring this summer.'

'When is the interview?'

'In two weeks on Friday, the twenty-fourth.'

'Well . . . good luck. You must have a good chance and it's what you wanted.'

'I was thinking that maybe we could go for a drink together on that evening.' I paused. 'Just a drink.'

'We could do that, Jack.'

'You can help me celebrate or commiserate.'

'I am sure you will do well. Don't undersell yourself. You're a wonderful teacher; a great deputy and loved by all the children and parents. They would be mad not to have you.'

Her enthusiasm was infectious. Maybe there was real hope for the interview . . . and possibly something else.

I decided not to sound too keen or push my luck. 'You're too kind but, either way, it will be good to see you and catch up on all your news.'

'I'll look forward to it, Jack. Shall we say eight o'clock at one of the local pubs? You choose. As it happens, Sherri will be at my mother's that night, so I won't have to rush home.'

'Great, see you then.'

I replaced the telephone receiver and smiled.

Chapter Eighteen

Clouds and Silver Linings

It was Friday, 24 June, the day of my interview, and when I awoke a low-lying mist shrouded the light of a pallid dawn. It had been a humid and sleepless night and the sound of thunder rumbled in the distance. A storm was gathering . . . a big storm.

Jim had given me the whole day off school even though I wasn't due in Northallerton until the early afternoon. So I spent the morning rehearsing possible answers to questions and just after 11.30 a.m. I walked out to my car for the journey to North Yorkshire. The air was already hot and the drone of bees in their never-ending search for pollen – the sound of summer – enveloped me. Cuckoo spit sparkled in the lavender leaves like milky white foam while above my head the raucous cries of crows disturbed my racing thoughts. As I drove out of the village I knew it was a day that would change my life . . . one way or the other.

It had been a surprise to discover the headship of Ragley village school had been readvertised. Clearly they hadn't found a suitable candidate. It was critical they found one today as the headteacher, Mr Pruett, was about to retire. I had made an extra effort to look smart and, with neat creases in my flared polyester trousers, polished shoes and a fashionable kipper tie, I hoped I would make a good impression. Yesterday I had shared the news with the rest of the staff and they had all wished me the best of luck. Jim was especially supportive and showed me a copy of the reference he had written for me.

I had lots of time so I made an early start with the intention of driving to Northallerton via York. The detour would give me an opportunity to see Ragley-on-the-Forest. The roads were clear as I drove through Harrogate and turned east. Eventually, in the distance, I glimpsed York Minster dominating the skyline of the beautiful, historic city. It was where I had trained to be a teacher and memories flooded back of carefree student days. Then to the north of the city I drove up the A19 where a cluster of pretty villages nestled near the foot of the Hambleton Hills. Before the market town of Easington I turned on to a country lane and drove slowly up the High Street of Ragley-on-the-Forest.

There was a row of shops, a village hall and The Royal Oak pub overlooking a large grassy triangle with a pond. I pulled up for a moment and stared at the school beyond an avenue of horse chestnut trees. It was a Victorian building with a bell tower and high arched windows. It looked solid and dependable, a school with history that had served countless generations of children. I wondered if, by the end of the day, I would be part of its journey.

*

Soon I arrived at the sprawling market town of North-allerton and parked outside the imposing building of County Hall. A stern-looking lady on reception checked a list of names on her clipboard. 'Follow me,' she said in a no-nonsense manner.

We walked past Corinthian columns beneath an impossibly high ornate ceiling and up a wide marble staircase. She gestured towards a funereal reception area dominated by a huge mahogany table and uncomfortable chairs. 'Wait here until you are called. The interview will take place in Room 109.' When she strutted away her heels clicked on the steps as she returned to her desk.

It was 1.30 p.m. and I watched the minutes tick by on the ancient wall clock with its faded Roman numerals. I was alone and wondered where the other applicants might be. It seemed like an eternity until, at precisely two o'clock, a door opened and a short, dapper man in a pin-striped suit appeared. 'Good afternoon, Mr Sheffield. I'm Bernard Pickard, Assistant Chief Education Officer. Come this way please.'

I sat facing a huge oval table behind which sat the chairwoman of the interviewing panel. She took off her steel-framed spectacles and polished them slowly and deliberately.

'Good afternoon, Mr Sheffield. I'm Miss Barrington-Huntley, chair of the interviewing panel, and you're here today to be interviewed for the post of headteacher of Ragley-on-the-Forest Church of England Primary School. We interview in alphabetical order and you are our fourth and final candidate today.' She glanced left and right to the four men who were staring at me intently. 'May I introduce Mr Richard Gomersall, our Senior Primary Adviser; the Revd Joseph Evans, the Chair of Governors; Mr Stanley Coe, the Vice-Chairman; and you have already met Mr Pickard. My colleagues will be invited to ask questions and, if you are unclear at any time, please feel free to ask for them to be repeated.'

The interview went surprisingly well. I felt confident answering the Senior Primary Adviser's questions concerning the curriculum and mixed-ability teaching. Miss Barrington-Huntley was particularly perceptive, often adding supplementary questions concerning the role of Social Services and the qualities required for effective leadership. On occasions she helped out the bluff and inarticulate Mr Coe, who seemed to believe children should be seen and not heard. The vicar, a skeletally thin and apparently gentle man, asked my views on Christian worship and the role of the Church and appeared content that I supported the work of St Luke's in Newbridge. For almost an hour the intense Mr Pickard made copious notes and never smiled.

At the end there was a pause and Miss Barrington-Huntley decided to sum up. 'Mr Sheffield, have you any questions?'

'Only to say thank you for the interview and when will I hear of your decision?'

'We have told the other candidates that we shall contact them by telephone but, given you are the last to be interviewed, you may wait outside if you prefer.'

'Thank you. I'll do that.' I stood up and left.

Once again I sat in the reception area watching motes of dust hover in a shaft of sunlight from a high window.

Time passed slowly and it was almost four o'clock when I was called back in. For the first time Miss Barrington-Huntley gave me a hint of a smile. 'Mr Sheffield,' she said, 'after careful consideration we have decided to offer you the very challenging post of headmaster of Ragley School. First, I must ask you formally, do you accept?'

I heard a nearby church clock chime the hour as I took a deep breath and said simply, 'I accept.'

There were brief handshakes and I told the Revd Evans I would contact the school to arrange a visit. Out in the fresh air I hurried to a nearby telephone box.

'Jim, it's me. I got the job.'

'Well done, Jack, I'm pleased for you.'

'I'm still in Northallerton. Shall I call in?'

'No, we can catch up next week and you can tell me all about it. In the meantime, drive safely and enjoy your weekend.'

'Thanks, Jim. I'll always be grateful.'

Shortly before eight o'clock I drove towards North Beck village. It was a gentle journey of cow parsley, celandine and the lowing of cows in the fields. I was feeling relaxed and looking forward to seeing Donna once again. Even at this late hour the day was still wringing with humidity. Kenny Rogers was singing 'Lucille' on the radio when I pulled up outside her cottage. The sun was warm on my back and the scent of roses hung in the air when the door opened. She gave me an expectant look. 'Are we celebrating or not?'

'I got it. They offered me the headship and I said yes.'

She smiled. 'That's great news. What was the interview like?'

'Rigorous but fair.'

'You deserve it, Jack. I'm pleased for you.'

I looked at Donna in her summer dress. She looked lovely. 'So . . . which pub are we going to?'

'I thought The Rising Sun in the next village. Makes a change.'

'Sounds good. Is Sherri OK?'

'Yes, at my mother's.' She picked up her silk scarf from the chair by the hall table and locked the door. As we drove off it reminded me of happier times and Donna was full of news about how well Sherri was doing at school. 'By the way,' she said as we drove into Oakfield village, 'remind me to return your coin collection when we get back. It's on the hall table.'

'Was it helpful for your project?'

'Yes, perfect. The children enjoyed examining the coins but I don't want to hang on to them. They must be valuable.'

'Yes, of course, that's fine.'

The quaint wattle-and-daub pub looked empty when we walked in. On this warm evening most of the customers were taking advantage of the beer garden. We ordered tall, cool drinks at the bar and carried them outside to a picnic table covered with a bright orange parasol. I was reminded of how it used to be as we sat there in the golden light and sipped our lime and lemonade.

'Tell me more about the interview. What were the questions like?'

'Well, as you would expect, the Primary Adviser asked the pertinent ones. It was the usual stuff about the curriculum and I was happy with that. Then he got on to gifted children and the need for individual programmes of work.'

'Interesting . . . What about the others on the panel?'

'You would have liked the chair, Miss Barrington-Huntley. She was a really sharp lady. I think I made good contact with her. The Chair of Governors from Ragley was there, a local vicar who seemed pleased I helped out in church from time to time. There was also the Vice-Chair from Ragley who was like something from the Dark Ages but he didn't say much.'

'What were the other applicants like?'

'I didn't see them. I was the last of four and they were interviewed in the morning.'

'You must have been excited when they offered you the job.'

'I was although it felt like an eternity while they were deciding. Eventually I was called in and I accepted. I'll be visiting the school at the beginning of the holidays.'

Donna looked thoughtful. 'So . . . lots to do before September.'

'Definitely – new job, new home. Anyway, what about you? Have you made any more plans?'

'I've looked at a couple of new teaching posts.'

'Anywhere in particular?'

'Nowhere specific and wherever I go will have to be within travelling distance of a good school for Sherri.'

'You're sure to find somewhere and you're a good teacher.'

'My head was disappointed when I told her.'

'I guess she would be.'

'But she thought I would have a good chance of a Scale Two post.'

'Why not? You're already leading girls' games and promotion is the next step up the ladder.'

'My head said she would give me a good reference so that will help.'

There was another rumble of thunder and we turned to look at the gathering clouds in the distance. 'You will let me know how you get on, won't you?'

She paused before answering. 'I will if I can . . . but it's not straightforward for me.'

'I understand,' I said quietly but, deep down, I didn't.

She finished her drink and sat back. 'And on that note, Jack, I could do with getting back. I've an early start tomorrow with Sherri and my mum. We're going shopping in Leeds.'

'Of course. It's been a long day.'

'Thanks for the drink, Jack . . . and well done.'

We chatted as we drove back to North Beck. It was midsummer, the time of the long days. However, the light of this one was beginning to fade as the sun sank behind the dark clouds gathering in the purple sky. Once again I pulled up outside her cottage. 'Shall I wait while you go in?'

'That's kind, Jack, but I'll be fine.'

'OK. Look after yourself.'

'Yes I will . . . and you too.'

As she stepped out of the car there was a flash of lightning in the far distance and a deep, ominous rumble of thunder. We both looked up at the sky. 'Storm's coming,' I said.

For a moment a flicker of sadness crossed her face and she shook her head. 'It always was, Jack . . . it always was.'

Then she turned and walked up the path to her front door. She didn't look back.

When I drove away I reflected on what might have been.

Donna walked into the hallway and locked the door. Then she hung her silk scarf over the chair in the hallway and walked into the kitchen. It was then she saw it. There was broken glass on the mat by the back door. For a moment she was too shocked to move. Then she turned slowly and looked back. In the doorway stood a vision from hell. It was Barty.

He grabbed her arm and forced her into the lounge. 'Sit down and shut up if you know what's good for you.'

Donna was too frightened to scream. 'If you don't leave I'll call the police.'

'No, you won't.'

'You've broken into my house.'

'The window locks your friend fitted don't stop me.'

'Why are you here?'

'You know why I'm here: to get back what's mine.'

'There's nothing here for you.'

He pushed her down on to the sofa and twisted her wrist.

'You're hurting me!'

'Like you hurt me.'

'Get out!'

'I want to see my daughter . . . and I want you.'

Donna was trying to regain her self-control. 'Barty . . . it was over between us years ago. Think about it. I was a schoolgirl when we met.'

'That's for me to decide. I'm here to take what I came for.' He leaned forward and grabbed her by the shoulders.

'Leave me alone,' she screamed and kicked out at him.

He slapped her face hard and laughed. 'The dog, the woman and the walnut tree, the more you beat them the better they'll be.'

Donna recalled the old proverb with utter disgust. 'Barty, please . . . please leave.'

He stood up, smiled and began to undo his belt.

It was when I reached the outskirts of North Beck that I suddenly remembered. I hadn't collected my coin collection. At the end of the High Street in the gathering gloom a small blue van was parked under a sycamore tree and I pulled up behind it. I wasn't sure whether to turn back or not.

Minutes passed.

Finally I made a decision.

Barty stank of cigarettes and beer as he pressed against Donna. 'Now,' he hissed. 'You will do exactly as I say.'

It was at that moment there was a knock on the door.

Barty held Donna's wrists tightly and stared into the hallway. 'Don't answer that.'

'I have to.'

'You don't and no one knows I'm here.'

Donna was desperate and tried to speak lucidly. 'It's probably Milly from next door. She's elderly. Calls in at all times of day or night, often for a cup of sugar. She's a bit of an eccentric. If I don't answer she will worry and tell another neighbour.'

Barty gradually released his grip. 'Get rid of her. I'll be here listening to every word. And remember if you try to make a run for it I know where Sherri goes to school. You don't want her hurt, do you?'

Donna walked unsteadily into the hallway. The door knocker rattled again.

She opened the door slowly.

I smiled and was about to speak when I saw the fear in her eyes and the red mark on her cheek.

She put her hand over my mouth.

'Milly,' she said loudly. 'I've got a visitor so can you come back tomorrow?' She pointed to the lounge door. There was a pause as she moved aside and I stepped in.

Then I saw him. He wore dirty jeans and a shabby leather jacket and was staring at a photograph on the mantelpiece. It was Sherri looking relaxed on a sunny day in the Yorkshire Sculpture Park. Donna came to stand behind me. I clenched my fists in anger and stepped into the room.

'What the . . . !' he cried and looked at Donna. 'You bitch!'

He launched himself at me and I fell back against the wall as he tried to get out past Donna into the hallway.

I grabbed his collar, spun him round and held him firmly in a headlock. He was struggling like a wild thing, kicking out and punching me in the ribs, but he was a skinny lightweight and I pushed him to the floor. The rancid stink of sweat and alcohol rose from him like a noxious cloud.

'Donna, ring the police.'

'You bastard,' he cried as I pinned his wrists behind him.

I looked up at her. 'RING THE POLICE!'

Her body was shaking as she dialled 999. 'Police,' she said, 'and please hurry. A man has broken into my home and attacked me.' The conversation was brief and to the point. Then she stood in the doorway. 'They're coming,' she said simply.

'Donna,' I said quietly, 'open the front door, then go in the kitchen and wait there until they arrive. You're safe. I've got him now.' I noticed her dress was ripped at the shoulder. 'Are you hurt?'

She seemed transfixed. Her hand touched her cheek and she shook her head.

Barty was groaning as I forced him to stay still. 'Make one move and you'll regret it.'

Within minutes a two-door Fiesta pulled up outside and two policemen ran into the house. 'What is it, Miss?' asked the taller of the two, a huge man well over six feet tall.

Donna was standing by the kitchen door. 'He broke in,' she said and pointed to the broken glass on the kitchen floor. She was ashen-faced and trembling and nodded towards the prostrate figure of Barty. 'Then he attacked me. My friend arrived just in time.'

The shorter one, built like a middleweight boxer, knelt down beside me. 'We'll take over now, sir.'

I stood up as the two policemen restrained Barty. He began to struggle again until, seconds later, his arms were pinned behind his back and his wrists were secured in metal handcuffs. They dragged him roughly to his feet as another car arrived. A man in a suit got out.

'Cavalry's here,' said the tall policeman with a wry smile.

His colleague nodded and turned to Donna. 'CID will take some details, Miss.'

The newcomer walked into the crowded hallway. He looked at Donna. 'I'm Detective Inspector Kirby. These are my colleagues, Sergeant Porterfield and Constable Montgomery.' He was a tall, athletic man who exuded calmness and professionalism. 'Take him away.'

Barty gave Donna a manic stare as he was marched out. 'You'll pay for this, bitch.'

Donna's face froze as she stared at him. It was a look of cold fire, almost visceral.

'Don't worry, Miss,' said the sergeant, 'he'll be under lock and key tonight.'

The detective looked at the kitchen with an experienced eye and then back to Donna. 'Shall we sit down?' He gestured towards the lounge and looked at me. 'And you are?'

'I'm a friend, Jack Sheffield. I arrived after he had broken in and restrained him. Thanks for coming so quickly.'

He looked at Donna, who was still pale and distressed. 'Would you like a cup of tea, Miss? Perhaps Mr Sheffield could make one while we're talking.'

I made myself useful in the kitchen while the hum of conversation continued in the lounge. I heard the detective ask if Donna had a friend who could stay with her tonight and she gave a cautious reply. I served the tea, sat down with them and listened carefully.

Eventually he turned to me. 'Looks like you arrived in the nick of time.'

'Yes.' I looked at Donna. 'How are you feeling now?'

'Better.'

I turned back to the detective. 'What about the broken window? Can I clear up the glass and do a repair job?'

He stood up and surveyed the kitchen once again. 'Yes, do that. I've heard the story and it's clear he was working alone.'

I had an idea. 'Donna, I could take you to your mother's.'

'Yes, Jack. Let's do that.'

Darkness had fallen by the time Donna had collected an overnight bag and I had tidied the kitchen. We stood in the hallway and I picked up my coin collection. 'Good job I came back for this.'

Donna's mind was elsewhere. It was as if she hadn't heard me.

As we drove away the storm finally arrived but, on this tempestuous day, it was not just from the heavens. More dark clouds had gathered in the west and a curtain of rain swept across the hills towards us. It was midnight before I finally drove back into Bradley village and a metallic crash of thunder blasted the heavens and lightning split the sky.

It had been a day of clouds and silver linings. After the interview my life had changed and a new pathway stretched out before me. As for Donna, I had seen the danger that would always be in the background and, more now than ever, I understood her fears.

Chapter Nineteen

A Long Goodbye

It was Friday, 15 July, the end of the penultimate week of the school year, and I awoke to a perfect morning. A pale sunrise caressed the sleeping land and the warm air held a breathless promise. On the radio the Jacksons were singing 'Show You the Way to Go' while I ate my breakfast cereal. It seemed appropriate as the time had come for me to move on with my life.

Changes were in store at school and Jim and I were discussing these shortly after I arrived. 'I think we're settled now, Jack. I've had a word with Rhonda and she's happy with the governors' recommendation that she will be Acting Deputy until a permanent appointment can be made.'

'That's good. You'll get excellent support from her.'

'She was pleased although I don't think she wants the job permanently – leading a department suits her.'

'I've worked with her for six years and she still frightens the life out of me.'

Jim grinned. 'Too true but she leads that team really well. There's plenty of Welsh fire in that lady.'

'Even though she's got a broader Yorkshire accent than me.'

'Takes all sorts to make a good team.'

'Well, that's true also.'

'Which reminds me, I thought we ought to have a meeting with Tom now that he's moving into the top juniors. You could pass on the benefit of your experience.'

'And Katy will keep an eye on him,' I added with a smile.

He sat back in his chair. 'So all change once again. Shame I missed out on Izzy. I would have offered her a full-time post if she hadn't been snapped up by Sun Hill.'

'Sorry, Jim. That was my fault, leaving it so late to apply for a headship.'

'No problem. It's an opportunity to make a new appointment, maybe a probationer like Tristan.'

'Have you noticed he's looked more settled these days?'

Jim nodded. 'Yes, it's encouraging. He seemed to go through a tricky spell, didn't he? Then suddenly he came out of it.'

'He's a good teacher.'

'That's right. Anyway, where are you up to with the sale of your bungalow?'

'Good news. There's a young policeman and his wife who are keen. They've offered seven thousand which amounts to a tidy profit. So, in the short term, I'll be renting a flat in York while I look for something new to buy in North Yorkshire.'

'Well, good luck with it all.'

'Thanks.' I glanced up at the clock. 'It's my assembly this morning so I had better get on.'

'By the way, Audrey said could she have a quick word.'

James Hunt's biggest fan was checking registers when I walked in. 'How are you, Jack?' She studied me for a moment with an experienced eye. 'You're looking a bit tired. Not burning the candle at both ends, I hope.'

'Just busy, Audrey. Selling my bungalow and finding somewhere to live in York is taking time.'

'Well, good luck. I shall miss you . . . and your tidy registers.' She passed over my attendance register. 'Excellent attendance figures once again, Jack.'

'Thanks . . . Jim said you wanted to see me.'

'I was wondering if you would like me to ring Ragley School for you about meeting the head.'

'Yes, if you don't mind. I'm happy to visit at a time of their convenience in the summer holiday. Officially I take over on the first of September but I'm keen to get in there well before that if only to prepare my classroom.'

'Fine, I'll get back to you.'

After registration I sensed the mood amongst the children in my class had changed. They were excited after their recent visit to The Ridge.

'It were great, sir,' said Billy Gubbins. 'They've got woodwork benches an' chisels an' saws.'

'We met a lady teacher who does Domestic Science, sir,' said Pauline Ackworth, 'and we told her 'bout Mr Wagstaff an' all t'bakin' we do.'

'An' she were really pleased, sir,' said Dawn Whitehead.

Hands were being raised everywhere except for Jeremy Prendergast, who was looking pensive. 'What about you, Jeremy?'

He shook his head and sighed. 'Well, it's just so *big*, sir, compared with our school. Long corridors, a maze of classrooms . . . but the library was brilliant, hundreds of books and lots of choice.'

'It's a wonderful opportunity for you, Jeremy. You can show what an excellent reader you are.'

Somewhat reassured, this shy boy smiled but I sensed the concern he was feeling and decided to have a word with his mother.

Claire Braithwaite had her hand in the air.

'Yes, Claire.'

'I met the netball teacher, sir, and she had heard of me.'

'And us, sir,' said Stacey and Tracey in unison.

They were clearly thrilled.

'There's a chance we might all get straight into their under-13 team,' said Claire.

It was reassuring that the preliminary visits had gone well. They certainly helped to smooth the transition to secondary school. I looked at their eager faces and knew they were ready for the next stage of their school journey, a new world of uniforms, forty-minute lessons and friends that could last a lifetime. I decided to hold back on our English lesson and spelling test while the discussion continued. Susan Verity was hoping to learn the clarinet; Pauline Ackworth was confident she would soon be bilingual after meeting the French teacher, David Lovelock; Gary Cockroft thought that their football pitch was like Wembley; and Danny Bishop said the jam roly-poly pudding was the best he had ever tasted.

Meanwhile, in the school office Audrey dialled the number for Ragley School.

'Good morning,' said a prim and polite voice, 'Ragley School.'

'Good morning,' said Audrey, 'it's the secretary here from Newbridge Primary School. Sorry to disturb you but I'm ringing for Mr Sheffield. He's hoping to visit your school at the outset of the summer holiday.'

'Of course, I'm sure Mr Pruett would be only too happy to oblige. He would want to talk to Mr Sheffield to arrange this. Could he call back at lunchtime?' There was a riffle of paper. 'Twelve thirty should be fine. I'm Miss Evans, by the way.'

'Hello, Miss Evans. I'll pass on your message to Mr Sheffield and thank you. I'm Miss Fazackerly.'

'I'm pleased to speak with you, Miss Fazackerly. We are of course very sad to be losing Mr Pruett after such long service but looking forward to welcoming Mr Sheffield.'

'May I say, Miss Evans, that you are fortunate. Mr Sheffield is a lovely man, hard-working and a good teacher. I'm sure he will be an asset to your school.'

'That's most encouraging to hear. However, I know you will understand when I say it is important there is an appreciation of my systems of administration. For example, I wouldn't want to change my filing system.'

'I couldn't agree more, Miss Evans. No one would

dream of changing *my* organization. If they did the school would no longer function.'

'My point entirely, Miss Fazackerly. We clearly think alike.'

'We certainly do, Miss Evans.'

'In that case I shall inform Mr Pruett to be here in the office at twelve thirty precisely.'

'Likewise, Miss Evans.

'Thank you, Miss Fazackerly. It has been good to speak with you.'

'My pleasure.'

When they replaced their respective receivers they both smiled.

Great minds think alike, they both thought.

The bell rang for morning assembly and the children filed into the hall. Neville had put one of his records on the turntable and he gently lowered the stylus. The soothing sound of Claude Debussy's 'Clair de Lune' added to the peaceful start to assembly, the last I would lead at New-bridge. The children settled cross-legged on the polished woodblock floor, the teachers sat on their chairs and we were ready to begin.

'Good morning, girls and boys.'

'Good morning, Mr Sheffield; good morning, every-body.'

I felt sad as I stared at all the young faces I knew so well. Izzy gave me a reassuring smile as I introduced our first hymn. 'We shall begin with number forty-four, "When a knight won his spurs in the stories of old". Let's hear you singing really well. Please stand.'

Perhaps I should have phrased it a little differently as Billy Gubbins decided to audition as a town crier with ear-shattering effect.

When they sat down again I read 'The Selfish Giant' by Oscar Wilde and you could have heard a pin drop. They were clearly fascinated by the wonderful tale of the giant who would not allow children to play in his beautiful garden. Suddenly Gary Cockroft raised his hand. I didn't want to stop the flow of the story but Gary looked really keen to share his thoughts.

'Jus' like Mr Bolinbroke, sir, when we went into his allotment. He chased us off.'

'Why did you go there, Gary?'

'Me an' Danny wanted to 'elp but we didn't get a chance to ask.'

'I'll have a word with Mr Bolinbroke, Gary, and tell him you mean no harm.'

'Thanks, sir, and mebbe say we weren't goin' t'pinch 'is rhubarb.'

He gave me that *butter wouldn't melt in his mouth* smile that I knew so well.

'Anyway, back to the story . . .'

At morning break I called in to see Jim. Katy and I had written detailed reports on all the children prior to them moving on to The Ridge and I wanted to discuss some of the issues with him. In particular, I knew it was important that the teachers were aware that Jeremy Prendergast was the brightest pupil I had ever taught. His scores on tests for English and maths put him in the *gifted* category and among those children in the top 2 per cent of the normal curve of distribution. He would need his aptitude to be nurtured if he wasn't to simply coast along in an introverted manner.

However, when I walked in it was clear Jim had other issues to deal with. He waved me to a chair as he continued his telephone conversation. 'Are you saying there's a danger of an epidemic?' He listened carefully to the response. 'Fine, I appreciate the information but it would be helpful if you could call in. It's important we progress this.'

When he replaced the receiver he looked across at me. 'One moment, Jack,' and he scribbled a note on his pad.

'Sorry to disturb you, Jim. This will keep.'

'No, stay. You need to hear this. That was the school nurse. She's worried about the numbers of children in the area with whooping cough. There's concern that not enough children are being vaccinated. She will be here later today. I'll keep you informed.'

It was another reminder that a headteacher's work is never done. Unexpected problems will emerge every day and you have to deal with them.

'Busy times, Jack,' he said with a smile. 'Your turn soon. It's a bit like juggling plates. Now . . . tell me what was on your mind.'

It was shortly before lunchtime and I was walking through the hall just as Frank was finishing putting out the dining tables. 'Sorry we were a bit slow finishing the television programme, Frank.'

'No problem, Mr Sheffield.'

At that moment Rita Starkey arrived to collect her dinner-lady overall from the kitchen. She stopped when she saw the Swithenbank twins, Tracey and Stacey, pushing the television back into the staff-room. She had always liked these assertive girls and was keen to pass on the benefit of her experience in all matters.

"Ello, Mrs Starkey,' they chorused.

"Ello girls. 'Ave y'been watchin' telly?'

'Yes, Mrs Starkey.'

'Well, remember not t'sit too close 'cause you'll get square eyes.'

'OK, Mrs Starkey.'

Rita looked at Frank. "Ow's yer leg, 'andsome?'

'Middlin',' said Frank with a smile. 'Can't complain.'

'Meks a change for a man,' said Rita, quick as a flash, as she stepped briskly into the kitchen.

'Quite a lady, that one,' said Frank with an admiring glance.

'Definitely,' I said.

'If she sez it's Thursday, it's Thursday. Y'don't mess wi' Rita.'

'Yes, I've gathered that.'

Frank shook his head, 'Sadly, 'er 'usband's not t'full shilling so she 'as t'work f'both of 'em an' 'old everything together. She's 'ad a 'ard life.'

'Quite a lady.'

'She is that an' ah'll tell y'summat f'nowt, Mr Sheffield. When she were young she were fit as a butcher's dog.'

I smiled and walked on. Sometimes it was best not to reply.

At afternoon break it was the usual eclectic mix of conversation in the staff-room.

Celestine was thrilled that Virginia Wade had won the Wimbledon Ladies' Tennis Championship; Tom was complaining that Don Revie had resigned as the England football manager in order to seek his fortune in the United Arab Emirates and Audrey was excited that Princess Anne and Mark Phillips would soon be moving into their new home.

Meanwhile, Rhonda was holding forth: 'You'll never guess where Bryn is taking me for our twenty-fifth wedding anniversary.'

'Cardiff,' said Katy quick as a flash.

'Or even Swansea,' added Tristan.

'Ignore them,' said Celestine. 'Come on, tell us.'

Rhonda took a holiday brochure from her shoulder bag. 'You could have knocked me over with a feather. Have a look at this. Three weeks in Florida for three hundred and six pounds.'

'That's fantastic,' said Tristan.

'Sounds great, Rhonda,' said Katy. 'Did you twist his arm?'

'Well, I did leave the brochure open at this page next to his lamb casserole last night.'

At the end of school I tidied my classroom and on my way home I stopped off at Snoddy's Stores to take advantage of Gilbert's frozen-food selection. By seven o'clock I was enjoying fish fingers, chips and peas with a large mug of tea. I had just finished rinsing the single plate when the phone rang. It was Donna.

'Hi. This is a surprise.'

'Jack, I was thinking about meeting up? It would be good to see you before the end of term.'

'That would be great. I've been thinking about you. Are you OK?'

'Yes, I'm fine. The thing is . . . I've got some news and I would like to share it with you.'

'Sounds interesting. Where shall we meet?'

'Sherri is staying with her friend this weekend. Why don't we have a day out? We never did get to York. Maybe a walk by the river. Tomorrow's forecast is good and I could bring a picnic.'

'Great idea. So shall I pick you up around ten o'clock?'

'Perfect. See you then.'

Later that evening I was watching *I, Claudius* on television. Derek Jacobi had found a friend in Herod and it struck me that friendships can be fickle.

On Saturday morning when I arrived at Donna's cottage the branches in the high elms stirred with a sibilant whisper and the air was humid and warm. After I knocked on the door she appeared carrying a wicker picnic basket and a large tartan rug.

'You've been busy.'

She smiled. 'We certainly won't go hungry.'

We packed everything in the boot and set off driving north. The miles flew by before I finally opened up a conversation. 'It's good to see you. How are you?'

'Fine now.' There was a long pause. 'It took a while to get over that incident with Barty.'

'I can understand that.'

'Thank you for being there, Jack. I don't know what I would have done without you.'

'You've been through a lot. I'm just glad the police took

311

him away. I heard his case went to court but don't know much else.'

'He's in prison now in Leeds. He got six months.'

'That seems pretty lenient.'

'Particularly as he had a previous record for drug dealing and burglary.'

'I didn't know that.'

'The first I heard about it was when the police told me he had been detained in custody because of the risk of further harassment.'

'That makes sense. You were lucky. At least he's off the scene for now.'

She was quiet for a moment. 'Yes . . . for now.'

We settled into our own private reveries until York came into sight.

We parked on Marygate by the ancient city wall and carried our picnic to the museum gardens. I spread out the blanket near the timber-framed Hospitium, built in the fourteenth century as a place for travellers to rest. It was good to sit in the warm sunshine.

Donna had packed a superb selection, including ham and cucumber sandwiches in fresh crusty bread, sausage rolls, ripe tomatoes, a fruit cake and crunchy apples. There was a bottle of white wine and cheese and crackers. 'This is delicious,' I said. 'A great idea and a perfect day to come to York.'

Finally the moment had arrived. 'So what's the news you wanted to share?'

She put down her plastic beaker of Muscadet and hugged her knees. 'Jack . . . I've got a job.'

'That's great: I knew you would. Is it teaching juniors?'

'Yes, third year juniors with responsibility for girls' games.'

'You will be brilliant. I'm so pleased for you. Did you find somewhere to live for you and your mum?'

There was a pause and she leaned back, stretched out her legs and sighed. 'I need to explain.'

'Yes?'

'My mother is staying here. It's just Sherri and me who are moving.'

'Oh . . . I thought . . .'

'I know but something came up that I hadn't considered before and it seems the perfect solution.'

'What's that?'

'It's a teaching post in a Service Children's Education School. They're the ones for the children of our armed forces.'

'I've heard of those but I didn't know there were any in England.'

Once again she gave me that familiar direct stare that I knew so well. 'Jack . . . the school is in Germany.' Her blue eyes never wavered.

'Germany?'

'Yes and there's a good school for Sherri as well as accommodation. So Mum isn't selling her house after all.'

I sat there trying to comprehend. There was only the sound of the breeze rustling the branches of the trees above our heads. A belligerent peacock strutted past towards the ruins of St Mary's Abbey.

'You've meant so much to me, Jack. I remember all those years ago how you helped me. If it hadn't been for you I would never have been a teacher.'

313

'You were born to be a teacher,' I said quietly.

'But it would never have happened but for you. Then you reappeared in my life just when I needed you.'

'That went for me as well.'

'I could never have got through all this with Barty if it hadn't been for you. You gave me the strength to cope.'

'You have more strength than you know.'

'Maybe. But heaven knows what would have happened if you hadn't come back that night.'

I smiled. 'Well, the coin collection *is* rather precious.'

'In more ways than one. I'm so pleased you left it behind.'

'And I still have to collect it.'

'I'll pass it over when you drop me off.'

Only when we were repacking the picnic basket did I look at her and say softly, 'It's no good saying *if only,* is it?'

'It wasn't meant to be . . . you and me. I wish it could have been different but as long as Barty presents a potential danger then no one can share my life. Even so, we have opportunities ahead of us. You in your new school and me in mine. We both need to move on.'

It was a strange feeling sitting opposite this beautiful woman and realizing it was truly finally over between us. We stood up, packed the hamper once again and walked back to the car. 'Come on,' I said. 'Let's enjoy the rest of the day. I love York.'

'So do I.'

I locked the car and took her hand. We walked up Marygate and on to Bootham Bar, one of York's great gateways. Donna stared up at the ancient limestone walls. 'Imagine if we could go back in time,' she said. 'This is the site of the Roman Porta Principalis.'

314

Go back in time, I thought and wondered if anything could have been different. 'I've not walked on the city walls for ages,' I said. 'Come on.' We climbed the steep stone steps and strolled side by side until we reached Robin Hood's Tower and looked down over Lord Mayor's Walk. 'St John's College,' I said wistfully, 'where I trained in the sixties. Special times.'

We carried on to Monk Bar where we descended and merged with the busy shoppers in Goodramgate. 'It would be a pity not to call into the Minster,' she said. Outside St William's College we stared up at the largest medieval Gothic church in northern Europe before following tourists of all nationalities who had travelled far to visit this special place. Soon we were speaking in hushed voices as we walked beneath the high arches and stared up in wonder at the magnificent stained-glass Rose Window that commemorated the union of the royal houses of Lancaster and York. For around half an hour we were steeped in history and following in the steps of countless generations. It was a humbling spiritual experience and when we finally emerged into the sunlight once again we both knew it was a memory we would treasure.

As we walked on I realized we were gradually coming to the end of our time together. It was a long goodbye and we were savouring the hours and minutes. In Stonegate we stopped outside The Olde Starre Inne, the oldest alehouse in York. 'A final drink?' I asked quietly. Donna smiled and we walked inside. We both selected a refreshing lemonade shandy and stood at the bar.

'Cheers, Donna.'

We clinked our glasses. 'Cheers, Jack.'

'So is there anything else you would like to do while we're here?'

'Perhaps a walk by the river.'

'Perfect. Let's do that.'

'Will you be sad when you leave Newbridge? Seven years is a long time.'

'A little. I have some great colleagues there but I'm excited about the headship.'

'A new chapter in your life, Jack. I'm sure you'll do well.'

'I'm meeting the retiring head at the beginning of the holiday. He's been there for thirty years so it will be a wrench for him.'

'He'll have a few stories to tell, no doubt. Every village has them.'

'I'm wondering what the staff will be like. It will be strange being the newcomer but also in charge.'

'I know what you mean and I feel a little like that myself. Germany will be a big step.'

'What does Sherri think about it?'

'She's excited and wants to learn the language.'

'The opportunity will be there for her. By the time she leaves school she'll be fluent.'

It was peaceful walking by the river and we watched the pleasure boats drift by. Finally we returned to the car and set off for home. 'So You Win Again' by Hot Chocolate was on the radio as we drove out of York but at that moment it didn't feel like it.

We pulled up once again outside her cottage. After we had unpacked the picnic basket she walked inside and came back with my coin collection. It was in a small canvas bag and she put it down by the gate. 'Yours again at last, Jack. Better late than never.'

'Thanks and just as well I forgot it last time.'

She smiled and stood closer. 'Goodbye, Jack. I'll never forget you.'

'I'm sad it came to this,' I said, 'but I understand.'

We held each other in a long embrace and then stood back facing each other. 'I wonder where we will be next year,' I said.

She smoothed the collar of my jacket and gave me that familiar level stare. I realized no reply was necessary.

'Goodbye, Donna. Good luck in your life.' I picked up the bag and put it on the passenger seat. As I drove away I looked in my rear-view mirror. Donna was standing by her gate and waving goodbye.

It was the last time we ever met.

Chapter Twenty

School Days

On this perfect morning, dawn had painted the eastern sky with a wash of pink and pearl, a soft hue that bleached the sapphire blue. It was Friday, 22 July, my last day at Newbridge Primary School, and with a mixture of sadness and expectation I set off for school.

Big Frank was, as usual, emptying litter bins in the playground when I arrived and he limped over to greet me. 'Mornin', Mr Sheffield. Las' day.'

'Good morning, Frank. Yes, mixed feelings.'

'Well, ah wish y'luck in yer new job. It's lovely up there in North Yorkshire. Ah tek my Pauline sometimes.'

'It's been good working with you, Frank, and I'm grateful for all you've done. The school is lucky to have you.'

'My pleasure. It's important to 'elp all t'kiddies in t'village.'

There was a black rubbish bag at his feet. 'By the way, did you ever find out who was leaving those bottles?'

'Yes, all sorted an' least said, soonest mended.'

He gave me a look that suggested I should probe no further. 'OK, Frank. Good to hear.'

'Anyway, good luck.' We shook hands. He had a grip like a vice.

'Thanks, Frank, see you later.'

Jim was wading through a pile of paperwork when I called into his office. He looked up at me and smiled. 'Morning, Jack. The advert's gone out for a new appointment so we'll be up and running again at the start of next term.'

'That's good. Do you need any help for morning assembly?'

'All in hand but thanks anyway.'

'I thought I would drop off my satchel and then walk down to the school gate to welcome the children.'

Jim nodded and glanced out of his window. 'It's always been appreciated by the parents so keep it going at your new school. It works wonders for relationships.'

When I went outside I found the playground was filling up with excited children. Six weeks of freedom stretched out before them. Mrs Brenda Lofthouse was the first to give me a wave. She was pushing a pram and smoking a cigarette. Her son, Colin, now seven years old, was growing fast. 'Go on,' she said and gave him a friendly push.

'Hello, Mrs Lofthouse, how are you?'

She stubbed out her cigarette on the school wall. 'Not looking forward to the 'oliday, Mr Sheffield. Our Colin's a real 'andful at t'best o' times. Mind you, if weather stays like this 'e can play out.'

319

'And how is Kimberly?'

'She's comin' up f'ten months now.'

I looked down at the rosy-cheeked girl. 'She looks the picture of health.'

'An' eatin' mashed food like there's no t'morrow. Anyway, good luck in yer new job, Mr Sheffield.' She wandered back to the High Street and lit up another cigarette.

Next to the school gate I spotted Billy Oldroyd and smiled. He was wincing as his mother gave him a hug and a big kiss as they parted. Some things didn't change.

It was then that a battered Austin 1100 pulled up outside and Mrs Swithenbank got out. 'Morning, Mr Sheffield. Just wanted to say a big thank you for all you've done for my girls.'

'All part of the job, Mrs Swithenbank.'

'I don't know how you do it; they're out of control at home.'

'It's been a pleasure teaching them and, if you get time, have a word with Miss Bell. She's done wonders for them with the netball.'

'I will, Mr Sheffield.' She glanced at her watch. 'Well, mustn't be late for work,' and she roared off as the twins ran on to the playground to join in a skipping game. Pauline Ackworth and Claire Braithwaite were winding a long rope while Susan Verity and Dawn Whitehead skipped and chanted:

> *'Little fat doctor,*
> *How's your wife?*
> *Very well, thank you,*

That's all right.
Eat a bit o' fish,
An' a stick o' liquorice,
O-U-T spells OUT!'

'Good morning, Mr Sheffield.' It was Mrs Prendergast with her son, Jeremy. 'Off you go and enjoy your last day at Newbridge.' She gave him a hug and he walked to a shady spot in the corner of the playground, took out a book from his duffel bag and began to read.

'I wanted to express my appreciation, Mr Sheffield. Jeremy has always felt safe in your class.'

I thought *safe* was a carefully chosen word.

'I'm sure Jeremy will do well at The Ridge, Mrs Prendergast. He's a bright boy and there are many opportunities for him.'

We looked across at her studious son sitting there in a world of his own. She removed her horn-rimmed spectacles and polished the lenses with the hem of her cardigan. 'He's always been like that, ever since he was tiny. It's a struggle for him to find a like-minded friend. I'm worried how he will cope at the big school.'

'I've had a word with a few of the teachers up there, Mrs Prendergast. So, never fear, there *will* be support.'

'I do hope so.' She opened her shoulder bag. 'Anyway, here's a card to say thanks for all you've done.' And she passed over a large lavender-blue envelope.

'Thank you.'

She smiled and walked away, pausing briefly to look at Jeremy who was still engrossed in Alan Garner's *The*

Weirdstone of Brisingamen. It was a poignant moment watching this gifted little boy sitting alone with his nose in a book and seemingly oblivious of the hurly burly around him.

Jim had requested an earlier assembly at ten o'clock, a full half-hour before morning playtime. There was a sense of expectation as the children settled and all the staff including Frank, Audrey and the kitchen ladies found seats around the edge of the hall. Grayson was in attendance to deliver the closing prayer and around thirty parents had managed to get time off work to attend and were seated at the back. It was the Leavers' Assembly when we said goodbye to our top juniors.

Jim was wearing a smart linen suit and looked calm and relaxed as he stood and surveyed the young faces before him. 'Good morning, boys and girls.'

'Good morning, Mr Patterson; good morning, everybody,' came the familiar response.

'This is a special day,' he said with a reassuring smile. 'The boys and girls in Miss Bell's class and in Mr Sheffield's class leave us today and in September they will start their secondary education at The Ridge. We know they are well prepared and will be a credit to Newbridge. There have been many achievements during this past year, not least in high standards of English and mathematics but also in sport, music and drama.'

He paused to let the import of this sink in. 'There have also been memorable times such as the excellent visit to the Eternal Peace Residential Home before Christmas and the many events organized by the Parent-Teacher Association that help our school in so many ways, not least the improvements to our school library and, of course, our wonderful audio system.' He glanced at Neville, who responded with knowing acknowledgement.

'We mustn't forget the moments that made us smile. Finding an escaped cat in Jesus's manger was definitely one of them!'

There was laughter from the children, staff and parents and a frown from our local vicar.

'We shall begin our assembly with one of our favourites, "Kumbaya". Please stand.' Izzy was at the piano waiting for her cue. 'Thank you, Ms Kowalski.'

The introduction was played, children opened their hymn books and the hall was filled with the sweet sound of many voices.

'Sit down again, please,' said Jim and waited for silence.

It was then he came into his own. I had never known anyone better at telling a story in school assembly. As always he didn't use a book but rather spoke from experience and the children were captivated. The theme was a simple one and involved trying your best. The magic was the way he involved children from all the year groups. He highlighted the achievements of every class and their teacher and, at the end, we all clapped.

'Now, before Mr Huppleby leads us in the Lord's Prayer, it's time to sing one of our favourites, "One More Step Along the Road I Go".'

I looked at Izzy when, for the final time, she played the introduction. There was a hint of sadness in her eyes as the children raised the roof with a rousing rendition of the popular song.

When everyone was seated once again silence descended

and Grayson led us in the Lord's Prayer. At the end there was a communal 'Amen' and everyone looked expectantly at Jim as he returned to the front of the hall.

'Thank you, Mr Huppleby, for joining us this morning and for your continued support throughout the year. It is much appreciated.'

Grayson gave an imperceptible nod of acknowledgement.

'Boys and girls, I have said well done to all of you for your hard work this year and now it's time to say thank you to all the grown-ups. So well done to all your teachers for being a wonderful team. We are lucky to have such dedicated teachers at Newbridge and their work each day helps all of us to learn and to grow.' The children turned to look at the reaction of their class teacher with eager faces.

'Also, I should like to thank our school governors and your parents for their support and, particularly, the members of the PTA who make our school a better place.' There were appreciative smiles from the parents while Mrs Clarissa Peacock on the back row gave a regal wave. 'Also,' continued Jim, 'the ladies in the kitchen work hard every day to provide you with excellent meals and we are grateful to them.'

Danny Bishop looked up at Rita Starkey and gave her a thumbs up and she grinned and responded with a wink.

'And where would we be without Mr Cannon, our caretaker, who, in all weathers, looks after our school with true dedication?' Big Frank smiled and I saw him scan the line of teachers and nod towards Tristan. 'And, finally, we are fortunate in having a superb secretary. Miss Fazackerly's organization is remarkable and we are all grateful for her dedicated service.' Audrey blushed and took a lace hanky from the sleeve of her cardigan and dabbed her eyes. 'So, boys and girls, let's show our appreciation to all the grown-ups.'

A thunderous round of applause followed.

'This morning is also an important day as we are saying goodbye to our music teacher, Ms Kowalski.' There were murmurs from the children and members of the choir looked sad. Izzy clasped her hands and looked down. 'Ms Kowalski has been a wonderful addition to our staff and has provided Newbridge with the gift of music. We congratulate her on her new appointment as a full-time teacher at Sun Hill Primary but shall miss her energy and enthusiasm. As a token of our appreciation we have a small gift to be presented by Claire Braithwaite on behalf of the school choir.'

Claire walked to the piano and gave Izzy a crisp white envelope. She opened it and everyone looked expectantly in her direction. 'Oh, thank you so much,' she said and held up a gift voucher for the music shop in Milltown. 'I shall buy a very special book of music with this and always think of you when I use it.' She looked tearful for a moment while applause rang out again.

Jim waited for it to die down and then spoke again. 'I said this was a special day and it is for our deputy head-teacher, Mr Sheffield. This is his last day at Newbridge before he takes up a new post as a headteacher in North Yorkshire.' I saw all the children turn towards me and felt emotion well up inside me. 'Mr Sheffield has been our deputy, our teacher and our friend for the past seven years. We are sad to see him go but grateful for all he has done for us and wish him luck for the future. I should like to ask Mrs Williams to present Mr Sheffield with a gift from the staff that I know he will appreciate.'

Rhonda collected a beautifully wrapped parcel from Audrey and brought it to where I was sitting. 'For you, Jack,' she said quietly.

'Open it, sir,' said the Swithenbank twins.

'Let's see, sir,' said Billy Gubbins.

I removed the red bow and the wrapping paper to reveal an elegant mahogany presentation box. I stood up so the children could see the contents. It was a writing set including a Platignum pen, a bottle of Quink ink and a leather-bound notebook.

'This is perfect,' I said. 'Very many thanks.'

There was more applause.

Jim could see I was struggling for words and stepped in. 'Mr Sheffield may wish to write a few stories in his spare time so I'm sure he will make good use of his gift. We also have a card signed by all the staff to be presented by Miss Bell.'

Katy passed over a card with a photograph of Newbridge School on the front. Inside were lots of cryptic messages. I looked around at all my colleagues and smiled.

'And now, boys and girls,' said Jim, 'I'm looking for the smartest class to leave assembly.' Row by row, the children walked out in complete silence to be replaced with an explosion of noise as the bell rang for morning playtime and they all ran outside to enjoy fresh air and freedom.

After chatting with some of the parents I carried my gift and card into a staff-room buzzing with conversation. It was then that Neville made a grand entrance carrying a huge and beautifully iced cake with the message 'GOOD LUCK JACK & IZZY' on top.

'Thank you,' said Izzy and gave him a hug.

'Great cake, Neville,' I said.

'Thanks, Jack. It's my Orange Gateau.'

'You must give me the recipe,' said Audrey.

'It's from my *Homepride Book of Home Baking*,' said Neville. 'The candied orange slices make such a difference, along with the American frosting,' he added with the merest hint of false modesty.

We all sat there enjoying coffee and a slice of cake while I read my card. Rhonda came over and pointed at her message. It read *'Pob lwc*, Jack'. 'It means: "Good luck, Jack",' and for the first time in seven years she gave me a kiss on the cheek to roars from Tom and Tristan.

Shortly before the lunchtime bell I was in the school office with Gary Cockroft. He had fallen on the playground and I had spotted the cuts and bruises on his elbows and knees. Significantly Gary had not mentioned this. Audrey had administered First Aid.

'Ah were tryin' t'score a goal, Miss Fazackerly,' said Gary, completely oblivious to his injuries.

'You should have been on the field, Gary, not the playground,' I said.

'You and your football,' muttered Audrey. She gave me an *I've seen it all before* look and I sent Gary back to class.

Rita Starkey was in conversation with Big Frank when I walked through the school hall. She called out, 'Good luck up in t'top end o' Yorkshire.'

'Thank you, Mrs Starkey.' I walked over and shook her hand. The skin on her palm was hard and her nails were broken, the product of years of hard work.

She glanced at the clock. 'Never been late for m'shift but it were close t'day.'

'Was there a problem?' I saw Frank raise his eyebrows and it occurred to me that maybe I shouldn't have asked.

However, Mrs Starkey was nothing if not direct. 'Ah've been chief cook an' bottle-washer all m'life, Mr Sheffield, but sometimes *enough is enough*.' She shook her head. 'It's my Keith. Sent 'im packing wi' a flea in his ear. Ah thought good riddance t'bad rubbish but then ah felt sorry for t'poor sod an' ah took 'im back again.'

'Oh, I see,' I said a little lamely.

'Good thing is ah've still got my Charlie.'

'Charlie?'

'Ah'd be lost wi'out 'im.'

'Really?'

'Ah've trained 'im an 'e's perfec' now.'

'Is he?'

'Anyway, got t'get m'pinny on,' and she hurried into the kitchen.

Frank was grinning. 'Y'don't know who Charlie is, do you?'

'No idea.'

'Charlie's a parrot. Rita's nex'-door neighbour, Betty, is a right pain in the bum. Allus puttin' it over 'er 'bout 'er 'usband earnin' big money as a foreman at 'Unter's Mill. So Rita taught Charlie t'sing that ABBA song "Money, Money, Money" an' puts 'im on t'windowsill to annoy 'er.'

'Inventive,' I said with a smile.

'Y'don't mess wi' Rita,' and he wandered off to put out the rest of the dining tables.

At afternoon break Audrey had brought in the local newspaper, the *Newbridge Chronicle*. 'This whooping cough outbreak is a worry. We're sending out a letter to parents.'

Rhonda looked across the room at Celestine. 'It might be an idea for us to go to the school gate at the end of school and speak to some of the parents.'

'Yes, good thought,' said Celestine.

'Mr Patterson has liaised with the school nurse,' said Audrey. 'It's important not to scare parents but the fact is not enough children are being vaccinated.'

The afternoon was spent playing games with the children in the hall and when the bell finally rang to mark the end of term it occurred to me that it was one of the best school days of my life. There were many cards on my desk from the children and I was looking through them when Katy called in.

'Well, this is it, partner,' she said. 'It's been good working with you, Jack. Now I'll have Tom next door. It'll be different.'

'Football instead of rugby.'

She grinned. 'There is that.'

'Just thinking,' I said. 'I never did see your dramatization of Jason and the Argonauts.' My comment was tongue in cheek.

'A blast from the past and just as well. The script was more *The Sweeney* than Greek legend and my hearthrug would have made a poor golden fleece.'

'Either way, don't give up on it. You've done some great drama with our top juniors.'

'Always a pleasure, Jack. Anyway, I'll leave you to your cards and packing. I've got a meeting now with Tom. We're coming in a week early before next term starts so we'll be well organized.'

'Good luck, Katy.'

'You too.'

We shook hands and she strode confidently out into the corridor.

A few minutes later I was collecting the last of my belongings from my desk when Neville walked in.

'Jack, a small gift from me.'

'Thank you, Neville. That's most thoughtful.'

It was an *Ace Golden Eagle Stamp Album* complete with maps of the world and pages listed alphabetically from Abu Dhabi to Zululand.

I smiled. 'Wonderful! An opportunity to rediscover an old hobby.'

'And a reminder of our time together,' he said quietly. I knew what he really meant. 'Best wishes for the future, Jack. You've been a good colleague and, more than that, a friend when I needed one most of all.'

'It's been a pleasure working alongside you and, of course, sampling your delicious cakes.'

He laughed and it was good to see the transformation in this sensitive man after the difficult times of the past. As I watched him walk away I hoped he had found true happiness with David Lovelock and that he would receive the appreciation he deserved as a caring man and a great teacher.

I was carrying the first of my belongings to my car when Audrey appeared from her study. I put the box down on the table in the entrance hall.

'Would you like a hand, Jack?'

'Thanks but I'm fine and not in a rush. Just collecting some of the things that are precious to me.'

She peered in the box. There was a globe on a stand and she spun it gently. 'New worlds in store.'

'Yes, sad to leave but looking forward to being a head.'

'I'm sure you'll do well. Just a thought . . . do keep on the right side of your new secretary. She sounds a caring and well-organized lady.'

'So . . . just like you.'

She smiled but there was a hint of sadness behind it.

'Hasn't he gone yet?' Jacket discarded and sleeves rolled up, Jim appeared in the doorway to his office with a big smile on his face. 'Have you finished with him, Audrey?'

Audrey shook my hand, 'God bless,' she said and walked back into her study.

'Quick word, Jack.' He beckoned me in and closed the door. Then he leaned back against his desk and looked me up and down. 'Long time since I interviewed you, Jack. I made a good choice.'

'Thanks.'

'No long goodbyes. I'm always here if you ever need to share a problem.'

'I know that. I couldn't have had a better mentor.'

There was a pause as we both reflected on the years we had worked together. No more words were needed and with a final handshake we parted.

I was making journeys to and from my car loading up the resources I had collected over the years when Izzy arrived by my side. 'Hi, Jack, I'm leaving with Katy in a few minutes. Thought I would come to say goodbye.'

We stood there on the playground and she looked at the school gate. 'That's where we first met,' she said and I recalled the day when she had captured my imagination with her zest for life.

She looked thoughtful. 'A lot has happened since. I've been lucky. The job here has given me a stepping stone into teaching a class of my own.'

'You've earned it.'

'Maybe . . . but I've a lot to thank you for and not just getting rid of my good-for-nothing boyfriend.'

'He's long gone and you're a good teacher, Izzy, and you'll do well at Sun Hill.'

'And you've helped me along the way. A new start for both of us.'

It reminded me of my last conversation with Donna. For a brief time these dynamic women had been part of my life. Now both were moving on. Then, without hesitation, she stepped forward and hugged me. 'I'll miss you, Jack.'

'You too,' I said quietly.

She turned back towards the car park and I watched her walk away, confidence in her step and her wavy black hair stirring in the slight breeze.

*

In Bradley village as I bumped over the canal bridge Rod Stewart was singing 'The First Cut Is the Deepest' on my car radio while I was deep in thought. Back in my bungalow I decided to busy myself and I packed a few more boxes with books.

Finally, after a simple meal, I opened the door to get some fresh air and stood there in the gathering darkness. It was an evening of night sounds, subtle yet insistent . . . distant traffic, a barn owl, discordant laughter, the keening of tree branches and the secret scurrying of small creatures. I stood there thinking back to a relationship that had briefly filled the empty part of my life.

Love was certainly a complex companion.

Different pathways . . . different destinies.

It was 10.15 p.m. when I finally settled down with a cool beer to watch BBC television. It was a documentary about the life of a village in Wiltshire and the locals seemed to be having the same problems I had experienced. Last week their church roof was about to collapse, cows were making a mess in the High Street and the village pantomime was a complete disaster. I wondered if this might be like Ragley village.

That night I picked up my leather-bound notebook and my pen from my bedside and began to write. The book was destined to be full of stories, both amusing and poignant, but I didn't know it then. Then I picked up my favourite novel, Tolkien's *Lord of the Rings*, and, once again, I reflected on Gandalf's words. He said that all we have to decide is what to do with the time that is given us.

We are the architects of our own destiny.

I had made my choice and I had no regrets.

*

It was Monday, 25 July when I drove slowly up the High Street of Ragley-on-the-Forest. The headteacher, Mr John Pruett, had been most obliging and suggested I visit the school at the beginning of the summer holiday in order for him to pass over the school keys. The next stage of my life was about to begin.

The sun was shining as I passed the row of village shops: the General Stores, Piercy's Butcher's Shop, the Village Pharmacy, Pratt's Hardware Emporium, Nora's Coffee Shop, Diane's Hair Salon and a tiny Post Office with a red telephone box outside. I paused as I reached the village green. On a tall flagpole a flag of St George was fluttering in the gentle breeze, a reminder of the Silver Jubilee celebrations.

The white-fronted public house, The Royal Oak, was in the centre of a row of cottages. I followed a side road that led past the avenue of horse chestnut trees to the school's tall, solid, red-brick Victorian building, and I parked alongside the waist-high wall of Yorkshire stone. Then I walked up the cobbled drive and under the archway to the huge oak entrance door. Out of the sunlight the hallway was dark and opposite me was a door with a small brass plate that read 'John T. Pruett, Headmaster'.

I tapped on the door and it was answered by a bespectacled man with a kindly face. He looked tired and careworn.

'Good morning,' I said, 'I'm Jack Sheffield.'

He smiled. 'Hello, Mr Sheffield, welcome to Ragley,' he said. 'I'm John Pruett.'

We spoke for an hour and it was clear this gentle, dedicated man was ready for retirement. He spoke at length about the school he loved and showed me the logbooks, huge leather-covered tomes. 'You'll be needing these,' he said. 'The whole history of the school is here, almost a hundred years. Now it's your turn. As headmaster, you have to keep an accurate account of everything that happens. Well, just the official stuff of course. Keep it simple.' Then he smiled. 'Whatever you do, don't say what really happens because no one will believe you.'

It was when I finally drove home again that I sensed an extraordinary life lay ahead of me. These were no ordinary days . . . these were school days.

And in a heartbeat it was time to move on.

Epilogue

Ysemay Kowalski had a successful career at Sun Hill Primary School. After a string of boyfriends she met a long-haired piano tuner from Liverpool and fell in love. They bought a cottage in the Lake District and made music.

Donna Clayton moved with her daughter Sherri to Germany. They live there still. She never married. Barty Withinshaw died in a road accident in 1979. He was high on cocaine when he drove into a motorway bridge.

Jim Patterson remained at Newbridge for the rest of his career. He spent his life giving children a love of learning and encouraging his staff. On retirement he was awarded a CBE for his services to education.

Big Frank Cannon retired as caretaker through ill health and opened a shop repairing shoes. His friend Nobby Poskitt made sure everyone in the village went to Cannon the Cobbler for their footwear to be soled and heeled.

Epilogue

After retirement Rhonda Williams returned to her childhood village in Wales where she worked hard to lose her Yorkshire accent.

Neville Wagstaff enjoyed a happy life with his partner, David Lovelock. They moved to Brighton in 1995.

Katy Bell married Mike Foster and they opened a highly successful fitness studio in Harrogate. Their daughter became an international heptathlete.

Tristan Lampwick became head teacher of a London primary school. As a local Arts Director his productions of Shakespeare plays became renowned in the capital. He remained teetotal for the rest of his life. Whenever he needed his shoes repaired he travelled north to Newbridge where he and Big Frank shared a pot of strong tea.

Audrey Fazackerly continued as school secretary at Newbridge until she retired. She met her hero, James Hunt, whilst on holiday in Wimbledon. He signed her tennis programme, posed for a photograph and kissed her on the cheek. It was a moment she treasured for the rest of her life.

In the summer of 1977 Jack Sheffield moved to North Yorkshire to begin life as a village school headteacher.

He hoped that one day he would meet the girl of his dreams.

About the Author

Jack Sheffield grew up in the tough environment of Gipton Estate, in north-east Leeds. After a job as a 'pitch boy', repairing roofs, he became a Corona Pop man before going to St John's College, York, and training to be a teacher. In the late seventies and eighties, he was headteacher of two schools in North Yorkshire before becoming Senior Lecturer in Primary Education at the University of Leeds. It was at this time he began to record his many amusing stories of village life as portrayed in *Teacher, Teacher!*, *Mister Teacher*, *Dear Teacher*, *Village Teacher*, *Please Sir!*, *Educating Jack*, *School's Out!*, *Silent Night*, *Star Teacher*, *Happiest Days*, *Starting Over*, *Changing Times* and *Back to School*.

School Days is his fourteenth novel and continues the story of Jack's early teaching career.

In 2017 Jack was awarded the honorary title of Cultural Fellow of York St John University.

He lives with his wife in Hampshire.

Visit his website at **www.jacksheffield.com**.